LADY OSBALDESTONE'S PLUM PUDDINGS

LADY OSBALDESTONE'S CHRISTMAS CHRONICLES
VOLUME 3

STEPHANIE LAURENS

ABOUT LADY OSBALDESTONE'S PLUM PUDDINGS

#1 New York Times bestselling author Stephanie Laurens brings you the delights of a long-ago country-village Christmas, featuring a grandmother, her grandchildren, an artifact hunter, the lady who catches his eye, and three ancient coins that draw them all together in a Christmas treasure hunt.

Therese, Lady Osbaldestone, and her household again welcome her younger daughter's children, Jamie, George, and Lottie, plus their cousins Melissa and Mandy, all of whom have insisted on spending the three weeks prior to Christmas at Therese's house, Hartington Manor, in the village of Little Moseley.

The children are looking forward to the village's traditional events, and this year, Therese has arranged a new distraction—the plum puddings she and her staff are making for the entire village. But while cleaning the coins donated as the puddings' good-luck tokens, the children discover that three aren't coins of the realm. When consulted, Reverend Colebatch summons a friend, an archeological scholar from Oxford, who confirms the coins are Roman, raising the possibility of a Roman treasure buried somewhere near. Unfortunately, Professor Webster is facing a deadline and cannot assist in the search, but along with his niece Honor, he will stay in the village, writing, remaining available for consultation should the children and their helpers uncover more treasure.

It soon becomes clear that discovering the source of the coins—or even which villager donated them—isn't a straightforward matter. Then the children come across a personable gentleman who knows a great deal about Roman antiquities. He introduces himself as Callum Harris, and they agree to allow him to help, and he gets their search back on track.

But while the manor five, assisted by the gentlemen from Fulsom Hall, scour the village for who had the coins and search the countryside for signs of excavation and Harris combs through the village's country-house libraries amassing evidence of a Roman compound somewhere near, where the coins actually came from remains frustratingly elusive.

Then Therese recognizes Harris, who is more than he's pretending to be. She also notes the romance burgeoning between Harris and Honor Webster, and given the girl doesn't know Harris's full name, let alone his fraught relationship with her uncle, Therese steps in. But while she can engineer a successful resolution to one romance-of-the-season, as well a reconciliation long overdue, another romance that strikes much closer to home is beyond her ability to manipulate.

Meanwhile, the search for the source of the coins goes on, but time is running out. Will Therese's grandchildren and their Fulsom Hall helpers locate the Roman merchant's villa Harris is sure lies near before they all must leave the village for Christmas with their families?

Third in series. A novel of 70,000 words. A Christmas tale of antiquities, reconciliation, romance, and requited love.

OTHER TITLES BY STEPHANIE LAURENS

LADY OSBALDESTONE'S
PLUM PUDDINGS

LADY OSBALDESTONE'S PLUM PUDDINGS
Copyright © 2019 by Savdek Management Proprietary Limited
ISBN: 978-1-925559-21-7

Cover design by Savdek Management Pty. Ltd.

First print publication: October, 2019

Savdek Management Proprietary Limited, Melbourne, Australia.
www.stephanielaurens.com
Email: admin@stephanielaurens.com

The names Stephanie Laurens and the Cynsters and the SL Logo are registered trademarks of Savdek Management Proprietary Ltd.

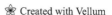 Created with Vellum

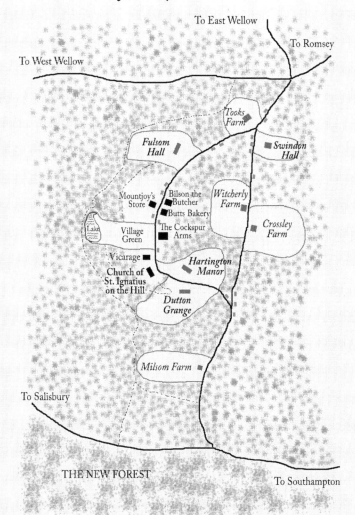

Little Moseley, Hampshire

To East Wellow

To Romsey

To West Wellow

Tooks Farm

Fulsom Hall

Swindon Hall

Mountjoy's Store

Bilson the Butcher

Witcherly Farm

Butts Bakery

Crossley Farm

Lake

Village Green

The Cockspur Arms

Vicarage

Hartington Manor

Church of St. Ignatius on the Hill

Dutton Grange

Milsom Farm

To Salisbury

THE NEW FOREST

To Southampton

THE INHABITANTS OF LITTLE MOSELEY

At Hartington Manor:

Osbaldestone, Therese, Lady Osbaldestone – *mother, grandmother, matriarch of the Osbaldestones, and arch-grande dame of the ton*

Skelton, Lord James, Viscount Skelton (Jamie) – *grandson of Therese, eldest son of Lord Rupert Skelton, Earl of Winslow, and Celia, née Osbaldestone*

Skelton, George – *grandson of Therese, second son of Lord Rupert Skelton, Earl of Winslow, and Celia, née Osbaldestone*

Skelton, Lady Charlotte (Lottie) – *granddaughter of Therese, eldest daughter of Lord Rupert Skelton, Earl of Winslow, and Celia, née Osbaldestone*

North, Amanda Charlotte (Mandy) – *granddaughter of Therese, eldest child of Reginald North, Lord North, and Henrietta, née Osbaldestone*

North, Melissa Abigail (Mel) – *granddaughter of Therese, second daughter of Reginald North, Lord North, and Henrietta, née Osbaldestone*

Live-in staff:

Crimmins, Mr. George – *butler*

Crimmins, Mrs. Edwina – *housekeeper, wife of Mr. Crimmins*

Haggerty, Mrs. Rose – *cook, widow*

Orneby, Miss Harriet – *Lady Osbaldestone's very superior dresser*

Simms, Mr. John – *groom-cum-coachman*

Daily staff:

Foley, Mr. Ned – *gardener, younger brother of John Foley, owner of Crossley Farm*

Johnson, Miss Tilly – *kitchen maid, assistant to Mrs. Haggerty, daughter of the Johnsons of Witcherly Farm*

Wiggins, Miss Dulcie – *housemaid under Mrs. Crimmins, orphaned niece of Martha Tooks, wife of Tooks of Tooks Farm*

At Dutton Grange:

Longfellow, Christian, Lord Longfellow – *owner, ex-major in the Queen's Own Dragoons*

Longfellow, Eugenia, Lady Longfellow – *née Fitzgibbon, older half sister of Henry*

Longfellow, Cedric Christopher – *baby son of Christian and Eugenia*

Hendricks, Mr. – *majordomo, ex-sergeant who served alongside Major Longfellow*

Jiggs, Mr. – *groom-cum-stable hand, ex-batman to Major Longfellow*

Wright, Mrs. – *housekeeper, widow*

Cook – *cook*

Jeffers, Mr. – *footman*

Johnson, Mr. – *stableman, cousin of Thad Johnson of Witcherly Farm*

At Fulsom Hall:

Fitzgibbon, Sir Henry – *owner, younger brother of Eugenia Longfellow*

Mrs. Woolsey, Ermintrude – *cousin of Henry and Eugenia's father, widow*

Mountjoy, Mr. – *butler, cousin of Cyril Mountjoy of Mountjoy's Store*

Fitts, Mrs. – *housekeeper*

Phipps – *Henry's valet*

Billings, Mr. – *Henry's groom*

Hillgate, Mr. – *stableman*

Terry – *stable lad*

James – *footman*

Visitors:

Dagenham, Julian, Viscount Dagenham (Dags) – *eldest son of the Earl of Carsely, friend of Henry from Oxford*

Kilburn, Thomas – *friend of Henry from Oxford*

Wiley, the Honorable George – *heir to Viscount Worth, friend of Henry from Oxford*

Carnaby, Roger – *friend of Henry from Oxford*

At Swindon Hall:
Swindon, Mr. Horace (Major) – *owner, ex-army major, married to Sarah*
Swindon, Mrs. Sarah (Sally) – *wife of Horace*
Colton, Mr. – *butler*
Colton, Mrs. – *housekeeper*
Mrs. Higgins – *the cook*
Various other staff

At the Vicarage of the Church of St. Ignatius on the Hill:
Colebatch, Reverend Jeremy – *minister*
Colebatch, Mrs. Henrietta – *the reverend's wife*
Filbert, Mr. Alfred – *deacon and chief bell-ringer*
Mr. Moody – *choirmaster*
Mrs. Moody – *wife of Mr. Moody, organist*
Hatchett, Mrs. – *housekeeper and cook*
Visitors:
Webster, Professor Hildebrand – *professor of antiquities, Brentmore College, Oxford*
Webster, Miss Honor – *assistant to Professor Webster, his niece*

At Butts's Bakery on the High Street:
Butts, Mrs. Peggy – *the baker, wife of Fred*
Butts, Mr. Fred – *Peggy's husband, village handyman*
Butts, Fiona – *Peggy and Fred's daughter*
Butts, Ben – *Peggy and Fred's son*

At Bilson's Butchers in the High Street:
Bilson, Mr. Donald – *the butcher*
Bilson, Mrs. Freda – *Donald's wife*
Bilson, Mr. Daniel – *Donald and Freda's eldest son*
Bilson, Mrs. Greta – *Daniel's wife*
Bilson, William (Billy) – *Daniel and Greta's son, Annie's twin*
Bilson, Annie – *Daniel and Greta's daughter, Billy's twin*

At the Post Office and Mountjoy's General Store in the High Street:
Mountjoy, Mr. Cyril – *proprietor, cousin of Mountjoy, butler at Fulsom Hall*
Mountjoy, Mrs. Gloria – *Cyril's wife*
Mountjoy, Mr. Richard (Dick) – *Cyril and Gloria's eldest son*

Mountjoy, Mrs. Cynthia – *Dick's wife*
Mountjoy, Gordon – *Dick and Cynthia's son*
Mountjoy, Martin – *Dick and Cynthia's second son*

At the Cockspur Arms Public House in the High Street:
Whitesheaf, Mr. Gordon – *proprietor*
Whitesheaf, Mrs. Gladys – *Gordon's wife*
Whitesheaf, Mr. Rory – *Gordon and Gladys's eldest son*
Whitesheaf, Cameron (Cam) – *Gordon and Gladys's second son*
Whitesheaf, Enid (Ginger) – *Gordon and Gladys's daughter*

At Tooks Farm:
Tooks, Edward – *farmer, keeper of the village's flock of geese*
Tooks, Martha – *Edward's wife, aunt of Dulcie, Lady Osbaldestone's housemaid*
Tooks, Mirabelle – *eldest daughter of Edward and Martha*
Tooks, Johnny – *eldest son of Edward and Martha*
Tooks, Georgina – *younger daughter of Edward and Martha*
Tooks, Cameron – *younger son of Edward and Martha*

At Milsom Farm:
Milsom, Mr. George – *farmer*
Milsom, Mrs. Flora – *wife of George, works part-time in the bakery with her sister Peggy Butts*
Milsom, Robert – *eldest son of George and Flora*
Milsom, William – *younger son of George and Flora*

At Crossley Farm:
Foley, Mr. John – *farmer, brother of Ned, Lady Osbaldestone's gardener*
Foley, Mrs. Sissy – *wife of John*
Foley, William (Willie) – *son of John and Sissy*
Various other Foley children, nephews, and nieces

At Witcherly Farm:
Johnson, Mr. Thaddeus (Thad) – *farmer, father of Tilly, Lady Osbaldestone's kitchen maid, and cousin of Mrs. Haggerty, Lady Osbaldestone's cook, cousin of Johnson, stableman at Dutton Grange*
Johnson, Mrs. Millicent (Millie) – *wife of Thad, mother of Tilly*
Johnson, Jessie – *daughter of Thad and Millie, Tilly's younger sister*

Various other Johnson children

Others from farther afield:
Goodrich, Mr. Callum Harris – *scholarly explorer and dealer in antiquities*
Pyne, Mr. – *woodcutter from East Wellow*
Hinkley, Mrs. – *housekeeper of Professor Webster's house in Oxford*

CHAPTER 1

DECEMBER 1, 1812. HARTINGTON MANOR, LITTLE MOSELEY, HAMPSHIRE

"*J* have a job for you, children. And for Mandy and Melissa as well." Therese, Lady Osbaldestone, halted in the middle of her private parlor and waved forward her butler, Crimmins, who had followed her into the room.

Crimmins was carrying two large glass jars filled with coins; he walked to the low table between the chaise and the armchairs before the fireplace and carefully set down both jars.

Therese's grandchildren, Jamie, George, and Lottie—the three older children of Therese's younger daughter, Celia—had delighted Therese and the manor staff by insisting on returning for the third year in a row to spend the weeks leading up to Christmas with their grandmama, the manor household, and the villagers of Little Moseley. Now ten, nine, and seven years old respectively, behind the restrained social façades all three were slowly perfecting as befitted their station in life, the trio remained the same scamps who had first burst on the village consciousness by tying together the ropes of the church bells and attempting to play a peal.

This year, the three stalwarts had been accompanied by the daughters of Therese's older daughter, Henrietta. The younger, Melissa, had joined the festivities in Little Moseley the previous year, and this time, Melissa's older sister, Amanda, known to all as Mandy, had insisted on coming as well.

Therese suspected Mandy had been intrigued by Melissa's reports of Little Moseley—and by the positive change in Melissa after her previous visit—and had come to see what was so special about a tiny village in Hampshire. As a significant factor in Melissa's improvement last year had been the impact of Viscount Dagenham, another visitor to the village, Therese had to wonder whether this year's events would live up to Mandy's—and Melissa's—expectations.

The five had arrived yesterday, all together in the Winslow carriage, which had traveled from Winslow Abbey in Northamptonshire—seat of the Earls of Winslow and Jamie, George, and Lottie's home—via London and North House, Lord North's residence in Mount Street, collecting sixteen-year-old Mandy and fifteen-year-old Melissa before rolling on to rural Hampshire.

Therese had been thrilled to welcome all five children and had been particularly pleased to see the smile on Melissa's face and the light of anticipation in her eyes.

Having learned from experience, Therese had organized a task to keep the children occupied, and with breakfast done and louring skies and an icy wind making venturing out unappealing, this morning seemed an opportune time to introduce her distraction.

As Crimmins stepped back, Jamie, George, and Lottie dropped to their knees around the table and, eyes wide, examined the jars. Lottie poked one. "What are these?"

George squinted through the glass. "They're pennies, I think."

Therese nodded. "Indeed. They're coins donated by the villagers to be used as good-luck tokens in the plum puddings the manor is making for the village."

That year's harvest had resulted in a bumper crop of damson plums—so many luscious plums that no one had known what to do with all the fruit, until Mrs. Haggerty, the manor's cook, had suggested using her special recipe for Christmas plum pudding, and given the quantity of fruit available, Therese had hit on the notion of making plum puddings for the entire village as the manor's contribution to the Christmas festivities.

The manor staff had embraced the idea, and when Therese had mentioned it to others, the villagers—many of whom were aware of Mrs. Haggerty's culinary skills—had leapt on the notion. The Whitesheafs, who owned and operated the Cockspur Arms Public House, just along the village lane, had insisted that, as the manor was providing the puddings, then the rest of the village should throw in their silver pennies to be used as the traditional good-luck tokens buried within each pudding.

Although Therese had been prepared to donate the pennies herself, faced with the insistence of the villagers and cognizant of the issue of pride, she'd acquiesced to the Whitesheafs' suggestion, and two large jars had duly been set out, one on the bar at the Arms and the other on the counter of Mountjoy's Store, farther up the lane.

"One jar is from the Arms, and the other, from Mountjoy's." Therese watched Jamie examine one jar, then carefully ease off the lid.

Jamie and Lottie peered inside.

Lottie dipped in her small hand, lifted out a handful of coins, and let the silvery discs slip through her fingers; they tinkled as they struck the others in the jar.

"What do you want us to do with these, Grandmama?" Jamie looked up at Therese.

Unable to hold back any longer, Mandy and Melissa—who'd been doing an excellent imitation of superior young ladies—dropped from the chaise to their knees on the other side of the low table. They, too, looked questioningly Therese's way.

She smiled, glanced around, and stepped back to allow Mrs. Crimmins, the manor's housekeeper, to ferry in a tray of cloths and assorted stiff-bristled brushes. The maids, Tilly and Dulcie, followed, each carefully carrying a basin of water—one sporting soapy suds, the other, clean, clear water.

Jamie and George slid the jars to the far end of the table, and Mrs. Crimmins and the maids arranged their supplies before the children, then, smiling, stepped back and retreated, leaving Therese to explain, "Before we can put any coins into puddings, the coins must be washed until they're clean, then dried and polished."

"Until they gleam!" Lottie grinned at Therese.

Therese graciously inclined her head. "If at all possible. It's always more uplifting to discover gleaming silver in one's pudding, rather than a tarnished coin."

Mandy had ducked her head to peer into one of the jars. "Do we clean them all?"

"As far as you're able," Therese replied. "With five pairs of hands, it shouldn't take too long. I would think you'll be done by the time the gong for luncheon sounds."

"Let's tip out the jars, then work through the coins." Carefully, with the others putting their hands on the table to contain rolling coins, Jamie upended one of the jars.

They mounded the coins into a stable pile. George drew several coins toward him, studied them, then looked at Therese. "They aren't all pennies." He glanced at the pile. "There are threepennies and sixpences as well."

Therese arched her brows. "It seems some in the village have been generous." She thought for a second, then said, "I suspect we'd better separate the denominations. Make stacks of each—pennies, threepennies, and sixpences. And keep any non-silver coins aside—they can't go into puddings."

"Yes, Grandmama," the five chorused.

Therese lingered long enough to see the five settle, remarkably amicably, to their task. Somewhat to her surprise, Mandy didn't attempt to translate her status as eldest into being the leader; that mantle clearly rested on Jamie's shoulders, as if by unstated acclaim. Under his direction, he, George, and Lottie washed and scrubbed the coins, while Mandy and Melissa dried and polished them.

"Once you've finished polishing the coins, stack them as pennies, threepennies, and sixpences," Jamie instructed his older cousins.

Sorting the drying and polishing cloths, Mandy and Melissa merely nodded.

Therese hid a smile and left them to it. She retreated to her writing desk beneath the windows overlooking the forecourt and settled to deal with her correspondence.

The clink of coins and the murmur of children's voices formed a pleasant backdrop as Therese scribed letters to her far-flung acquaintance. At one point, Crimmins entered with mugs of cocoa and biscuits for the workers and a small pot of tea for Therese. Pausing in her industry, she remained at the desk, sipping and observing.

The children barely paused to gulp down their cocoa and munch the shortbread biscuits before returning to their task; they'd made it a game to see how well they could clean each coin—how silvery they could make it —not in competition with each other but rather as a united force determined to eradicate the bane of tarnished coins.

Smiling to herself, Therese set aside her empty cup and returned to her letters.

She finally signed and sealed her fifth and last missive and placed it with the others for Crimmins to take to the post office, which was part of Mountjoy's Store.

Therese rose and looked down the room at the handsome onyx clock on the mantelpiece, then lowered her gaze to the activity on and around the low table before the fire. "My dears, it's nearly time for luncheon. How are you progressing?"

"We're almost done!" Jamie glanced up and grinned, then returned to roughly sorting the coins. "The stacks got mixed up. George and Lottie have the keenest eyes, so they're checking each coin and putting it in the right pile."

Therese noted that George and Lottie were peering closely at each coin before placing it in one of the three clusters of stacked coins before them.

"And these"—Mandy swished her hand in the rinsing bowl and fished out four silver pennies—"are the last of the scrubbed coins."

"We just need to dry and polish them"—Melissa reached for two of the coins—"and give them to George and Lottie, and we'll be finished."

"Excellent! As soon as you are, tidy up here, then come through to the dining room." Therese turned toward her writing desk. "I'm going to give my letters to Crimmins. I'll see you at the table."

She left behind her a flurry of activity as George and Lottie, frowning in concentration, verified the washed and polished coins as fast as they could, with Jamie passing the coins he'd sorted to them for a final verdict.

On the other side of the table, Melissa and Mandy grinned at each other as they dried and rubbed the remaining coins, pausing to hold each up to check its cleanliness and its gleam, then rubbing and polishing some more.

Finally, they pushed the last coins across the table to Jamie. "That's it!" Mandy declared.

"Now to tidy up." Melissa collected the used rags and cloths and placed them on the tray with the brushes.

Mandy peered into the basins, noted the lowered levels in both, then carefully tipped the water from one basin into the other.

Jamie nudged the final coins toward George. "Here," he said to Mandy, "I'll help." He gripped the almost-full bowl and raised it, allowing Mandy to slide the empty bowl beneath.

"That," Mandy said, as Jamie lowered the full bowl into the empty one, "will make it easier for Crimmins."

"What's this?"

They all looked at George, who was squinting at a coin—one of those Jamie had just passed him.

"It isn't a penny." George shook his head. "Not like any silver penny I've ever seen."

Lottie leaned closer, then reached out and took the coin from George's fingers. She turned it in hers, scrutinizing one face, then the other. "It's not a sixpence or a threepenny, either. And it doesn't have any of the usual people on the back."

"Let me see." Jamie held out a hand, and Lottie surrendered the coin.

She returned to the six coins she had yet to sort into their appropriate pile. She quickly worked through them, then paused with one coin in her fingers. "Here's another one."

"Really?" George leaned over to look, then nodded. "It's the same or as near as makes no odds." Immediately, he bent over the last four coins on the table before him. "Penny, penny, sixpence, and..." He hesitated, then held up the last coin. "Another odd one, but not the same."

Jamie frowned. "So we have three silver coins that aren't pennies, threepennies, or sixpences."

"Coins of the realm," Mandy put in.

Jamie nodded. "Yes—three silver coins that aren't coins of the realm. Two are alike, and the third is different again."

The five exchanged glances.

The resonant *bong* of the gong summoning them to luncheon reverberated through the house.

The children's gazes met again, then they scrambled to their feet.

"Let's go and wash and tidy ourselves," Mandy said, "then show the coins to Grandmama."

Six minutes later, the five filed into the dining room.

Already seated at the table's head, Therese took in their expressions—ones of puzzled curiosity—and arched her brows in mute query.

In reply, while the others slipped into their seats about the table, Jamie approached and laid three coins on the snowy-white cloth beside Therese's plate. "Among the last coins, we found these."

"Did you, indeed?" She peered at the coins. After a second, she groped for her lorgnettes, found and deployed them, and examined the coins more closely.

Jamie slipped onto the chair to her left.

"Of all the coins we cleaned," Melissa said from her place on Therese's right, "those three are the most worn away."

"We couldn't make out the writing." George tipped his head. "Well, other than to know it isn't like what's on any of our normal coins."

"We wondered," Jamie said, "if these coins might be old."

"Hmm—I rather think you're right." Therese straightened. Her gaze still on the coins, she snapped her lorgnettes shut, then released them to hang on their ribbon about her neck. "I suspect these might be Roman coins. They're certainly foreign. As for how old they might be...I fear I can't even hazard a guess."

The door opened, and Crimmins came in, bearing a steaming tureen from which a tantalizing aroma issued forth.

Noting the sudden focusing of the children's attention on the tureen and the platter of freshly baked rolls Mrs. Crimmins brought in, Therese hid a smile. "Let's eat first—after all your hard work this morning, you must be quite ravenous. After the meal, we can decide what to do with your discovery."

With murmurs of agreement, the children applied themselves to the soup, the rolls, and the pies that followed.

By the time the empty platters and plates had been cleared and the five turned expectant gazes once more on Therese, she had their way forward worked out. "I don't know enough about the field of numismatics." She looked at Jamie and George. "Do you know what that is?"

The boys exchanged a glance, then George guessed, "The study of coins?"

Therese smiled. "Indeed. And I know even less about ancient coins, so I suggest we seek some scholarly advice."

"From whom?" Jamie asked.

"Is there someone in the village who knows about old coins?" Mandy's tone signaled both surprise and hope.

"Not that I'm aware of," Therese replied. "But in seeking such a person, there is someone we can ask. Someone who, most likely, will be able to steer us in the right direction." She let her gaze circle the table, touching each eager face. "However, before we set out with these odd coins in hand, we should deliver the fruits of your morning's labors—the cleaned and polished coins for the puddings—to Mrs. Haggerty or at least into Crimmins's keeping."

The children nodded and pushed back their chairs. "We washed and dried the jars," Melissa said. "We can put the coins back for safekeeping."

Therese held up a hand, staying the exodus. "Before you return the coins to the jars, might I suggest you make one last careful check, to make sure there are no more strange and alien coins in the collection?"

Already on their feet, Jamie and George exchanged a glance. "We'll check," George said.

"I'll hold these." Therese swept the three coins into her palm. "Go and deal with the other coins, then come and find me, and we'll take these odd ones to the vicarage and see what counsel Reverend Colebatch has to offer."

The five hurried out of the dining room, leaving Therese smiling. Her holiday distraction was bidding fair to being more diverting than she'd anticipated.

∼

Lottie's and George's keen eyes hadn't played them false; the children unearthed no additional odd coins lurking among the pennies, threepennies, and sixpences.

With the rest of the collection delivered into Crimmins's care, the five donned their coats, scarves, boots, and mittens and joined Therese in the front hall. She surveyed them critically—it was threatening to sleet outside—but reassured all five were well rugged up, she held out the three coins they'd left with her. "One of you should carry your find."

She'd expected Jamie to step up, but together with George, Lottie, and Melissa, he looked at Mandy—who was looking expectantly at Jamie.

He shook his head. "Not me—you're the eldest, and you're part of our group. You should carry our discovery."

Mandy blinked, and a touch of color tinted her cheeks. She hesitated, then said, "If you're sure?"

"We're sure you're the eldest," George said, "so yes, we're sure."

Mandy pinked a touch more, then stepped forward and drew out her handkerchief. She laid the lawn square over her gloved palm, and after Therese set the three old coins on the fine fabric, Mandy carefully knotted the ends to form a small bundle. "There." She tucked the bundle into her pocket. "Now they'll be safe."

With everyone satisfied—and Therese quietly proud of Jamie and the others for making Mandy's acceptance as one of them so plain—they set out to negotiate the drive and the short walk to the vicarage.

Given the threatening weather, they kept to the lane rather than taking their usual route up the church drive and through the graveyard. Being devoid of distractions—such as gravestones—the way via the lane was quicker, and in no time at all, Therese was nodding at Jamie to tug the vicarage's bell chain, which he did with enthusiastic vigor.

Henrietta Colebatch opened the door. Her face lit when she saw Therese and her brood.

Therese returned her smile. "Good afternoon, Henrietta."

"Good afternoon, my lady—and to all your young ones, too!"

The children immediately chorused "Good afternoon, Mrs. Colebatch" and bobbed and bowed.

Henrietta beckoned them inside. "Do come in out of the cold—such a nasty wind today."

They quickly filed over the threshold and were soon ensconced in the shabby yet comfortable vicarage sitting room. The fire had been built up and threw out welcome heat.

Henrietta waved at the lighted lamps. "I've had to close the curtains—when the wind rushes in from the northeast, it worms its way past the window frames, and the drafts are horrendous."

Therese introduced Mandy, who rose and bobbed a curtsy. Therese continued, "And you will remember the others, although I daresay the boys, at least, have grown several inches over the past year."

"Indeed, they have," Henrietta replied. "And little Lottie has grown, too." She smiled on all three and exchanged nods with Melissa. "It's lovely to see you all back again, my dears. The rest of the village will be delighted as well—indeed, our new choirmaster, Mr. Moody, is hoping to put together a special choir for the carol service in the same way that Mr. Mortimer did last year. Mr. Moody was hoping more of our regular visitors would arrive to swell his numbers."

Therese looked at her grandchildren and noted that the four who had formed part of Mortimer's memorable choir looked keen, while Mandy looked curious and hopeful. "I believe you can inform Mr. Moody that the manor can supply five reasonably well-trained voices." Her grandchildren threw her encouraging looks, and she smiled, then turned to Henrietta. "But the choir and general village events are not what has brought us to your door. By any chance, is Reverend Colebatch available?"

"Jeremy's in his study." Henrietta pushed to her feet. "Let me see if I can winkle him out."

"Tell him we're here to pick his brains regarding old coins," Therese said.

Henrietta's brows rose. "I suspect that will bring him running."

Her words were prophetic; while Reverend Jeremy Colebatch didn't quite run, he certainly strode into the room with a spring in his step.

"Well, then." He clapped his hands together and beamed. "What have we here?" After exchanging nods with Therese, he greeted Jamie, George, and Lottie with genuine pleasure, acknowledged Melissa and Mandy, then sank into the worn armchair beside Therese. "I have to admit I've been wrestling with my Sunday sermon for hours and would welcome any distraction. So!" He widened his eyes at Therese, then glanced at the children. "How may I be of assistance?"

Therese gestured to Mandy, who had pulled out her handkerchief and was loosening the knot. "As you know," Therese said, "the village has been collecting coins—silver pennies, with the occasional threepenny and sixpence thrown in—for use in the plum puddings. While cleaning the collected coins this morning, the children discovered these."

With the handkerchief spread on her palm, the coins shining against the white, Mandy leaned forward and held out her hand so the reverend could examine their find.

He looked, then reached into his pocket and drew out a pair of pince-nez. After balancing them on his nose, he peered again, then picked up one of the coins and studied it—first one side, then the reverse.

Reverend Colebatch blinked. "Good heavens!" He squinted again, then returned the coin and picked up another.

The children exchanged excited glances and waited, their gazes following the reverend's every move, every twitch of expression crossing his face.

Finally, Reverend Colebatch returned the third coin to Mandy's palm, glanced briefly at Therese, then looked at the children. "Am I to take it you found these coins mixed in with all the rest?"

Jamie nodded. "Do you know what they are?"

"Yes and, sadly, no. I strongly suspect all three are Roman, but while I've heard of the like, I've never actually seen Roman coins myself. I can't tell you anything of what type of coin they are or what period or reign they're from." The reverend held up a finger. "However, I know of an antiquities scholar who, I believe, will be able to tell you all you wish to know about these coins."

"Who?" George asked.

"An old friend from my university days—Professor Hildebrand Webster of Brentmore College in Oxford. He has a sound reputation, established over many years, in the field of ancient artifacts, and these coins, I believe, fall firmly within his area of expertise." The reverend glanced at Therese, then looked at the children. "If you wish it, I would be happy to write to the professor and tell him of your discovery and ask his advice as to how best to proceed."

Therese looked at the children and arched her brows.

The five exchanged glances, then Jamie—who, when it came to Reverend Colebatch, appeared to be the elected spokesman—nodded. "That sounds like an excellent idea. Until we know what the coins are, we don't even know if there's anything to be excited about."

"Exactly so!" Reverend Colebatch clapped his palms on the chair's arms and pushed to his feet. "I'll write straightaway—although I warn you, even if my letter goes out in tomorrow morning's mail, it'll be the better part of a week before we can hope to hear back..." He paused, head cocking in thought, then went on, "Of course, knowing Hildebrand, it's most likely he'll come himself." Reverend Colebatch refocused on the children and grinned. "I can't imagine he won't want to examine these coins in person."

To Therese's eyes, the children looked a trifle less enthused at the notion of an erudite professor descending on them and their find, but all five managed a grateful smile.

"Perhaps," she said, "while we're waiting for the professor to write back, the children might attempt to learn how the coins found their way into our collection. Once we know who put the coins in the jar, presumably, we'll be able to learn where that person found them."

"Indeed!" Reverend Colebatch clapped his hands together and gripped, as if to restrain his building excitement. "If Hildebrand comes to examine the coins, that, undoubtedly, will be the very first thing he'll want to know." He looked at the children. "This could lead to a very important discovery for the entire village." With a last nod to them all, he swung on his heel. "I'll take myself off and write that letter forthwith."

Mrs. Colebatch insisted on serving them afternoon tea, and as the scones of her cook, Mrs. Hatchett, were a legend in the village, everyone readily acquiesced.

Once the scones were devoured and the teacups drained, Therese and her tribe took their leave of Mrs. Colebatch, who, given the reverend hadn't reappeared, promised to ensure that the vital letter was completed, properly addressed, and sent out for the post first thing in the morning. "Never fear," Mrs. Colebatch said and waved them on their way.

The sky was darkening ominously, and the wind had risen, howling through the treetops as they made their way along the lane and up the manor's drive.

Therese walked with the children around her, Jamie and George solicitously flanking her, instinctively behaving as their very correct father would.

"Where should we start our search?" Lottie asked.

"How should we search?" Mandy looked at the others.

George glanced back along the lane. "Perhaps we should pop along to the Arms and Mountjoy's Store before the store closes for the day and ask if anyone there knows about our odd coins."

It was already after four o'clock, and the light was swiftly fading. "I suggest," Therese said, "that in this case, a logical approach will serve you best. I would advise spending the evening planning, then you may commence your hunt in the most effective manner in the morning."

Her pronouncement met with ready agreement; none of them truly wished to forsake the warmth of her private parlor for the increasingly frigid darkness.

"We'll draw up a plan," Jamie declared. "A campaign to discover the source of our coins."

CHAPTER 2

$\mathcal{T}$he following morning, Jamie and Mandy led the way into Mountjoy's Store. Mrs. Mountjoy was serving behind the counter; the five children waited to one side until she was free of customers. When she looked inquiringly their way, Jamie and Mandy stepped forward.

"Good morning, Mrs. Mountjoy," Jamie politely said.

"Good morning, your lordship." Mrs. Mountjoy smiled. "And what can I do for you and yours today?"

"We've come about some odd coins we found in the jars, mixed up with the pennies for the plum puddings." Jamie glanced at Mandy. "This is another of my cousins, Melissa's sister, Mandy."

Mandy nodded to Mrs. Mountjoy. "Good morning, ma'am." Mandy showed Mrs. Mountjoy the coins, once again displayed on her handkerchief.

"We think the coins are old," Jamie went on. "Possibly very old."

"Reverend Colebatch is writing to an Oxford professor about them," George put in, "and in the meantime, we've volunteered to help by finding out where the coins came from."

"If we could find out who put them in the jar," Lottie piped up, "we could ask them."

Mrs. Mountjoy, who had been peering at the coins, straightened and smiled at Lottie. "I see. But I'm afraid I don't know who that was." The shopkeeper looked at Jamie. "I've never seen coins like that before. Are you sure they were in the jar from here?"

Jamie pulled a face. "We can't say. We only found them after we'd tipped out both jars and cleaned all the coins."

"We wondered," Melissa said, "if you would mind asking your customers when they stop by if they'd noticed having any odd coins. Coins that looked old and not like our normal coins."

Mrs. Mountjoy pursed her lips, but after a moment, she nodded. "No harm in asking. I'll speak with Cyril and our sons and daughter-in-law— they mind the shop, too—about asking all our customers." She nodded at Mandy as she retied her handkerchief with the coins inside. "It's possible someone will remember handling strange coins."

"If you don't mind," Jamie said, "we'll call in every day to see if anyone has remembered the coins."

Mrs. Mountjoy smiled. "Eager as ever, I see." She tapped the counter. "If any of us hear anything, we'll be sure to leave a message for you here."

They thanked Mrs. Mountjoy and left the shop.

"Next stop, the Cockspur Arms," Jamie declared.

They started walking down the lane toward the public house, which faced the village green.

"How often do the villagers come into the store?" Mandy asked.

Jamie glanced at her, then grimaced. "It might be a week or more before all the regular customers stop by."

"And there are some who live farther out," George mused. "They might only come into the village every few weeks—not every week."

Melissa sighed. "So even if the Mountjoys ask everyone who enters the shop over the next week, they still might not speak with the person who put the coins in the jar."

"We don't even know if the jar from the store was the one the coins were in," Mandy pointed out.

"Hoi, the manor tribe!"

The hail had them halting and turning to look back up the lane.

A group of five young gentlemen had, apparently, been ambling into the village; now, the group lengthened their strides. The gentleman in the lead was of medium height and stocky build, with curly blond hair framing a pleasant face, currently wreathed in a beaming smile.

Jamie, George, and Lottie beamed delightedly in return. Melissa smiled more shyly.

"Henry!" Jamie raised a hand in salute—only to have Henry seize it and shake it vigorously.

"Well met, young Skelton." Releasing Jamie's hand, Henry nodded to George and Lottie. "And George and Lottie, too. And Miss Melissa." Henry sketched a bow; as he straightened, he looked curiously at Mandy. "We'd wondered if you lot would come again this year. It wouldn't be the same roll-up to Christmas without the whole gang, what?" Before Jamie could answer, Henry smiled at Mandy. "And who's this? Another cousin? Pray introduce us."

Jamie grinned. "Yes, this is another cousin—Miss Amanda North, Melissa's older sister. Mandy, this is Sir Henry Fitzgibbon of Fulsom Hall, which lies at the northern end of the village."

Mandy extended her hand to Henry. "I'm delighted to meet you, Sir Henry."

Henry grasped her gloved fingers and bowed over them. "The pleasure is mine, Miss North." He released her and waved to the gentlemen flanking him. "Allow me to present my chums. Viscount Dagenham."

The dark-haired gentleman standing on Henry's right dragged his pale-gray gaze from Melissa and bowed to Mandy. "A pleasure, Miss North."

Mandy bobbed a curtsy. "My lord."

Henry waved at the tall gentleman on his left. "This is Mr. Thomas Kilburn. And beyond him is Roger Carnaby, and the last in line there is George Wiley."

Bows and greetings were exchanged, with Henry adding, "Roger missed the festivities last year, so he and Miss Melissa haven't met, either."

Jamie performed the required introductions, and Melissa shifted her attention from Dagenham long enough to bestow a smile on Roger.

The next five minutes went in learning what everyone had been up to since their last encounter the previous year. "Fun and games, that was," Henry reminisced with a fond smile. "Searching high and low for that blasted book of carols, but we triumphed and found it in time." He focused on Jamie, then glanced at George, Lottie, Melissa, and Mandy. "I say, you don't have a hunt on these holidays, do you?"

Jamie looked smug. "As a matter of fact..." Then he grinned and, with interjections from George and Lottie, related their discovery of the strange, old, probably Roman coins in the jars of pennies collected for the plum puddings.

"Plum puddings?" Thomas looked puzzled.

Henry explained about Lady Osbaldestone's offer to supply plum puddings for the entire village. "So we all chipped in our spare pennies for the good-luck tokens."

"They were collected in two jars," Melissa said. "One in the Arms, the other in Mountjoy's Store."

"Reverend Colebatch thinks that the coins are Roman," Jamie said, "and he's written to a friend of his—a professor of antiquities in Oxford."

"He—the reverend—thinks the professor will come to see the coins and will want to know where they came from," Lottie said, "so that's what we're trying to find out."

Jamie explained their current tack of trying to learn who put the coins in the jars by asking if anyone in the village remembered doing so or even remembered handling strange coins.

"If we can find out who put the coins into the jars," Melissa added, "hopefully, they'll be able to tell us where they got the coins."

Henry and his friends exchanged eager glances, then Henry turned to Jamie and the others. "It sounds as if you've another quest on your plate, and as usual, we're at loose ends. Can we help?"

Jamie exchanged a swift glance with his siblings and cousins, then smiled brightly at Henry. "I can't see why not—the more the merrier."

Henry clapped him on the shoulder. "Good man. So—what's our plan?"

Jamie and Melissa related the outcome of their discussion with Mrs. Mountjoy. "So that's Mountjoy's Store covered." Jamie swung to look down the lane. "We were just on our way to ask at the Arms."

"Good-oh!" Henry waved onward. "We'll all come and lend our weight."

It was midmorning when their company, now ten strong, pushed through the door of the Cockspur Arms. Ginger Whitesheaf was polishing tables while her brothers, Cam and Rory, were wiping and stacking glasses and mugs behind the long bar.

All three Whitesheafs smiled on seeing Henry, Jamie, George, and Lottie and nodded politely to Melissa and Mandy as well as the four visiting gentlemen.

"Good morning, Ginger," Henry said.

"Sir Henry." Ginger nodded to Jamie. "Your lordship. What can we do for you today?"

Jamie glanced into the tap. There were two old men playing a board game by the fireplace, but no one else. "We came to ask," Jamie said, "if you know of anyone who mentioned odd coins that they put into the jar of silver pennies."

Ginger's brow furrowed. "Odd coins?"

They explained, and Mandy drew out her handkerchief and showed off the coins, to the immediate interest of Henry and his friends as well as Cam and Rory. Mandy finally laid the lawn square and the coins on the bar counter so everyone could poke and prod and examine the three worn silver discs.

"Well, I never." Eventually, Cam straightened. "But to answer your question, I haven't heard anyone mention odd coins—not in any way."

"Nor me." Rory stepped back as well. "But we can ask everyone who comes in." He nodded toward the far end of the counter. "The jar was down there, by the till. Easy enough to ask every time someone pays."

"Let me speak with the pair by the fireplace." Ginger crossed to the table before the hearth, but the men shook their heads, and she came back shaking hers. "They haven't had any odd coins, and they haven't heard of anyone who has."

Jamie explained that it might be a week before the professor from Oxford arrived. "We thought if you and the Mountjoys can ask everyone who comes in over the next week, there's a decent chance we'll find whoever had these coins."

The Whitesheafs agreed. "I'll tell Ma and Pa," Rory said, "but they're not in much these days. It's usually the three of us run the place now."

The group nodded, and Jamie thanked the Whitesheafs.

While Mandy picked up the coins and her handkerchief, Henry looked at the others. "So what's next? Shall we sit and discuss whether there's anything else we can do?"

All were in favor. Henry called for jugs of mulled cider and water and ten mugs, and they repaired to a long table by the window.

Once they'd all settled about the long board, Mandy spread her hand-kerchief and the coins in the middle of the scarred surface, then Ginger arrived, balancing a tray with the requested jugs and mugs. Henry poured, watering down the cider for the younger children, and passed around the mugs.

The group sipped and stared at the coins.

Dagenham had squired Melissa to the far end of the table. She'd sat on the bench beneath the window, and he'd drawn up a chair to the table's end, by her elbow. They'd accepted mugs of cider and had sipped. Now, his voice low, Dagenham asked, "Will you be here for long?"

Melissa met his gaze. "Until the twenty-second. Apparently, the carol service is on the twenty-first—we leave for Northamptonshire the morning after."

Their muted conversation and their focus on each other served to cocoon them from the rest of the company, but George and Lottie noticed and exchanged a knowing look, then George reached out and tapped one of the old coins. "Is there any other way we might learn who had these?"

The others frowned, then Thomas asked, "Is it possible to determine which of the two jars the coins were in?"

Jamie explained what they'd done in emptying the jars to clean the coins. "So no, we can't even guess."

"Actually," Mandy said, "I can't remember there being any way to tell the jars apart—they were identical, weren't they?"

Jamie, George, and Lottie agreed.

George Wiley, sitting opposite Lottie, humphed. "What about how far down in the jars the old coins were? That might give us some idea of when they were added."

After a moment of thinking, Jamie glanced at George, then at Mandy, seated opposite. "I tipped up one jar, then the other."

"But," George said, "the coins were right at the bottom of the combined pile—they were among the very last coins cleaned."

Mandy nodded. "Which means"—she mimicked upending a jar on the table—"that these three coins were close to the top of the first jar you emptied."

"So the coins were high in one of the jars." George Wiley leaned forward. "That means they were put into the jar only a little while before the jar was collected."

"When were the jars taken to the manor?" Henry asked.

Jamie didn't know, but George piped up, "I heard Crimmins say he'd picked them up on Monday afternoon."

"Right, then." Henry rubbed his hands together. "So most likely the coins were put into the jar on Sunday or Monday—but the Arms doesn't open until noon on Monday, so there wouldn't have been much time then."

Roger Carnaby nodded. "Most likely Sunday afternoon or evening—

lots of people who don't come in at other times during the week will drop by village pubs then."

"But," Thomas said, "if the coins were in the jar from Mountjoy's Store, the coins would most likely have been put in on Monday morning."

Those actively discussing the issue nodded, while at the end of the table, Dagenham and Melissa remained in a bubble of their own.

"You said you were down from Oxford?" Melissa prompted.

Dagenham turned his mug around and around between his long fingers. "Yes. I've finished my studies." He paused, his gaze on the mug. "My parents are encouraging me to take a post with the Home Office, at least for a little while. Get some experience of government and governing under my belt and all that."

Melissa sipped, then volunteered, "My father's in the Foreign Office, so I know quite a lot about that sort of life."

Dagenham glanced at her, then carefully said, "I expect to be in town during the upcoming Season." He paused for a second, then asked, "You?"

"We live in town, in Mount Street, so yes, I'll be there, but I'll still be in the schoolroom, of course."

Dagenham glanced down the table at Mandy. "Is your sister out yet?"

Melissa shook her head. "She's only a year older." Melissa hesitated, then confided, "We're thinking of asking Mama and Papa to allow Mandy and me to come out together—perhaps in another three years. Mandy will be nineteen, but she says she doesn't want to rush and wouldn't mind waiting the extra year until I'm eighteen."

Dagenham blinked and stared at nothing. "Three years."

Melissa dipped her head and raised her mug.

"Strangers!" Roger Carnaby's exclamation had all at the table looking his way. He saw and reiterated, "Strangers—what if a stranger put those coins in the jar?"

Lottie looked puzzled. "Why would they? The pennies were for the village's plum puddings, not just anyone's."

Roger shrugged. "Perhaps he knew the coins were odd and wanted to be rid of them."

Henry snorted. "I suppose that's possible. We can certainly ask the Mountjoys and the Whitesheafs. The villagers tend to notice strangers, even if they're just passing through."

Ginger approached to collect their now-empty mugs and the jugs.

Jamie turned to her. "Have there been any strangers in the village recently—say, since Saturday?"

Ginger shook her head. "Not in here. Only person I haven't recognized in weeks is your cousin." She nodded at Mandy. "And she's not a stranger in the way you mean." Gathering the mugs and setting them on her tray, Ginger tipped her head toward the window. "It isn't the season for strangers wandering the countryside."

They all glanced at the window to see the glass being peppered by sleet.

"Ugh." Lottie wrinkled her nose. "I think we'd better head back to the manor. Grandmama will be watching for us."

"Well," George Wiley said, as they donned gloves and scarves, "I think we can rule out the coins being donated by a stranger. Strangers stop in at pubs—if none looked in here, it's unlikely they went to Mountjoy's."

"True." Henry rose and wound his knitted scarf about his throat. He glanced at Jamie, who was also getting to his feet. "What else can we do to determine where these coins"—Henry nodded to where Mandy was retying the coins into her handkerchief—"came from?"

At the other end of the table, Dagenham pushed to his feet. He tipped his head to Jamie. "As you said earlier, we'll need to check with both Mountjoy's and here for a full week at least to be sure the coins weren't put in by one of the villagers or a worker from one of the nearby farms."

"It's possible," Melissa said, tugging on her gloves, "that just asking at Mountjoy's and the Arms will identify who it was."

"Unless," George said as he stepped back from the table, "the person didn't know." When, puzzled, the others frowned at him, he elaborated, "When the coins were all mixed together, only Lottie and I spotted the odd ones. They're alike enough to silver pennies for anyone not paying close attention—or anyone with poor eyesight—not to notice the difference."

Jamie stared at George, then his shoulders slumped. "That means we might not get any answer at all from asking at Mountjoy's and the Arms. If the person never knew…"

George grimaced apologetically.

"Yes, well," Henry said in rousing fashion, "we're not going to let such a possibility stop us, are we?" With the others, he turned toward the door. "So how else can we find out where the coins came from?"

"Why did the coins turn up at all?" Thomas looked at the others. "How long do people—villagers especially—keep coins in their pockets? Not long, would be my guess."

George Wiley was nodding. "So they had to have got them recently—found them, perhaps?"

"Exactly," Thomas said. "We're out in the country—perhaps someone was digging holes for a new fence and found the coins in the dirt?"

"Or plowed a field," Mandy suggested.

"Not at this time of year," Henry said with a smile. "The ground's close to frozen, so no plowing, but"—he nodded at Thomas—"the point is a good one. Digging for any reason would do."

They'd reached the door and could hear the wind whipping past outside. They paused and looked at each other.

"Right," said Henry. "While we're waiting to hear from the Mountjoys or the Whitesheafs over the next week, we'll also investigate whether we can find any spot where the ground has been dug up."

"Or," Jamie said, "where there's been a landslide."

"Or a sinkhole!" George added.

Henry grinned. "That's the ticket! There are lots of possibilities." He met Jamie's eyes. "So—where should we search first?"

Four days later, the searchers were all present at Sunday service at St. Ignatius on the Hill, when, after the last hymn, Reverend Colebatch paused on the altar steps and pulled a sheet of paper from beneath his cassock. "It falls to me to announce the dates for the events with which our village traditionally celebrates Christmas."

After beaming upon his eager congregation, the reverend consulted his list and declared, "Dick Mountjoy assures me that the ice on the lake is already thick enough to be certain that the village skating party can go ahead next Thursday at two o'clock."

Eyes twinkling, the reverend waited for the children's excited whispers to fade, then went on, "Subsequently, on Wednesday, December sixteenth, the Christmas pageant will take place as usual on the village green." He glanced around the church. "We'll announce who is to be Mary and Joseph and those chosen for all the other roles next Sunday."

Speculative whispers swept around the church.

"Finally," Reverend Colebatch proclaimed, "the highlight of our festive celebrations, the carol service, will be held on the evening of Monday, December twenty-first. As you are all aware, this year, the village has welcomed to our hearts our new choirmaster, Mr. Moody, and his delightful wife and talented organist, Mrs. Moody"—the reverend inclined his head to the Moodys, who were standing beside the organ —"and on behalf of them both, I wish to extend an invitation to all our festive-season visitors"—Reverend Colebatch's gaze sought out Lady Osbaldestone's grandchildren as they sat flanking her in the front pew, then shifted to Henry and his friends, sitting two rows back on the other side of the aisle—"to join with the Moodys and our regular choristers to add depth and vigor to our choral offerings."

Reverend Colebatch looked down, consulting his notes.

Jamie, George, and Lottie shot eager, expectant glances at Mandy and Melissa, both of whom hesitated, but then nodded. Melissa turned her head and looked across the aisle at Dagenham, seated at the end of the row, next to Henry.

Dagenham had been waiting to catch her eye. He arched a brow, and Melissa arched one back, then, it seemed almost reluctantly, Dagenham inclined his head.

Beside him, Henry, Thomas, George Wiley, and Roger were grinning happily and nodding, too.

Wondering at Dagenham's resistance—wondering if she'd imagined it —Melissa faced forward as Reverend Colebatch said, "Ah, yes—here we are. The Moodys ask that all parties interested in joining the special choir for the carol service meet with them on the lawn before the church at the conclusion of this service to discuss times for practice."

Smiling, Reverend Colebatch raised his head. "And I can assure everyone that, this year, the Moodys already have the book of carols in their hands."

A chuckle circled the church, then the reverend signaled it was time for the final prayer. After he'd intoned it and the benediction, everyone made their way out of the church.

On reaching the winter-brown lawn, Therese inspected her brood. "I take it you all wish to sing in the choir again."

They assured her she'd read their eagerness correctly, although she noted Melissa looked faintly uncertain.

Mandy studied the others. "Is it really such fun?"

"You like to sing, don't you?" Lottie asked.

Mandy paused, then admitted, "Yes, I do."

"Well, this is one time you get to sing for others." Taking Mandy's hand, Lottie tugged. "Come on. I can see Mr. and Mrs. Moody over there."

The children looked at Therese for permission, and she nodded regally. "I'll return to the manor with the staff. I'll expect you for luncheon as soon as the Moodys have finished with you. Don't dally, or Mrs. Haggerty will be displeased."

"We won't!" the younger three chorused, then Jamie and George rushed off, and Lottie, Mandy, and Melissa walked after them.

Therese considered her granddaughters—Lottie and Mandy transparently eager, Melissa... Therese narrowed her eyes. "Not reluctant to sing," she murmured. "She's not sure about Dagenham."

The crowd gathering about the Moodys—a jolly-looking couple who were quick with their smiles—was sizeable. In addition to the five from the manor and the five gentlemen from Fulsom Hall, many of the villagers who sang in the regular choir were volunteering for the special choir as well. Johnny and Georgina Tooks were there, along with the Bilson twins, Annie and Billy. Also joining were Jessie Johnson, Willie Foley, plus Robert and William Milsom, ensuring the group had a good spread of children's ages as well as voices. As for adults, just as Henry and his friends ambled up, Ginger Whitesheaf and Fiona Butts came huffing along, towing Ginger's older brothers, Rory and Cam, with them.

"There's no reason you can't sing as well as these toffs," Ginger informed her brothers.

Henry grinned at the Whitesheaf brothers; Cam was the same age, and Henry had known him since birth. "Bit of friendly rivalry never went astray. Let's see what you're made of, Whitesheafs—put your voice where your mouth is, so to speak."

Battling a grin, Cam made a scoffing sound. "The congregation won't be able to hear you lads, not with Rory and me singing along."

Mr. Moody was quick to take advantage. "Right, then, gentlemen. How many basses do we have?"

While her husband sorted out the male voices, Mrs. Moody gathered the girls and divided them into sopranos and altos. While Lottie, Georgina, and Annie were much of an age, and all had high, sweet voices, Mandy and Ginger proved to have similar ranges and were deemed sopranos as well. Melissa was joined in the alto section by Jessie and Fiona.

"Well, now." Mr. Moody turned from sorting the males. "Let's put this all together, shall we?"

He directed the boys—Jamie, George, William, Robert, Willie, and Johnny—to stand with the sopranos, then lined up the three altos, followed by two tenors in Dagenham and Cam, and the baritones— Henry, Roger, and Thomas. "And lastly," Mr. Moody said, guiding his last two participants, George Wiley and Rory, into the line, "we have our two basses."

Mr. Moody stepped back. Clasping his hands before him, he surveyed his troops. "This is quite an impressive assembly. I believe we'll be able to put on a carol service to rival anything that's gone before. Even though I've heard the rapturous praise of last year's event, that is our ambition"—his eyes twinkled—"and I hope you will all join us in attempting to make it so."

They all grinned.

"So"—Mrs. Moody moved to stand beside her husband—"as to practice times, most of you will know the carols already, but blending your voices to ensure a truly great performance will require work. We've only two weeks in which to weld you into a brilliant and cohesive singing force, so if you please, we will meet here for practice on Tuesday, Thursday, and Saturday afternoons, promptly at three o'clock, and practice will last for approximately two hours. Can you all commit to that?"

Most nodded eagerly, but the Whitesheafs exchanged glances, then Rory said, "We'll need to get our parents to agree to cover our shifts behind the bar, but most likely, they will."

Mrs. Moody nodded. "Good." Like her husband, she surveyed their ranks, then beamed. "In that case, it's off to your luncheons, and we'll see you all here on Tuesday at three."

Those who lived farther afield scampered off. The manor five joined Henry and his friends, and the group ambled down the church drive.

Melissa and Dagenham fell back; together, they brought up the rear.

Silence held them—not fraught, yet not quite comfortable.

Eventually, his gaze on the path before his boots, Dagenham somewhat diffidently inquired, "Do you think the Moodys will ask us to sing 'The Holly and the Ivy' again?"

Melissa lightly shrugged. "Who's to say?" After a second, she added, "They might."

A heartbeat passed, then Dagenham asked, "If they do, will you agree?"

Melissa thought for several seconds, then tentatively ventured, "It was…special, singing that duet last year." She glanced briefly at Dagenham's face. "Wasn't it?"

He drew breath and nodded. "Yes. It was a…special moment."

Melissa straightened and raised her head. "I enjoyed it, so if they ask, I'll agree to sing it again."

Dagenham nodded. "I will, too."

The others had reached the lychgate and had halted in its shelter. As Dagenham and Melissa joined them, Jamie grumbled, "It's not encouraging that despite the Mountjoys and Whitesheafs asking everyone who has been into the store or the pub, no one has remembered handling any odd coins. I really thought we would have heard something by now."

"We have one more day," Henry pointed out. "And as the coins were at the top of one of the jars, whoever put them in might only come into the village today or tomorrow. Perhaps the Whitesheafs will find someone who knows about the coins among their customers this evening—there's always a decent crowd then."

Mandy nodded. "We can hope. But we haven't found any sign of digging or holes or any other sort of turning of the soil, so…" She grimaced. "Perhaps we should pray."

"I wonder," George Wiley murmured, "how far afield the coins might have come from."

The others stared at him, then Dagenham humphed. "That's the definition of an unanswerable question."

The wind was whipping up, its cutting edge honed with ice. The group parted with promises to send word to the others if anyone learned anything of the coins, then Melissa and Mandy hurried after their cousins up the manor drive.

Late on Monday afternoon, with the light fading, Therese stood at the window in her private parlor and, through flakes of whirling snow, peered at the steadily whitening drive.

The children had insisted they had to meet Henry and his friends and check if the Mountjoys or Whitesheafs had found anyone who remembered handling the three odd coins, hoping against hope that someone had visited the inn the previous evening or the store that morning, someone who only came into the village once a week.

For her part, Therese hoped the group weren't drowning their sorrows in mulled cider in the inn and forgetting to look out of the window. The swirling snow was thickening; given the heavy skies, they would have a decent covering by morning.

She was about to draw the curtains when she noticed three figures emerging through the veil of snow. She recognized the lanky length of Reverend Colebatch, walking alongside a heavier man. "The professor must have arrived."

The third figure was a lady, which piqued Therese's curiosity.

She rang for Crimmins and met her butler in the hall. "Reverend Colebatch is coming up the drive with two others. I'll await them in the drawing room."

"Very good, ma'am."

She'd barely taken up her stance before the fireplace when the doorbell jangled. A minute later, Crimmins announced, "Reverend Colebatch, Professor Hildebrand Webster of Brentmore College, Oxford, and Miss Webster, my lady."

Therese smiled and went forward. "Do come in and warm yourselves by the fire." Crimmins had already collected their heavy coats. Therese nodded to Reverend Colebatch, who was in the lead. "Jeremy." Then she inclined her head to the burly gentleman following. "And Professor Webster, I presume." She held out her hand, and the professor clasped it and bowed. "I must thank you for coming all this way and in such weather."

"Not at all, my lady—it's only just closed in. Our journey down was clear enough." Professor Webster's voice was growly and gruff. He was a heavyset man with a barrel chest and a paunch over which his waistcoat strained. Steel-gray curls wreathed his head, and his complexion was ruddy, but of the sort that signaled a life spent out of doors rather than an overfondness for drink. His most notable features were a pair of shaggy gray eyebrows that perched above a rather bulbous nose.

The professor waved to the young lady by his side. "Allow me to present my niece, Miss Honor Webster. She acts as my amanuensis and keeps me in line."

Therese turned to Miss Webster and was pleased to encounter a direct look from a pair of fine hazel eyes. Of average height and slender build, Honor Webster was sensibly gowned in a warm woolen carriage dress, and her golden-brown hair was restrained in a neat bun, although teasing tendrils had worked loose to bounce in corkscrew curls beside her cheeks.

Her features were pleasing, with wide eyes, arched brown brows, and delicately tinted lips. All in all, on first sight, Therese approved; she offered her hand with a smile. "It's a pleasure to make your acquaintance, my dear."

Honor Webster lightly clasped Therese's fingers and sank into a graceful curtsy. "Thank you for your welcome, my lady." Straightening, Honor glanced at her uncle, then looked inquiringly at Therese. "As soon as Uncle Hildebrand learned of your coins, nothing would do for it but that he had to come and examine them himself."

Miss Webster's tone was affectionate and indulgent, while her words were to the point.

Therese waved them to the armchairs. "Please sit, and I'll endeavor to appease your understandable curiosity. I won't be a moment."

She left the room and returned to her private parlor and her writing desk. After church yesterday, Reverend Colebatch had warned her that he expected the professor to arrive today, and that knowing the man, he would be eager to examine the coins. Understanding that academics frequently had one-track minds, Therese had ensured that the coins had remained at the manor. She released the secret drawer in her writing desk, lifted out the small pile, shut the drawer, and carried the coins to the drawing room.

The professor and Miss Webster expectantly watched as Therese entered and crossed to the low table between the armchairs they occupied, to one side of the hearth.

"These are the three coins my grandchildren stumbled across." Therese placed the coins in a row on the tabletop and stepped back.

Professor Webster leaned forward. He peered at the coins, then withdrew a jeweler's loupe from his pocket, fitted it to one eye, and picked up one coin.

Therese retreated to her favorite armchair on the other side of the fireplace and watched as, in a silence punctuated by soft grunts, the professor examined each coin.

Finally, he set the third coin back on the table and angled a shrewd look at Therese. "Where were these found?"

Rather than answer, she countered, "What are they?"

"Two Roman denarii and a siliqua, most likely from the period of occupation—I would say around 400AD. There were Roman settlements in this area around that time." He huffed and amended, "Although I suspect the denarii were minted well before that."

"Are they valuable?" Therese asked.

The professor straightened, burgeoning enthusiasm lightening his expression. "Valuable enough in their own right, but if they're indicative of a hoard, as they might well be, then *that* is truly exciting."

Therese heard the front door open, and the chatter of young voices reached them. "Ah—that will be my grandchildren." She raised her voice. "My dears, please join us. The professor has arrived, and he has information to share about the coins."

She didn't need to call twice. The drawing room door swung wide, and her brood of five trooped in, closely followed by Henry and his friends.

The professor looked taken aback by the unexpected company. Therese hid a smile and obliged with introductions, including titles and sufficient connections to ensure that the professor didn't make the mistake of imagining this group would be easily dismissed.

"Well met, Professor." Henry was the last to shake his hand. "We—indeed, the whole village—are keen to hear your verdict."

Everyone looked expectantly at Webster.

He harrumphed and repeated his assessment of the coins; describing them again clearly escalated the excitement he was fighting to contain. He concluded with an openly eager "So what I need to know now is where the coins came from."

The group of ten exchanged glances, then at Jamie's nod, Henry turned to the professor and replied, "As to that, we can't yet say. The coins were discovered mixed in with a collection of silver pennies in two jars that had been placed about the village for donations for the village's plum puddings."

Webster blinked. "Plum puddings?" He glanced at Therese. "Jars?"

Therese explained her scheme of supplying the village with plum puddings and how the villagers had insisted on donating pennies to be used for the traditional good-luck tokens. "Consequently, a jar was placed in the village store, and another was left on the bar in the local public house. Both jars were close to full with silver coins when my staff collected them on Monday afternoon."

"When we"—Jamie waved at his siblings and cousins—"cleaned the coins, we found the three odd ones." With the help of Henry, Melissa, and Dagenham, Jamie recounted their efforts thus far to learn who had put the three coins in the jar. "But although the Mountjoys and the Whitesheafs have asked everyone who has come in during the past week, no one has remembered having any strange coins."

Henry sighed. "We're at a temporary standstill. We haven't noticed any unusual earthworks—any holes or digging that might have unearthed the coins—either."

Dagenham added, "We're starting to wonder if whoever put the coins in the jar didn't even realize they were odd—that they weren't just overly worn pennies."

The professor's expression was one of frustrated impatience. "I see." He stared at nothing for several moments, then refocused on the group. "In situations such as this, there are two critical questions that need to be answered. First, where did the coins come from? And beyond that, are there any more—specifically, have they come from a hoard?"

Amused, Therese saw the entire group nod in eager fascination.

"To answer those questions," Henry said, "we need to find whoever put the coins in the jar."

"Certainly, that's the most obvious way forward," the professor acknowledged, "and I commend your efforts thus far." He glanced at his niece, then looked at Reverend Colebatch and grimaced. "I would dearly love to lead the charge myself, but I fear I have a treatise that I absolutely must complete by the end of the year."

"Indeed, you must." Honor Webster had been training a distinctly warning look on her uncle. She shifted her gaze to Therese and Reverend Colebatch and explained, "Uncle Hildebrand has been honored by one of the leading antiquarian societies and asked to write a treatise on Viking artifacts for their journal. The treatise must be submitted by the end of the year, and he has a long way to go." Her gaze returned to the professor. "He really shouldn't have come charging down to Little Moseley, but the lure of a find proved too much temptation."

The professor grumbled, "I would be a poor scholar if I didn't follow up the report of such a find."

Honor's expression softened. "I grant you that, but you really must buckle down now, uncle. It won't do to miss the deadline."

Professor Webster heaved a put-upon sigh. "You're right, of course." His gaze swung to the group of earnest searchers. "So I can't be actively involved in the search."

"But you will be staying in the village." To the rest of the room, Reverend Colebatch explained, "I've arranged for the professor and Miss Webster to use one of the church cottages." He waved to the east. "The one near the Romsey lane that Mortimer used last year. It's vacant at present."

"Indeed, indeed—the quiet here will help me concentrate." From under his bushy eyebrows, the professor slid a look at his niece. "I'll work faster here than in Oxford." Webster returned his gaze to the searchers. "So when you find any clue, I'll be available for you to consult."

Henry and Jamie were quick to assure the professor that the group would happily forge on with the search. "We'll scour the area," Henry declared, "and leave no stone unturned in hunting down where the coins came from."

"And," Jamie solemnly said, "we'll keep you informed of anything we learn."

"Excellent." The professor smiled encouragingly. "And if you need any further information, you can—"

"Ask me," Honor Webster firmly interjected. She shot her uncle a fond yet strict look. "You'll need to keep your nose to the grindstone. Those searching can report to me, and if they need to pick your brains, you may be sure I'll pass the message on. But while I can liaise with the searchers and assist you with your research, I can't write your treatise for you."

The professor looked as if he wanted to argue, but knew he had no leg to stand on. Instead, he harrumphed and grudgingly conceded.

Therese decided she approved of Honor Webster.

Reverend Colebatch beamed at the youthful crew. "I can assure you, Hildebrand, that you're leaving the search in good hands. Our group here has succeeded in quests before, and I'm sure they'll give this latest endeavor their best."

The children, Henry, and his friends confirmed that was so.

Then Reverend Colebatch glanced out of the window and blinked. "Dear me—it's coming down even faster now. We'd best be off."

Therese rose, waited while farewells were said, then accompanied the professor, his niece, and the reverend to the door.

The ten searchers trailed behind her. After closing the door on the three adults, Therese turned to see the younger group sporting frowns of varying degrees.

Dagenham summed up their dilemma. "All very well to say we'll search, but how should we proceed?"

Henry grunted. "We need to stop and think. Something will occur to one of us—it usually does."

"We have choir practice tomorrow afternoon," Melissa pointed out.

Jamie nodded. "Let's all wrack our brains and meet at choir practice tomorrow and formulate a proper plan."

Therese hid a fond smile as the others agreed. Her grandson was well on his way to becoming an experienced leader of men.

CHAPTER 3

*T*he next day dawned bright and clear, with the morning sun transforming the world into a magical place, draped in white and scattered with diamonds.

While Mandy and Melissa were content to spend the hours after breakfast reading novels by the fire, Jamie, George, and Lottie were incapable of allowing such a day to pass without doing *something*.

Something active.

Midmorning saw them rugged up against the cold and tramping through a thin blanket of snow, heading southward on the track that ran from Tooks Farm, around the rear of Fulsom Hall, past the lake, and on to the dilapidated cottage at Allard's End, at the rear of the Dutton Grange estate.

They'd gone to Tooks Farm to consult with Johnny Tooks, reasoning that if any of the village lads, who roamed far and wide through the woods, had seen unexpected digging or a landslide or anything of that nature, Johnny would have heard of it.

Johnny had been agog to learn about the three Roman coins. Sadly, he knew of no digging or disturbance of the earth, but had promised to alert the other lads to keep their eyes peeled.

Johnny was now walking with Jamie, George, and Lottie; he had to check on the village's flock of geese, which were in the final stages of fattening themselves on the fallen fruit in the abandoned orchard behind old Allard's deserted cottage.

The four had agreed that animal burrows might be places of interest, and as they walked, they scanned either side of the path, hoping to spot tracks in the snow, while idly speculating on their chances of discovering the ruins of a Roman fort, or a camp where legions had rested, or—as voiced by Lottie—the remains of a villa with a pretty mosaic floor like one she'd seen in a book.

They were rounding the western shore of the lake when George stopped and pointed up the slope. "What about a fallen tree?" They all looked at where he was pointing; a huge old tree lay on its side, wedged between two others five yards above the path. "Perhaps there's a hole where the roots came up."

"Let's take a look." Jamie started scrambling up the slope, and the other three followed.

They reached the tree and clambered over it, but even though they brushed aside snow and leaves, there was no sign of any hole or even disturbed earth.

With disappointed huffs, they straightened and brushed off their gloves.

The sound of whistling reached their ears, then Lottie looked southward, in the direction they'd been heading. "There's someone coming along the path."

Seconds later, the others heard the regular thud of boots on the path. They remained behind the fallen tree, leaning on the trunk as they waited to see who the walker was.

A stranger in a greatcoat worn open over a tweed jacket, breeches, and boots came striding into view. He was tall, and his coat fell from broad shoulders. He'd thrust his hands into his coat pockets, and his gaze was fixed on the path before him. His hair was a light brown with blond streaks scattered through it, and the planes of his face were long. Even though he'd yet to see them, his features were set in relaxed, almost-smiling lines.

Lottie shifted, and the crackle of leaves beneath her boots had the man glancing up. He spotted them, and his lips eased into a true smile. He halted and surveyed them. "Hello. What are you doing up there? Exploring?"

His likeable face and open expression were of the sort to encourage confidences.

Johnny replied, "We're searching."

"Oh?" The man arched his eyebrows. "For what?"

Jamie, George, and Lottie exchanged glances, unsure how much they should reveal, but Johnny readily volunteered, "Roman coins."

The man's eyes widened. "Really?" Rather than look disbelieving, he appeared impressed. He glanced at Jamie, George, and Lottie, then returned his gaze to Johnny. "Have you found any?"

"Three," Johnny proudly said, then amended, "Or at least, Jamie, George, and Lottie here did."

Still clearly impressed, the man looked at Jamie. "Did you, indeed?"

Given Johnny's revelations, there seemed little point in refusing to reply, and the man seemed genuinely interested and entirely unthreatening. Along with George and Lottie, Jamie nodded. "We found three Roman coins mixed in with a collection of silver pennies."

George added, "A professor from Oxford told us they were two denarii and a siliqua."

Lottie piped, "We think they might have come from a *hoard*."

That gave the man pause. After a second, he said, "There is quite a history of Roman occupation in this area."

Jamie blinked, and George asked, "Do you know much about it?"

"A bit." The man stepped back to the edge of the path and leaned his shoulders against the bole of a tree. "Ancient history is something of a hobby of mine."

He paused as if dredging his memory, then said, "I've heard about the remains of possible Roman settlements at Fordingbridge, which is not that far to the west of here, and there's been even more bits and pieces found around Twyford and Otterbourne, to the east. Nothing major yet, just bits of pots and such—no hoards—even though many people have looked." He seemed to mull over those facts, then added, "With finds to the east and finds to the west, and Roman towns at Clausentum, just north of Southampton, and Venta Belgarum—that's Winchester—and Noviomagus Reginorum, which is Chichester, all within easy reach, I would say there's a decent chance this area played host to, at the very least, the villa of a wealthy Roman, possibly even of a Roman general."

He pushed away from the tree and refocused on the children. "When coins such as yours are found, it's always possible there's an as-yet-undiscovered hoard somewhere near, and the history of the area being what it is makes that even more likely."

The gentleman—from his clothes and his diction, let alone his knowledge, it seemed fairly clear he was a gentleman—studied the children. "I realize this might seem a bit forward, but I'm staying in the village." He waved toward the northern end of the lane. "I'm renting a cottage just up from Swindon Hall, and I'm at something of a loose end." He smiled in self-deprecatory fashion. "As I've just demonstrated, ancient history—Roman history—is an interest of mine, so I wonder if might I help you search. My name is Harris."

Jamie exchanged a glance with George and Lottie. Johnny was plainly ready to agree, but Jamie felt they needed to act responsibly and exercise caution—yet there was no denying Harris had been helpful; he'd already told them more than the professor had. He also appeared entirely trustworthy, on top of being gentry-born, well-dressed, and well educated.

Before Jamie could respond, Lottie, who had been staring at Harris and biting her lower lip, asked, "If we let you help us, you won't try to steal the hoard away for yourself, will you?"

Harris grinned. "A fair and wise question." He placed his hand over his heart and stated, "I swear on my honor that if we find a treasure of any sort, I will not keep even a single coin for my own."

Then he smiled unrestrainedly, and they were all charmed.

"So what do you say?" Harris looked from one to the other. "Do I pass muster?"

His good humor over Lottie's blunt question vanquished Jamie's reservations. He smiled back. "Welcome to the search party—there's ten of us, all told. Well, not counting Johnny and the other village lads, but they have chores so can't search all the time."

The four children scrambled over the fallen tree and slithered down to the path.

"I have to get on." Johnny waved along the path. "I have to check the geese." He looked at Jamie, Lottie, and George. "I'll see you at choir practice." Johnny dipped his head to Harris, then turned and hurried on.

"So." Harris studied Jamie, George, and Lottie. "How and where did you come upon these coins?"

Between then, they related the story of the jars of silver pennies, how they'd discovered the coins in one of the jars, and their efforts thus far to determine who had donated, wittingly or unwittingly, the three Roman coins. "So far," Jamie concluded, "no one has remembered handling the coins or seen anyone else with them, either."

Harris had listened closely. A frown wrinkling his brow, he asked, "Have any strangers visited the village recently?"

Jamie and George shook their heads, and Lottie said, "Other than you, the only strangers who have come for weeks are the professor and his niece, Miss Webster, and they came because Reverend Colebatch wrote and asked them to visit and tell us about the coins."

"The professor is a friend of Reverend Colebatch—he and Miss Webster are staying at the cottage past the church." George waved in that direction.

"But the professor has to write some treaty by the end of the year," Lottie said, "so he has to work on that all the time and can't *actively* help us search, but if we find anything, he'll help us then."

"I see." Harris nodded understandingly. He glanced at the fallen tree they'd been checking. "So what stage of searching are you up to now?"

"Well," Jamie said, "as no one who's come into the store or the Arms over a whole week has known anything about the coins, and we've heard of no obvious digging or such anywhere around, we all agreed to think about what to do next and meet this afternoon after choir practice to make a plan." He looked hopefully at Harris. "Do you have any suggestions, sir?"

Harris lightly frowned. After a moment of thought, he said, "You've covered the obvious avenues—that was sound thinking." He glanced over his shoulder in the direction of Mountjoy's Store. "I was on my way to the store to pick up a few things. Let me see if they have a map."

"The store is the post office, too," George said. "They have maps on the wall."

Harris nodded. "Good. A map will give my brain a place to start—with fresh eyes on the area, I might see something those more familiar with the place won't."

The sound of a bell tolling rolled over the snowy fields.

"That's the church clock striking twelve." Jamie glanced at George and Lottie. "We'll have to hurry if we don't want to be late for luncheon."

"And we don't want to be late," Lottie informed Harris. "Mrs. Haggerty, Grandmama's cook, gets cross."

Harris grinned. "She sounds like the cook at my parents' home. You'd better get going. I'll take a look at the map and see what I can think of. I'm sure I'll meet you somewhere about the village."

Jamie, George, and Lottie—thinking of roast beef, gravy, and golden potatoes—chorused a goodbye and rushed off along the path.

A smile on his face, Callum Harris Goodrich watched them go. "What a refreshing trio."

It seemed he'd fallen on his feet in coming to Little Moseley, and the news that Webster was largely if not wholly keeping to a cottage at the far end of the village only added to the feeling. Presumably, it would be safe for Callum to venture into the village stores.

No one but Webster would recognize him.

Swinging on his heel, Callum resumed his progress along the path skirting the lake. He would leave the path at the lake's northern end and cut through the village green to the lane. From the roofs he'd glimpsed, it seemed likely the store the children had mentioned—Mountjoy's—would be somewhere along there.

He settled into a ground-eating stride. He'd been right to follow the prod of his instincts when, after appropriately girding his loins, he'd knocked on Webster's door in Oxford and had been informed by the housekeeper that the professor had up and left with barely a moment's notice for some little village in Hampshire. To Callum's mind, Webster upping and departing in an unplanned rush meant only one thing—his erstwhile mentor had learned of some discovery. Webster's housekeeper remembered Callum fondly and had been happy to tell him the name of the village to which Webster had decamped.

"And so here I am." Callum smiled with satisfaction. With Webster holed up in a cottage, composing some treaty—treatise, Callum supposed —Callum's way was clear.

And his first stop would, indeed, be the post office. He was eager to study their maps.

The following afternoon, Callum returned to Mountjoy's Store to buy more eggs and also to check the map on the wall that he'd been directed to the day before.

Memorizing maps at a glance was a necessary skill in his line of work, but after he'd spent the previous evening cogitating, there were several features he wanted to check.

He bought six eggs and a slab of bacon and placed them in the basket he'd found in his rented cottage. After chatting amiably to the man presiding behind the counter, Callum walked past the shelves of goods running down the middle of the store to the side wall on which several maps were displayed. There was a map of England, Scotland, Wales, and Ireland, and another of Hampshire, but the one Callum halted before was a detailed map of the village and surrounding area, including topographical features.

He knew the Romans had tended to build on land elevated above its immediate surroundings—on top of a low hill or on a shelf on the side of one. In the period during which the Romans had occupied the area, adopting defensive positions had been the norm.

A quick scrutiny of the map confirmed his memory; there were several rolling folds—such as the one on which the church stood—that would likely have provided suitable positions for the Romans to build upon.

He was staring at the map, trying to match possibilities with what he'd seen on his walks about the village, when he heard the bell above the store's door jingle.

Seconds later, Callum heard the murmur of voices at the counter; he paid no attention until the man serving raised his voice.

"You'll find the baking soda in the far corner, Miss Webster—above the salt, nearly against the side wall."

Miss Webster? Callum's eyes widened. Had he ever met Webster's niece? He wracked his memory—and forced himself to remain unmoving as light footsteps approached.

The footsteps halted to his right.

He eased back just enough to slide a glance in that direction.

Miss Webster had her back more or less to him as she looked up at the shelving hugging the front wall alongside the corner with the side wall. She had gleaming, golden-blond hair, arranged in a knot on the top of her head; the topmost curl was high enough it might just tickle Callum's nose. He couldn't see her face, only the curve of a porcelain-like cheek and the neat but determined line of her jaw. She was wearing a woolen pelisse in a bright shade of blue. He watched as she stretched up a gloved hand, trying to reach a box on the highest shelf. Her fingertips barely brushed the front of the box, which had been pushed toward the rear of the shelf.

Callum saw "Baking Soda" inscribed on the box. "Here. Allow me."

He hadn't made a conscious decision to step forward, but he'd never met Miss Webster; she wouldn't recognize him.

She glanced over her shoulder at him, then smiled and stepped back. "Thank you." Her voice was low, her tone warm.

She had lovely hazel eyes.

Callum reached up, grasped the box, and offered it to her, along with his most charming smile. "My pleasure."

She eyed his smile with a degree of repressive wariness, but accepted the box and settled it amid various other purchases in the basket on her arm—while from beneath long brown lashes, those bright hazel eyes swiftly raked from his head to the toes of his boots.

Emboldened, still smiling, he offered, "I'm Harris—I'm new to the village."

Her fine brows arched. "Indeed?" After a second's pause, during which Callum plainly waited hopefully, she relented and admitted, "So are we."

"We?"

"My uncle and I." She hesitated, then said, "As you're staying in the village, you'll hear about it soon enough. My uncle is a professor of history with an interest in antiquities, and I act as his amanuensis. He was summoned here to examine and verify some Roman coins a group of children discovered."

She turned toward the counter.

With an insouciant grin, Callum fell in beside her. "I've already heard about the find," he admitted. "I met the three imps yesterday. I understand they're searching for the source of the coins, and I've volunteered to assist as I can." He tipped his head toward the side wall. "That was why I was studying the map."

"Oh." She glanced over her shoulder at the map. "I see."

They'd reached the counter, and she gave her attention to Mr. Mountjoy, referring to the man by name. Callum stood back and shamelessly eavesdropped as she and the shopkeeper briefly chatted while her purchases were totted up, then Callum drifted toward the door.

He was waiting to open it and hold it for Miss Webster when she was ready to depart. She primmed her lips just a touch as she approached, but when he swung the door open, she gracefully inclined her head and stepped out, into the lane.

He followed and pulled the door closed behind him. He felt compelled to keep her with him for at least a few minutes more. "Have you been in the village for long?" Chatting with her was, undoubtedly, the definition of "playing with fire," but apparently, it was a risk he was willing to take.

She glanced his way, met his eyes, and after a moment's debate, replied, "Only since Monday. We live in Oxford—my uncle is a professor at Brentmore College."

Callum nodded as if that was news to him. "The imps said he wasn't able to actively assist in the search for the source of the coins."

She sighed. "He can't—he has an academic treatise he absolutely must complete by the end of the year. He really shouldn't have come, but there was no argument strong enough to keep him away. So as things stand, he'll willingly confirm anything the searchers find, but he cannot spare the hours to be active in the field—much to his disgust."

I can imagine. They'd paused in the lane outside the store. Callum glanced at the shops opposite—Bilson the Butcher and Butts Bakery. "I only arrived yesterday—I was getting my bearings when I ran into the children. I'm still working out where everything is."

She tried to hide a smile and failed. "It's not a large village. I'm sure it won't take you long."

"Mr. Harris!"

Callum turned and saw a group of young people, including the children he'd met yesterday, hurrying up the lane toward him and Miss Webster. It was the youngest child—the little girl—who had called and was leading the charge.

She fetched up in front of him and fixed him with huge blue eyes and a satisfied smile. "We're very glad to have found you." The rest of the group reached them, and the little girl turned, waved at him, and said, "This is Mr. Harris."

In short order, Callum found himself introduced to the rest of the crew. They were an interesting group; he hadn't foreseen the caliber of those involved and was quietly impressed.

He noted that they were already acquainted with Miss Webster, with whom they exchanged polite greetings.

Eventually, Sir Henry Fitzgibbon—apparently, the local squire and vaguely in charge—said, "Young Jamie, George, and Lottie told us you have an interest in history—in Roman history, specifically—and that you might have some insight into how best to proceed with our search for the source of these coins."

Viscount Dagenham added in a faintly bored drawl, "Any suggestion at all would be welcome—we've spent the last twenty-four hours bemoaning our lack of success."

Callum resisted the urge to glance at Miss Webster. She was hanging back on the periphery of the group, silently watching and assessing, no doubt waiting to see if he would, indeed, rise to the occasion—if he could perform as he'd led the children to believe.

To become openly involved in such a search—one run under Webster's very nose—was the definition of reckless. The last thing Callum wanted to do was confront the man over another treasure. That would be akin to tossing a lit taper into a pool of oil.

Yet if Webster remained holed up in his cottage, then given Miss Webster didn't know who Callum was...

The truth was, no more than his erstwhile mentor was he capable of resisting the lure of buried treasure.

He glanced around the circle of earnest faces. "Jamie, George, and Lottie filled me in to some degree, but it would help if you told me exactly what you've done so far."

They sighed, but obliged; Callum listened closely and posed several questions, which quickly put them on their toes. He was distantly aware of Miss Webster watching—ultimately, it seemed, with approval.

"So, to be clear," Callum concluded, "you can confirm that everyone who has called at Mountjoy's or the Cockspur Arms over the past week has been asked about the coins, and no one knows anything about them."

Jamie frowned. "Well, other than you and Miss Webster, but you both arrived after the coins were found."

Callum nodded. "Indeed. But everyone else who called in at either place has been asked?"

A chorus of "Yes" answered him.

"And you're confident that word has spread through the wider village community, yet no one has remembered handling such coins or knows anything about them?"

"Yes" came again.

"And although we haven't yet searched exhaustively," Henry stated, "we've neither found nor heard of any holes being dug or similar thing that might have turned up old coins."

"No excavation as yet found." Callum nodded. "Very well—that's where the search stands." He paused, ordering his thoughts, then said, "I haven't seen the coins in question, but could someone have put them into one of the jars without noticing that the coins were unusual?" He glanced around the faces. "Thinking they were just silver pennies?"

Several of the group grimaced.

"That's possible," Henry admitted, and nods of agreement came from all quarters.

"All right." Callum drew in a breath and plunged in with both feet. "It seems to me that the first thing to do is to finalize the search you've *almost* completed—that of asking everyone in the village who might possibly have put those coins in the jars whether they recall doing that or handling odd coins at any time. For instance, have you eliminated any strangers who passed through?"

The group exchanged glances, then one of the older girls, Melissa, replied, "We haven't asked over the whole village, but we have asked the Mountjoys and at the Arms, and as you and the Websters don't count, then no strangers have been sighted at either place."

Callum held up a finger. "If we're seeking to eliminate a stranger as the source of the coins, then to be thorough, you need to ask over the whole village. For instance, someone from a neighboring village might have visited someone here, brought the coins with them, paid their local friend for turnips or something with the odd coins, and the local then dropped the supposed pennies into the jar without realizing the coins weren't normal." He looked at the earnest faces surrounding him. "In order to trace the source of the coins, it's important we establish absolutely that the coins couldn't have come from farther afield. So that's something that needs to be followed up."

Henry nodded. "We can do that."

"Good." Callum wasn't finished. "The next point to explore—or devise a way around—is that a local put the coins in the jar, but didn't realize the coins weren't pennies. Currently, that's shaping up as the most likely scenario."

The younger George frowned. "But if they didn't realize the coins were different, they're not going to know, even if we ask."

Callum grinned. "Exactly. So the question shifts to: How did someone local come to have such coins in their pocket?"

After a second, the other older girl, Mandy, suggested, "Perhaps they got the coins in change while shopping in Southampton?"

The older George grunted. "That's not going to be easy to trace."

Everyone paused, then Melissa waggled her head. "There are not that many people in the village who would buy things in Southampton, or even in Salisbury or Romsey, and those who would are easy enough to ask, surely?" She looked at the others. "It won't be that hard to ask around again."

Callum nodded. "Do. I can't see any other way to address that point. So that's one potential angle covered." He looked inquiringly at the circle about him. "What other way could some local have ended with those coins in their pocket?"

They'd been searching too long; they looked momentarily stumped.

Then a faintly amused voice supplied, "Presumably, someone might have picked up the coins from somewhere—in the lane or a field—as one occasionally does."

Callum shot a grin at Miss Webster. "Just so." He looked back at the group he was fast coming to regard as his crew. "So another question you need to ask everyone—absolutely everyone in the entire village—is whether they recall coming across and picking up any coins over the past...shall we say, month?"

Several groans greeted the suggestion. "We should have thought of that earlier," Thomas said.

"Never mind." Henry sounded determined. "We didn't ask before, so we'll just have to go around again."

"We need to go around again, anyway," Jamie said. "We need to cover the whole village again and ask if people had visitors, or if they went shopping outside the village, or if they found coins on the ground anywhere over the past month."

"That's correct." Callum smiled approvingly. He hesitated, then by way of encouragement, offered, "As I understand it, in locating hoards and treasures, perseverance is held to be the key. If everything was easily found, there wouldn't be much satisfaction, let alone triumph, in unearthing a treasure, would there?"

"Actually"—little Lottie spoke up—"it's the village skating party tomorrow afternoon." She looked at the others. "Almost everyone will come, won't they?"

"Good thinking!" several exclaimed.

Henry beamed at Lottie. "You're right—that will be the perfect time to ask our questions. We'll be able to canvass most of the village in an hour or so."

"That's an excellent notion," Callum said. "If, earlier in the day, you can manage to ask those who won't attend the party, then by the end of tomorrow, you'll have most of what we need to know before formulating our next step."

Lottie turned her big blue eyes on him. "Will you be there—at the skating party?"

Callum glanced sidelong at Miss Webster. "I'll try to come." The professor wasn't a fan of skating. Callum looked at the others. "We can meet and share our progress then."

Transparently re-enthused, the group broke up, and with a polite bow to Miss Webster—earning a definitely approving nod in reply—Callum turned and walked north along the lane. He felt quietly satisfied with his afternoon's achievements—he'd met an intriguing lady and managed to impress her while claiming the reins of the search for the source of the three Roman coins and steering it onto the right track.

CHAPTER 4

*C*allum heard the shrieks—ones of joy and delight—long before he could see the frozen lake. With his gloved hands sunk in his greatcoat pockets and his breath misting in the icy air, he trudged up the rise of the village green. They hadn't had any more snow, but the cold had turned intense. The white blanket covering the grass crunched with every step he took.

His skates were hanging by their knotted laces about his neck; he'd packed them assuming that, from Oxford, he would have gone to his parents' home in North Yorkshire for the usual family Christmas gathering and would be skating with his nephews and nieces on the village pond there. He would still go north; as long as he arrived at Guisborough Manor by Christmas Eve, all would be well.

On gaining the crest of the rise, he paused to catch his breath and take stock of the scene before him. It was a bucolic winter picture. Viewed from where he stood, the lake was longest running left to right, with the solidly frozen ice reflecting the grays of the clouds massing in the sky above. The surrounding land—to either side and up the rising bank of the ridge behind the lake—was painted in a palette drawn from the browns of bare branches and the greens of firs and pines. Embraced as it was by dense woodlands, the expanse of the lake resembled a magical clearing in which a host of sprites were cavorting.

Callum grinned at the fanciful thought. It seemed that most of the village children were already whizzing about on the ice, with a handful of their elders more restrainedly circling. Callum searched for the three children with whom he was familiar, only to realize they weren't yet indulging, but together with the older members of his unexpected crew, the trio were wending their way among the adults gathered on the lakeshore, stopping at each group to speak—asking their questions and eliciting answers.

"They're dedicated and diligent," Callum murmured.

As Lottie had prophesized, most of the village appeared to be in attendance. Callum saw all those he'd already met as well as many he hadn't, including quite a few older members of his own class. With any luck, he would be able to avoid them; one never knew when someone might recognize him, even if he had no idea who they were. Such was the nature of ton connections; one never knew when they might surface.

Although he swept the gathering once more, just to be sure, he felt confident he needn't fear coming face-to-face with the professor. Webster would have no use for such an unproductive activity; he would label it a frivolous waste of time.

For his part, Callum believed there was a place in life for frivolous wastes of time.

Without conscious direction, his gaze had settled on a figure in a bright-blue pelisse. Today, Miss Webster's golden hair was tucked beneath a fur hat, and she carried a muff.

"And," Callum murmured, "she's brought skates, too."

He grinned and started down the snowy slope. Trading amiable nods with those who recognized him, he made his way to where Miss Webster stood with the older girl, Mandy. He'd just reached the pair and had exchanged smiles and greetings when Mandy's sister, Melissa, joined them, along with Viscount Dagenham.

After exchanging nods with Callum and Miss Webster, Melissa and Dagenham reported that they'd asked all those they'd come across the three agreed questions—about visitors from outside the village, shopping beyond the village, and finding coins on the ground—to no avail.

"Absolutely no one seems to know anything at all about any strange coins." Melissa sounded thoroughly dispirited.

Dagenham, his gaze on Melissa's face, leaned closer, his shoulder lightly brushing hers. "The others might have had better luck."

Callum had noticed that the young viscount was particularly attentive toward Melissa, although she seemed too young to be, as the term went, fixing her interest. But what did Callum know?

The rest of the crew wandered up, their expressions making Callum's "No luck?" redundant.

Every head shook in a negative.

"No one's gone shopping anywhere beyond the village since before harvesting," Jamie reported.

"And everyone seems very sure they haven't picked up any coins lying about, either," Thomas said.

Henry huffed. "We've asked everyone about visitors, and on top of that, we asked all the shopowners and their assistants and all the grooms and ostlers at the Arms whether they'd sighted any stranger about, and the only ones mentioned were you and the Websters."

George Wiley looked at Callum. "That seems to make it certain that the coins were put in the jar by some local who didn't realize they weren't just silver pennies."

Callum digested that, then looked at Henry. "Is there anyone local— who you view as local—to whom you've yet to speak?"

Henry opened his mouth, a "No" clearly on his tongue, but stopped before he uttered it. His brow gradually furrowed, and eventually, he said, "There are a few people—men who live alone, mostly in small cottages tucked away farther out from the village. They use the village shops for their necessities, but for various reasons, they only occasionally come into the village. They're not exactly villagers as such—they won't be here today—but every now and then, they'll come into Mountjoy's or to the bakery or the butcher or spend an evening at the Arms." Henry glanced around at all the crew. "One can never tell when they'll be around, and they're not always at home, either. Quite a few travel for work, although they rarely move out of the county."

Dagenham straightened. "We could drive out tomorrow and see if they're at home and ask our questions."

The suggestion was approved by the rest of the older members of the search crew and arrangements swiftly made for three curricles—Henry's, Dagenham's, and Kilburn's—to ferry the five young gentlemen as well as Melissa and Mandy on a circuit of the countryside around the village, stopping in at the isolated cottages to ask their questions and see what they could learn.

The prospect of action lifted the spirits of those involved, and they visibly brightened.

Callum had been thinking. "While you lot take care of that, I'll see what more I can glean about Roman settlements in the area." He caught

Henry's eye. "Are there any old maps or books about the history of the village, or even of the locality more generally, available anywhere near?"

"I know there are books on the history of the village in the Fulsom Hall library," Henry replied. "You're welcome to look through those. And there are sure to be more tomes in the library at Dutton Grange—they've a larger collection overall. M'sister's married to Lord Longfellow, who owns the Grange. I can introduce you, and you'll be able to search there as well." Henry grinned. "Better you than me."

"The Swindons at Swindon Hall might have more books as well," Jamie said. "Major Swindon is interested in history."

"I know Grandmama—at Hartington Manor—doesn't have any," Melissa said. "I asked last year, and Grandmama told me the Grange library would be the best place to look."

"Reverend Colebatch will have some history books, too," the younger George said. "But I suspect they'll mostly be churchy stuff, and the Romans weren't Christians, were they?"

Callum grinned and nodded at Henry. "I'll start with your library and see how far it gets me."

"What are you looking for?" Miss Webster asked.

Callum had—almost—forgotten she was there, hovering beside him on the edge of the now-eager group. Choosing his words carefully, he replied, "Sometimes, there are references to Roman camps or the sort of clearings or old ruins that might indicate a Roman presence. If there's any site noted within the village boundaries, that would be a reasonable place to attempt a ground search." He looked at the others. "If I can find something—some reference pointing to a particular place—that will give us an avenue to explore directly, in case, despite all your questioning, we fail to pick up a clue as to where the coins came from."

That notion buoyed the group even more.

"Right, then," Henry declared, and positivity and determination rang in his voice. "Now we have our next steps settled, who's for the ice?"

"Me!"

"Us!"

They'd all been carrying their skates and quickly found logs to sit on; several had been placed close by the lakeshore specifically for that purpose. Once each member of the group had attached their skates, they hobbled the last foot to the frozen lake, and then they were off.

Callum held back, letting the youthful crew launch themselves onto the ice with gay abandon. All were confident and accomplished; they skated off in groups, chatting and exclaiming, and laughter soon bubbled forth as they encountered other villagers enjoying the communal celebration.

He glanced at Miss Webster, who'd remained beside him. "This—having a village celebration on the ice—is a novel yet obviously excellent idea. I must mention it to my parents—there's a good-sized pond in their village."

"Oh?" Bright hazel eyes signaled interest. "Where do your parents live?"

There was no harm he could see in sharing that. "In Guisborough. It's in North Yorkshire, not that far from the coast. It's usually very cold at this time of year."

She looked out at the skaters. "Are you going to be heading north for Christmas?"

That rather depends on what happens in Little Moseley. "I hope to." He glanced at her face; her expression appeared faintly wistful as she gazed out at the other skaters.

It hadn't escaped his notice that she was holding a well-worn pair of skates by her side.

He summoned his most charming smile. "Miss Webster?" When she glanced his way, he gestured to the lake. "Can I tempt you out?"

She studied him for a second, then her lips curved, and she inclined her head. "I might be a trifle rusty," she warned him as she moved with him to a nearby log.

He sat beside her, lifted his skates from about his neck, and untied the laces. "It'll come back to you once you're on the ice. Never fear." And he'd be there to catch her if it didn't; this was shaping up better than he'd hoped.

Sadly, his words of encouragement proved well founded; the instant they stepped onto the ice, she found her balance, and with a look of wonder gradually dawning and, ultimately, lighting her face, she proceeded to lead him a merry dance through whirls and swirls and elegant loops.

After catching up to her in the center of the lake, he grasped her outstretched hands and swung her around; they looked into each other's faces, and he laughed. "You're an accomplished skater, Miss Webster."

"I was," she admitted as she slipped her gloved hands free and whirled away. "And it appears I still am!"

Laughing, she turned and streaked away from him, and he grinned broadly and shot off in pursuit.

They circled, they raced, then they weaved and whirled. Others passed them and called delightedly, enjoying their impromptu exhibition. She blushed, but didn't falter, sweeping into another complex turn.

He found it difficult to drag his eyes from her; indeed, he didn't try. And if her focus rarely shifted from him, that seemed only fair.

Elsewhere on the ice, Melissa vacillated between, on the one hand, wanting to turn aside with Dagenham while the others skated on in a rowdy group and, on the other, pushing to keep up, clinging to the company of Mandy and the others and denying herself and him the chance to enjoy what amounted to moments of privacy while in full view of the entire village. In the end, she compromised and dropped back a yard or so, but no more; by unstated accord, she and Dagenham remained within easy hailing distance of the others—a separation that had become habitual over recent days.

The distance wasn't so great that they could be said to have stepped apart, as a courting couple might, yet the separation was sufficient to allow them to exchange private comments, to share smiles and looks weighted with meaning far beyond their easy words.

And throughout, they skated, moving gracefully and easily in the wake of the others. With her gloved hand firmly clasped in his long fingers, Dagenham led her in a series of loops and swirls...as if they were dancing.

She wasn't yet allowed to waltz, yet to her mind, this was just a waltz in a different setting—their eyes still lingered, their hands touched and brushed, and as he drew her in to skate close beside him, her heavy skirts flared over his legs.

It was a magical time—an hour during which they were part of their world, yet not, where being on the ice set them free, even though the constraints of society lingered in their minds.

Then Annie Bilson and her twin brother, Billy, came racing up, Annie chortling and waving Billy's knitted hat, and Billy in hot and determined pursuit. As the pair whizzed past Melissa and Dagenham, Billy grabbed his sister's flying hair and tugged.

Annie shrieked, flung the hat high, and flailed to keep her balance.

Billy released his sister's hair, dived for the hat, scooped it up, and cheering, raced away.

Instinctively, Melissa lunged to catch Annie, and the little girl's desperately waving hands clutched Melissa's coat.

"Oh!" Melissa tipped sideways—only to feel Dagenham, his long frame steely and strong, beside her. His arm clamped about her waist, and he steadied her against him, and Annie caught her balance, flashed Melissa a gap-toothed smile, and pushed off again in pursuit of her brother.

Leaving Melissa in Dagenham's arms.

She turned to him and met his gaze as her senses rioted.

His gray eyes seemed darker, more turbulent, but that might have been a reflection of the clouds.

She breathed in—and so did he.

Then, slowly, as if he were having to direct each muscle to move, he released her.

They stared at each other; they were standing near the middle of the lake, surrounded by others, yet in that moment, they seemed alone. Just him and her and...whatever lay between them.

"Melissa! Dags! Come on!"

They turned their heads and saw Henry beckoning; the group were skating on down the lake.

Melissa looked at Dagenham, and he looked at her, then a faint, almost-mocking smile lifted the ends of his lips, and with a graceful gesture, he waved her on.

He fell in beside her, and they glided toward the others.

Together with Harris, Honor had taken possession of the center of the lake. She couldn't recall ever feeling so exhilarated—so free. She'd always loved skating, but skating with a partner as accomplished as Harris was a pleasure she hadn't previously enjoyed.

She was enjoying this—to the top of her bent. She felt as if sheer happiness was filling her up and bubbling free—lighting her eyes and her smiles and infecting her laughter.

His grip on her hands was rock-steady, his judgment of speed and turn perfectly aligned with hers. Sometimes, he led, and at other times, he stepped back and followed. As the minutes passed, and they grew more accustomed to each other's foibles, entirely attuned to each other, she felt as if they were approaching that state where, instead of being two separate entities, their bodies moved as one.

It was a heady feeling, one she'd never before experienced.

Put simply, skating with Harris was a joy. They glided in concert; they experimented and explored—and through every moment, they gloried.

She could see his enjoyment in his face, in his sparkling blue eyes, and it mirrored her delight. Setting aside all reservations, she gave herself up to the magic.

Callum found his senses locked on his partner, his mind a willing captive to the moments, to the sensuous movements as they circled and swirled, then came together to pace and power along.

There was something about skating that had always drawn him, but skating with Miss Webster transformed the activity into a consuming pleasure. When, greatly daring, he gripped her waist, lifted her high, swung her in a perfect arc, and brought her down into a smooth glide, he could barely breathe for the emotion that locked about his heart.

For uncounted seconds, he couldn't drag his eyes from hers.

The applause from those on the shore seemed to come from a great distance.

How long they danced—for that was what it was—on the shushing ice, he honestly couldn't have said, but eventually, the crowd about them thinned, and the air grew more chill as the gray day faded into shadows.

They were among the last to skate back to the shore. When they halted at the edge of the ice, they were both breathing rapidly. Most of the villagers had already toiled up the slope and vanished from sight. Only a few stragglers remained.

Callum grasped his partner's gloved hand, bowed extravagantly over it, then, straightening, raised her knuckles to his lips. He captured her arrested gaze and, still a touch breathless after the prolonged exertion, simply said, "Thank you for your company, Miss Webster. This was a truly delightful interlude."

That was a massive understatement; her bright eyes confirmed she thought so, too.

Despite balancing on her skates, using his grip on her hand for balance, she managed a creditable curtsy. "And I most sincerely thank you, Mr. Harris. This afternoon transformed into an unexpected pleasure."

For an instant, Callum was lost in the brilliance of her hazel eyes. Without any real thought, he said, "My given name is Callum. I would be honored if you would use it."

She blinked, and her gaze grew more serious. She considered him for a heartbeat, then her lips curved, and she dipped her head in acceptance and said, "My name is Honor, and I make you free of it—and before you ask, yes, you are absolutely bound to act honorably in any and all dealings with me."

He laughed and inclined his head in acknowledgment, but there was a thread of steel underlying her words that he didn't miss and of which he took due note.

He retained his hold on her hand, and together, they hobbled to the nearest log and sat to remove their skates. That done, he gave her his arm, and she took it, and side by side, they made their slow way up the increasingly icy rise and on over the village green to the lane.

He paused on the narrow verge. His impulse was to see her to her door—quite aside from all else, prolonging his time with her—but he didn't dare; if Webster were to look out or, worse, open the door...

Instead, he trained his best smile on her face and allowed her arm to slide from his. "I believe we part ways here." He tipped his head northward. "My cottage is that way."

She smiled and inclined her head to him. "In that case, I'll bid you a pleasant evening...Callum."

He kept his smile in place and fervently hoped she wouldn't speak his name in her uncle's hearing.

With nods of farewell, they turned from each other and walked away.

As he strode up the lane, Callum couldn't escape the reflection that Honor would almost certainly regard what he was presently doing—concealing his identity so he could slide under her uncle's very nose in pursuit of the source of the three coins that had brought them all to Little Moseley—as the very antithesis of "honorable."

The following afternoon, Honor stepped out of Bilson's Butchers, pleased to have secured three nice lamb collops, of which her uncle was particularly fond. She and the professor had a dinner to attend that evening, but she would cook the collops and leave them in a pot for the next day.

She settled her purchases in her basket, wedging the collops between the vegetables she'd bought at Mountjoy's Store, and was about to start back to the cottage when the sound of firm footsteps approaching had her glancing up the lane.

Callum was striding toward her, his face set in an abstracted frown.

Honor recognized the expression—it was one her uncle often wore—

and knew Callum's near scowl wasn't directed at her. Indeed, she doubted he'd even noticed her.

Then his gaze drifted her way, and he saw her. His face lit, the scowl banished by a spontaneous smile of delight.

Honor felt her heart flutter; he really was a handsome devil, and when he smiled like that...

When he reacted like that to the mere sight of her...

She tried to tell her heart not to be stupid; she was too old to be dazzled by a smile.

Yet she was smiling delightedly in reply as she nodded and said, "Good afternoon, Callum. I imagine you've been studying the history books at Fulsom Hall."

"Indeed, I have." Still smiling, he halted beside her and reached for her basket. "Here—let me help you with that."

She quashed an impulse to protest that the basket wasn't heavy and, instead, relinquished it readily. He waved her forward and, when she stepped out, fell in beside her. "Have you discovered anything?" she asked.

"So far, nothing but teasing allusions. However, there are quite a few tomes that have sections on local history, so I haven't yet given up hope." He looked ahead. "As I said to the others, perseverance is a requirement in searches such as this."

There were times he sounded remarkably like her uncle, but she wasn't about to tell him that. Instead, she asked, "So where are you away to, with such a determined stride?"

She was charmed to see him lightly blushing. He cast her a sheepish look. "I'm afraid I got so caught up in my search that I missed luncheon. I'm on my way to the Arms to rectify the situation."

She laughed and surrendered to what was plainly inevitable. "You remind me of my uncle—that's just the sort of thing he does when his thirst for knowledge gets the better of him."

Callum looked ahead. "Yes, well—it's probably a ubiquitous male habit, forgetting the time when in pursuit of a goal."

The skies were gray and had been threatening snow, but thus far, the clouds had held off. Luckily, the wind had fallen; although icy, the air was still. Callum shortened his stride and reduced his pace to an amble, the better to prolong the time in which he could bask in the simple joy of Honor's presence.

They rounded the slight curve in the lane and drew level with the village green; the snow blanket of yesterday had melted slightly, and patches of winter-brown grass showed through.

The Cockspur Arms lay just ahead when they came upon two older ladies walking in the opposite direction.

Both ladies fixed their gazes on Callum and Honor. A swift glance at Honor's face showed her smiling in recognition.

He would have preferred not to pause, but the two ladies halted and waited, and Honor veered in their direction.

Obediently—having no other choice—he halted with Honor before the older ladies.

"Good afternoon, Miss Webster." The older of the pair, a haughty, black-eyed lady—a grande dame of the ton if Callum had ever seen one —smiled regally on Honor, then shifted her gaze to Callum and arched an inquiring brow.

"Lady Osbaldestone." Still smiling and relaxed, Honor bobbed, then nodded to the second lady. "Mrs. Colebatch." Honor gestured to Callum. "This is Mr. Callum Harris, another visitor to the village with an interest in history." As if sensing Callum's sudden alarm, Honor threw him an encouraging glance. "Mr. Harris is helping the search party organize themselves as well as assisting by trawling through the available history books for any mention of Roman sites in the neighborhood."

"Is he, indeed?" Lady Osbaldestone intoned, her gaze steady on Callum's face.

Instinctively, he increased the charm in his smile, but he'd recognized her name—she was, indeed, a grande dame—and he knew enough to be quietly terrified. He bowed to both ladies. "Ladies, it's a pleasure to make your acquaintance."

"Lady Osbaldestone is the grandmother of Jamie, George, Lottie, Melissa, and Mandy and lives at Hartington Manor," Honor explained. "Mrs. Colebatch is Reverend Colebatch's wife."

The children had referred to their grandmother as "Grandmama"; Callum had had no idea he'd walked into the orbit of the redoubtable Lady Osbaldestone. Had he known she lived in Little Moseley, he would have given the village a much wider berth.

He had to work to keep his mask of relaxed bonhomie in place while Mrs. Colebatch questioned him as to whether he'd gleaned anything useful from his searches, and feeling somewhat on his mettle, he found himself describing the vague hints and incidental comments he'd come across that, taken together, implied a Roman settlement of some sort in the general locality of the village.

"I see." Mrs. Colebatch sounded genuinely enthused.

Callum slid a glance at Lady Osbaldestone; she was watching him closely, studying his face. He found her unwavering black gaze distinctly disconcerting; he couldn't tell if she'd even heard his words. "I can't as yet be certain, of course"—he looked back at Mrs. Colebatch, by far the less threatening of the pair—"but I hope to find corroborating evidence in other histories, and with luck, one will give me some clue as to the actual location of the settlement."

Therese listened as Honor asked a further question, and Callum Harris responded, growing more animated and passionate the deeper he fell into his subject.

There was genuine commitment there—sincere dedication toward locating the source of the recently discovered coins.

The only problem was that she couldn't place the man before her as a Harris. She knew the family well, and to a man, they were dark and stocky. Indeed, from Callum's jawline and the way his hair framed the long planes of his face, she would swear he was a Goodrich. One of the Goodriches of North Yorkshire. Now she thought of it, she recalled mention of a Callum Goodrich—one of the Guisborough branch of the family, if she was remembering correctly. What had that mention been about? It hadn't been that long ago.

She fought to keep her eyes from narrowing; there was no sense in tipping him off. But she continued to observe closely and took especial notice of the way he and Honor interacted.

He was, she had to admit, a handsome rogue, especially when in the throes of expounding on his pet subject. Unsurprising, perhaps, that Honor was caught in his web.

Therese returned her gaze to Callum and wondered if he was trapped, reciprocally, in Honor's.

Therese watched and listened and elected to say nothing at this stage. Although, naturally, she waxed cynical about the motives of a gentleman who was not who he claimed to be, she nevertheless trusted the evidence of her eyes and her ability to discern true connection between a couple.

Given all that, she needed to think before taking any action.

As Callum reached the end of his exposition, a gust of icy wind whistled down the lane, bringing all four of them to an abrupt awareness of the time and the worsening weather.

Honor shifted. "I must get back—my uncle will wonder where I am."

Callum blessed the impulse that had prompted him to take her basket. He raised it slightly, in excuse to the older ladies, then waved Honor on. "I'll walk with you."

To his immense relief, Lady Osbaldestone inclined her head in gracious dismissal. "Indeed, and we must be on our way to Mountjoy's."

Mrs. Colebatch wished Callum luck in his search, then reached out and lightly squeezed Honor's arm. "Her ladyship and I will look forward to seeing you and the professor at dinner this evening, my dear."

Callum knew a moment of sheer panic as he half bowed to the older ladies. "It's been a pleasure to make your acquaintance, your ladyship. Ma'am." Then Honor smiled and nodded to the reverend's wife and Lady Osbaldestone, and the older ladies walked on, leaving Callum to swallow his trepidation and escort Honor briskly along.

Therese waved Henrietta Colebatch into Mountjoy's Store, then paused on the stoop to peer back down the lane. In the distance, just before the lane curved in front of the church, she could just make out the bright-blue splash of Honor Webster's pelisse.

Of Callum Harris, there was no sign. Therese scanned the scene, but the only likely explanation was that he'd gone into the Cockspur Arms. Perhaps he was meeting his crew of searchers there?

Regardless, she felt it was telling that Harris—or whoever he was—hadn't seen Honor all the way to her door. She recognized his type, the stratum of society from which he hailed; he would have been brought up better than that. "Then again, perhaps he's simply not yet ready to face her uncle."

That, she had to admit, was a possibility. She hadn't missed the flare of alarm in Callum's blue eyes over the news that she and Henrietta Colebatch would be meeting Honor's uncle that evening, which supported the notion that Callum wasn't yet ready to meet Honor's guardian.

"Hmm." Facing forward, Therese entered the shop.

The door clicked shut behind her—just as her busy mind found the right connections in her capacious memory. She halted. "Of course!" she muttered. "The *Devonshire* Harrises." The branch of the family that possessed a daughter who had married into the Guisborough Goodriches; Harris was Callum Goodrich's mother's family name.

Having completed her purchases, Henrietta had been walking toward Therese and had heard her. "Oh? Do you know the family?"

Therese smiled intently. "Indeed, I do. Quite an old family," she added, to allay Henrietta's curiosity. "Now, my dear, I rather think we had better hurry back. The weather's closing in."

Henrietta was only too ready to hurry out of the shop and back down the lane.

Therese, taller and with a longer stride, easily kept pace, all the while wondering why Callum Harris Goodrich was deliberately using only half his name.

CHAPTER 5

*T*herese doubted that even she could have planned events better. By that evening, when Professor Webster and his niece joined Therese, Mrs. Woolsey, Major and Mrs. Swindon, and the Colebatches in the vicarage's sitting room, Therese was ready to subtly probe the substance of Honor Webster's life.

Before she interfered with anyone's destiny, she always did her best to glean every last detail of their hopes and dreams.

Matchmaking was not a superficial task nor one to be undertaken lightly.

Therese bided her time while Honor and the professor were introduced to Mrs. Woolsey and Major and Mrs. Swindon, whom they hadn't previously met. She waited a trifle longer, until the company had settled on the sofas and in the armchairs and the three gentlemen had fallen into a discussion of the changes the major had noted during the Swindons' recent trip to the capital, before turning to Honor, seated in the corner of the sofa beside the armchair Therese had claimed, and airily remarking, "I noticed you and Mr. Harris on the ice yesterday afternoon. You both seemed to be enjoying yourselves."

Ermintrude Woolsey, Sally Swindon, and Henrietta Colebatch had all been at the lake and witnessed the performance. They looked at Honor with unfeigned interest.

Honor blushed and glanced at her hands, loosely clasped in her lap. "Mr. Harris proved to be an accomplished skater."

"As are you, my dear," Therese remarked. "It was refreshing to see the pair of you indulging in such simple pleasure—you transparently enjoyed the interlude."

Honor looked up, a smile touching her lips. "I did, although to be truthful, I hadn't skated in ages and feared that I had forgotten how, but as Callum—Mr. Harris—predicted, the knack came back to me the instant I stood on the ice."

Therese smiled encouragingly. "Is there some reason you've avoided skating recently?"

"Sadly, there's no good skating pond at Oxford, and the river rarely freezes sufficiently these days, so..." Honor lightly shrugged.

Therese frowned. "So your parents live in Oxford as well?"

"No—they live outside, close to Banbury. That's where their house is, and I learned to skate there, on the village pond."

"But surely you visit your parents—for instance, over Christmas? The distance between Oxford and Banbury isn't great, after all."

Honor dipped her head in agreement. "We—Uncle Hildebrand and I —will be going there for Christmas." She glanced at her uncle, but he was absorbed in the conversation now raging between the reverend and the major, and she continued, "But for much of the year, Uncle Hildebrand requires my active support, so I spend most of my days with him in Oxford."

Allowing her puzzlement to show, Therese shifted to regard Honor more directly. "How did that come about? You'll forgive the question, my dear, but it is passing strange to discover a young lady acting as a professor's amanuensis."

Honor inclined her head in acknowledgment.

When she paused, clearly marshaling her words, Therese shot a look at their three avid listeners and mentally blessed their sense in keeping their lips shut, even though they, as much as she, wanted to know more.

Eventually, Honor said, "My uncle...parted from his previous assistant on rather bad terms. After that, he didn't trust anyone to work alongside him—helping with his research and so on. But he got in such a muddle—he's really not good at keeping to any sort of schedule or timetable—that my father, who is my uncle's older brother and another professor, although in a different field, suggested that it would benefit all involved if I became Uncle Hildebrand's assistant."

"I see." Therese could read between the lines. She knew academic salaries weren't large. After a second, she ventured, "I take it you have several brothers and sisters."

Honor nodded. "Yes. Six." A fond smile lit her face.

And that, Therese thought, was the crux of Honor's story. She had left home to take the position with her uncle to ease the financial burden on her parents.

With that much clear, Therese pressed on. "Do you find your uncle's work personally fascinating—truly engrossing?"

Honor's lips twisted, half grimace, half self-deprecatory smile. "Well..." She shot a glance at her uncle—one both affectionate and yet clear-eyed. He was still engaged with the other men. She drew breath and, lowering her voice, confessed, "To be perfectly candid, fully half my time goes in keeping Uncle Hildebrand in line, and that is more irritating and aggravating than anything else. And while assisting with his work is more interesting, getting every last detail correct—as one must in academic work—is a constant challenge, one which requires obtaining frequent and ongoing guidance from him, and extracting pertinent and timely facts from Uncle Hildebrand has never been an easy task."

Therese sat back. "I can well imagine." She rapidly revisited what she'd thus far learned. Honor Webster wasn't her uncle's amanuensis because such a position satisfied her hopes and dreams. Indeed, if Therese was reading the situation correctly, Honor's position with her uncle was effectively quashing—at the very least stifling—her hopes and dreams.

Of course, Therese still had to confirm what Honor's hopes and dreams actually were.

Deciding to risk a direct approach, Therese fixed Honor with a level look and asked, "If Fate offered you romance and a chance to marry and have a family of your own, while simultaneously satisfying your family's and uncle's needs, would you seize it?"

Honor blinked. Then, slowly, she turned her head and looked at Therese as if seeing her clearly for the first time. She hesitated, then lightly frowned and said, "Yes, of course. But—"

"Such things happen, you know." Sally Swindon, seated beside Honor, could hold back no longer; she leaned forward and patted Honor's knee. "Why, just last Christmas, we had Horace's niece, Faith, to stay, and the dear girl was quite convinced she'd left all chance of marrying—well, of a marriage she would wish to have—behind her, but here in Little Moseley, she found her sweetheart. They're expecting their first child, Therese—did I mention it?"

Perfectly satisfied with the results of her interrogation and very ready to shift tacks, the better to avoid further unsettling Honor, Therese smiled benignly. "No, you didn't. Do tell."

Indeed, Therese couldn't have chosen a more appropriate distraction. She wasn't at all averse to discussing babies, especially in the company of a young lady who, in Therese's opinion, ought to be thinking along similar lines. Being the amanuensis of an Oxford professor was laudable as far as it went, but in this instance, Therese now felt comfortable in concluding that Honor Webster remaining as nothing more than that would be a waste of a promising life.

Therese did her part to encourage the conversation into wider spheres, allowing Honor to relax once more. Eventually leaving the other ladies to keep the conversational ball rolling, Therese reviewed the challenge before her. Should she promote a romance between Honor Webster and Callum Goodrich?

Such a connection would be perfectly acceptable to both families and society at large *assuming* Callum wasn't up to no good—that his aim in concealing his full name wasn't something nefarious. Given he was a Goodrich and all members of that family were universally acknowledged as honorable to the back teeth, Therese felt reasonably confident that Callum's reason for withholding his name would prove justified.

She just needed to learn what that reason was.

Consequently, over the dinner table, she turned her sights on Hilde-brand Webster. She'd recalled that Callum Goodrich had been a highly regarded student at Oxford and, as it seemed his interest lay in ancient history…perhaps the reason for Callum hiding his true identity while in Little Moseley was staring her in the face.

Over the soup course, she allowed the conversation to drift where it would. Having cut her eyeteeth in the hothouse of the ton, at formal dinners where one conversed only with those on either side, she appreciated the more relaxed ambiance of country dinners such as this, where speaking across the table was not just accepted but embraced.

After the main course was served and the company had had a chance to savor the roast spatchcocks, Therese caught the professor's eye. "Tell me, Professor, do you spend much time teaching, or is research your principal focus?"

Webster swallowed and replied, "On occasion, I'm delegated to lecture to our undergraduates, but these days, I spend more time mentoring graduate students. I suppose"—he glanced at Honor as if seeking confirmation—"I would spend roughly half my time with students of one level or another and the rest on research."

Honor smiled. "More like a quarter of your time with students and three-quarters on research."

The professor looked faintly surprised, but then said to Therese, "She's probably right."

"I see." Therese smiled encouragingly. "And have you come across any particularly promising students over recent years?"

The professor's gaze grew distant, then he pulled a face and shrugged, as if to imply that he couldn't think of any.

At the head of the table, Reverend Colebatch leaned forward. "What about that fellow Goodrich, Hildebrand? You held high hopes of him."

Instantly, a choleric flush suffused the professor's face. He set down his knife and fork and almost venomously growled, "Don't mention the name of that traitor to me."

Therese blinked and widened her eyes. "Traitor?"

That was all the encouragement the plainly aggrieved professor required to launch into a diatribe over what he labeled the defection of his once-star pupil to the shady side of the antiquities trade. "If he gets his hands on artifacts, he sells them! I was never more deceived in my entire life."

Frowning, the major ventured, "I take it he does so for personal gain?"

"What else?" The professor flung up his hands. "He's clever and astute, and God forgive me, I trained him. He finds antiquities, seizes them, and seeks out the highest bidder among the wealthy collectors. He's a traitor to the scholarly cause—there's no other way to describe him."

Therese was utterly taken aback. Could she have misread the situation? Was Callum Goodrich the exception that proved the rule of his family's honor?

Was he making up to Honor in order to inveigle details of the Little Moseley discovery from her?

But no—that didn't ring true. Honor wasn't directly involved in the search, and Therese knew what she'd sensed burgeoning between the pair. She hadn't been wrong about that.

Yet could Callum Goodrich be a villain in disguise? Was he helping her grandchildren and Henry and his friends with their search purely so he could step in at the last minute and seize the find and make off with it?

To Therese, that didn't ring true, either, but she had to own that such a scenario was possible.

Throughout the rest of the evening, she hid her troubled state; she was more than capable of maintaining a calmly serene façade in far more demanding circumstances.

But she could now see that Callum Goodrich might have a much stronger motive for hiding his identity than simply to avoid the professor.

To her mind, Callum Goodrich had a very large question mark hanging over his head—and he was here, in Little Moseley, consorting with her grandchildren, involving himself in the ongoing search for the source of the Roman coins, and intentionally or otherwise, inducing Honor Webster to fall in love with him.

It was, Therese acknowledged, time she took matters in hand.

At nine o'clock the following morning, Therese called her coachman-cum-groom, John Simms, to her private parlor and handed him a sealed missive. "Please convey that to Mr. Harris, Simms. He's staying in the northernmost cottage opposite Swindon Hall. Make sure you place it in his hand."

"Aye, ma'am." Simms took the note. "Will there be a reply?"

"It's a summons, so I expect he'll return with you."

"Very good, ma'am." Simms bowed and left.

Therese stared at the closed door for a full minute, then huffed and turned back to her correspondence.

As she'd expected, half an hour later, Crimmins knocked and announced that Mr. Harris had arrived.

"Please show him into the drawing room, Crimmins. I'll join him in a moment."

"Yes, ma'am."

She took her time tidying away her writing implements, then rose, straightened her skirts and her spine, and walked regally out of the parlor, across the front hall, and into the drawing room.

Crimmins, who had opened the drawing room door for her, closed it behind her.

Therese wasn't surprised to find Callum pacing rather nervously before the fire. On sighting her, he stopped and tried to assemble a suitable expression, but he clearly couldn't decide how contrite he needed to be and ended up looking faintly sheepish.

Therese walked to her favorite armchair and waved Callum to its mate. "Please, sit down."

He hesitated, then obeyed. However, he didn't relax in the chair but sat forward, clasping his hands between his knees.

Therese studied him for several seconds while he watched her through wary, mid-blue eyes.

The professor's claim that Callum sold artifacts to wealthy collectors had jarred loose several until-then-disjointed facts from Therese's extensive memory, and they, in turn, had led to other connections, associations, and realizations. The picture she now had in her mind of Callum Harris Goodrich and his deeds—based on information from people whose opinions she trusted—incorporated the professor's assertions, yet facts, nuances, and subtleties the professor hadn't mentioned colored Callum in a very different light, at least from society's perspective.

Holding Callum's gaze, she arched a brow. "Well, Mr. Harris—or should I say, Mr. Goodrich?"

He sighed and hung his head. "You know."

"Of course I know. How many Callum Harrises—Goodrich or otherwise—graduating from Oxford with a deep and ongoing interest in antiquities could there be?"

"If it wasn't for you, no one here would guess."

She tipped her head. "True. But it wasn't a guess on my part—I do know quite a lot about you. So"—she settled herself in her armchair and looked at him expectantly—"I now want to know why you are here—what brought you to Little Moseley and why you've remained."

Callum held her gaze for a full minute, plainly ordering his arguments, then said, "I came here because I first went to Oxford. I was on my way to Guisborough and stopped in to meet with several friends."

Therese arched a brow. "Including two of the curators of the Ashmolean Museum?"

He blinked, then inclined his head. "Indeed. We were in college together." He blinked again, amazed, and stared at her. "How did you know I was meeting two curators?"

"That," she admitted, "was a guess. One of them is one of my godsons. He's mentioned a treasure hunter who has been assisting in expanding the museum's collections."

He grimaced. "They insist on calling me that—I wish they wouldn't."

"So you met with your friends the curators, and...?"

He refocused. "Our meeting was purely touching base, but later, I thought..." His gaze drifted to the window beyond Therese, and he drew in a breath and let it out on a sigh. "Well, it was the festive season, the season of goodwill, and I thought it was time to see if Webster had calmed down enough to hear me out. But he wasn't there. The housekeeper told me he'd upped stakes and left in a rush, and she gave me the Colebatches' address."

Callum returned his gaze to Therese's face. "That's what brought me to Little Moseley. If Webster left in a rush like that, it could only mean he'd learned of some find. So I came to see what it was."

Therese nodded. She swiftly debated how to phrase her next question. "I've heard that you have been engaged in selling artifacts you've found to wealthy collectors. Explain to me how that works."

He huffed cynically. "You've been speaking with Webster. He's never got beyond that step—every time I try to explain what comes next, he erupts and refuses to hear me out."

"I'm listening."

He regarded her as if assessing the truth of that statement, then nodded and went on, "Artifacts—treasures of whatever sort—are valuable in many ways. Not just in their monetary worth but in their inherent ability to teach us of the past and also to inspire artists, scientists, and the like. In my view"—his jaw hardened—"such valuable artifacts belong in museums, where the greatest number of people can view, study, and appreciate them. That's what I work toward—what I've *always* worked toward. But the critical point to understand is that it's not simply a matter of finding a treasure and handing it over to a museum. Taking care of treasures and properly displaying them costs money, and in many instances, our museums lack appropriate funds. So without a sum of modern-day cash going to the museum along with a major treasure, the museum is forced to hide the treasure away."

Callum paused and met Therese's eyes. "I saw a way around that problem. You know my family—my background, the circle into which I was born. I had the connections—I knew whom to approach, and they would agree to speak with me. I had the entrée to wealthy, aristocratic collectors, and I knew which of them were more interested in using their collections to make a name for themselves, rather than hiding their acquisitions away from all others. I sell only to those wealthy, well-born collectors who see acquiring treasures in their chosen fields as part of their legacy to future generations and are therefore more than happy to see their names on plaques beside displays on show to the wider public."

Therese felt thoroughly vindicated—and not a little impressed. "So you find treasures."

He dipped his head in agreement. "Sometimes, on commission."

"And once you've found one, you sell it to a wealthy collector with the proviso...?"

"With the proviso that they gift—or at the very least, permanently loan—the treasure to an appropriate museum. I then hand eighty percent of the sale price to the museum to fund the care and display of the antiquity, and I keep the other twenty percent to both live on and fund my next expedition."

Therese considered him, then stated, "That's quite ingenious. I thoroughly approve."

His features relaxed, and he muttered, "Thank God for that."

She smiled. "Indeed. As it happens, I had heard something of your efforts from Lord Longridge—you recently brought back a Grecian vase for him, I believe?"

Callum nodded. "It's now gracing the Acropolis display in the British Museum."

"Very well. With your bona fides established, you may now explain to me the professor's stance."

He pressed his lips together and, after a moment, said, "You should ask him."

"But I'm asking you, and I would appreciate having your view."

He hesitated, then, plainly reluctant, said, "The professor holds that all treasures—for want of a better word—belong in the learned colleges, available only to dons and professors and possibly selected students to study. As I'm sure you know, that's the way it's been for decades, possibly centuries. The colleges sometimes loan items to the museums for display, but many of the best and, archeologically speaking, most important pieces remain hidden away, under lock and key, and are never seen by the public." He fell silent, then shifted and said, "That's really all I can say."

She inclined her head in acceptance; she had to give him credit for refusing to say a word against his erstwhile mentor. "How long were you with the professor?"

"About seven years in all—through my undergraduate and graduate studies, and after that, I was his assistant for several years, until just over four years ago." He glanced down at his clasped hands. "We first argued about where an Egyptian urn should go—Webster got his way, of course, and it's now buried in the cellars of Brentmore College, and no one other than him and his colleagues can gain access. Not even the Ashmolean curators have been able to view it—at Webster's behest, the dean insists it's too precious for general viewing and can only be studied by those in the college." He sounded disgusted.

"Correct me if I'm wrong, but under your system of placing treasures in museums, scholars like Professor Webster can still gain access for study, can they not?"

"Yes—by arrangement with the museum. It's all quite straightforward." He paused, then went on, "Subsequently, while on a break—my first solo excursion—I discovered a bronze figurine with links to Stonehenge. When I refused to hand it over to Brentmore, as Webster assumed I would, he saw red."

"I see." Indeed, she felt confident she now saw it all. Professor Webster's favored path might have been the one that had existed for centuries, but the course espoused by Callum Goodrich was undoubtedly the way of the future. Sadly, it appeared Professor Webster was too set in his ways to accept that.

Therese considered, then fixed Callum with a direct look. "Should our search for the source of the three Roman coins bear fruit and we discover something that qualifies as a treasure—a Roman hoard, for example—assuming you were given the chance to place the artifacts with a collector, who would you approach?"

Immediately, he replied, "Lord Lovett or Lord Lynley." He tipped his head consideringly. "Or possibly both, depending on the size and composition of the hoard."

Therese knew both gentlemen. Each commanded significant wealth and was an avid collector of coins and ancient gold and silver artifacts.

"And as we're talking of Roman artifacts, I would stipulate the Ashmolean as the museum to which the treasure should be gifted." Callum smiled faintly at Therese. "I happen to know that the curators there are looking to expand their Roman collection."

Therese allowed her lips to curve. "That sounds a wise and sensible plan."

Callum gazed at her, and his smile faded. "So what do you intend to do now?"

An excellent question. Sobering as well, Therese studied him; he bore her scrutiny without flinching. Eventually, she nodded, more to herself than him. "I won't reveal what I know of you, at least not yet. *However*"—she held up a finger and forced her expression into stern lines —"regardless of the outcome of our hunt for a Roman hoard, you must promise to reveal your true name and your connection to the professor to Miss Webster by..." She paused and counted the days, then said, "The evening of Monday next—the twenty-first."

He frowned. "Why by then?"

"Because that's the evening of the carol service, and I and my brood will be departing the village first thing the next morning, and I will not leave while that poor girl is falling in love with you while you're using an assumed name."

Therese felt rather pleased by the stunned look that overtook Callum's features. After he'd spent several seconds staring mutely at her, his lips formed the words "falling in love," but no sound came out.

She struggled to keep her lips set in a severe line and bent a commanding, demanding look on him.

Eventually, he refocused on her and blinked. Then he straightened, cleared his throat, and inclined his head. His voice sounded slightly strangled as he said, "By the evening of the carol service. You have my word."

"Excellent!" Therese beamed at him and rose.

He got to his feet, still looking as if she'd taken a plank to his head. "I'll, ah, be on my way, then."

She continued to smile as she showed him to the front door.

Closing it after him, she turned and stated, "And that was an *excellent* morning's work."

CHAPTER 6

*M*r. Moody tapped his baton on the top of his music stand. He'd spent the first hour of Saturday's practice putting the choir through their paces with "The First Nowell," "Hark, the Herald Angels Sing," and "This Endris Night." Jovially encouraging, he beamed at his choristers. "Now, as we discussed on Thursday, I see no reason not to take advantage of the additional choristers we've been blessed with and perform the same duet and solo sections as were sung last year. So many of the congregation have commented on how much they enjoyed 'The Holly and the Ivy' especially"—Moody beamed at Melissa and Dagenham—"that I'm sure you won't want to disappoint them."

Melissa cut a glance at Dagenham; as he was a tenor and she sang alto, they were standing side by side.

His gaze briefly touched hers; they'd already agreed that, if requested, they would perform the duet again. "Miss North and I will be happy to oblige," Dagenham stated.

"Excellent!" Moody looked toward the organ. "Mrs. Moody has been polishing the accompaniment. Perhaps we can use this moment to allow the rest of the choir a brief break and run through the duet." Moody beckoned, and Melissa and Dagenham stepped forward. "Do you remember the words?"

They're inscribed in my memory. Melissa nodded, as did Dagenham.

"Right, then." Moody tapped the top of the music stand, then raised his baton. "On the count of three."

Melissa heard the opening chords, and it was as if she'd stepped back in time to the carol service of the year before. She filled her lungs and opened her mouth, and her voice followed the notes, then Dagenham's tenor joined her alto, and their voices twined.

The buoyant power of his voice was, to her, almost tangible; she laid hers over it, like a woman relaxing into the arms of her lover.

And it was like that. Much more like that than it had been the year before. Their voices hadn't changed so much as matured—grown richer, fuller, more capable of carrying the emotive power of their hearts.

Despite being set at ease, no other chorister so much as shifted a finger as they sang; only Moody's baton kept time, and Mrs. Moody steadfastly played as they rolled through the verses, in the last, their voices blending seamlessly in the final chorus:

The rising of the sun
And the running of the deer,
The playing of the merry organ,
Sweet singing in the choir.

They held the last note, then let it fade.

Silence fell, and they both drew in deep breaths and half turned to each other. Their eyes met as the rest of the choir burst into spontaneous applause, and Moody and Mrs. Moody beamed and called their bravos.

Abruptly, self-consciousness engulfed them, and both turned aside to their peers.

Melissa heard Lottie say to Mandy, "That was even better than last year."

Mandy flashed Melissa a bolstering smile. "It was truly lovely."

Moody tapped firmly on the music stand. "Well, we now have a standard for all the rest of our singing to aspire to." He beamed upon them all. "So if you would re-form again?" He waved them into their lines, then glanced down at his notes. "I believe the next piece we should run through is 'O Come, All Ye Faithful.'" He looked up, his eyes bright. "Let's try it in all the different parts this time, shall we?"

Melissa was grateful that, this year, Jessie and Fiona were there to help strengthen the alto section; she felt as if her lungs had tightened in the wake of the duet.

No—in the wake of the power it had made manifest.

She was, she decided, starting to sound like her grandmother.

She wasn't sure if that was a good thing or not.

Regardless, she wasn't about to glance Dagenham's way. She could hear him singing beside her as if nothing the least discombobulating had occurred, so she raised her chin, ignored the vise about her chest, and sang along as well.

Callum slipped into the church. The sound of the choir had lured him in. He closed the door quietly and made his way to the rearmost pew. He slid onto the wooden seat, relaxed, and let the music swirl about him.

He'd come to waylay the crew after practice, to learn if, in visiting the outlying cottages, they'd unearthed any clue as to where the Roman coins might have hailed from.

Somewhat to his surprise, he found the carols comforting; the familiar strains took him back to his childhood, to singing the same songs on snowy Christmas mornings in the church in Guisborough, then pelting his brothers and sisters with snowballs in the graveyard after the service.

He realized he was smiling in a silly fashion and glanced around the shadowed nave, but there was no one near enough to see.

Honor certainly wasn't present; he'd assumed she wouldn't be. If she was acting as Webster's amanuensis, he would keep her busy—increasingly busy the deeper he got into his treatise and needed more references checked. And in truth, Callum was avoiding her, at least for the moment —until the shock of hearing Lady Osbaldestone assert that Honor was falling in love with him faded.

He hadn't expected that, and given the statement had been made by an arch-grande dame renowned for her matchmaking skills, it was difficult to discount—to wave aside and dismiss.

Especially when he didn't want to.

Yet in light of Lady Osbaldestone's declaration, he wasn't sure how he should now approach Honor—how to interact with her, much less confess the truth to her.

In the matter of someone falling in love with one, knowing was better than not knowing, but in this case, *knowing* pricked and prodded at his conscience and made him squirm.

The choir started another carol, and he refocused on the music, letting it flow into his mind, drown out his thoughts, and soothe him.

Finally, the church clock struck five times, and Moody called an end to the session and dismissed the choir. In short order, the choristers came rolling up the aisle, tugging on gloves and tossing scarves about their necks, rugging up to hurry home through the deepening darkness.

Callum rose, and the crew, as he now thought of them, saw him and gathered around. "Any news?" he asked.

He listened as they reported a complete lack of success in finding anyone with knowledge of the coins. Their spirits had transparently been uplifted by their singing, but the recitation of their unproductive doings saw them grow despondent and rather morose.

"It's as if the coins materialized from thin air." Henry shook his head. "No one remembers seeing or handling them at all."

"And no one had any visitors," Kilburn said.

"Or picked up any coins over the last month," Wiley glumly added.

After a moment, Dagenham stirred and looked at Callum. "Did you find anything useful in the historical record?"

Callum met Dagenham's eyes, then swept his gaze over the group; they needed bucking up. "Yes and no. What I have found are mentions of a Roman settlement—a villa or merchant's outpost, something of that nature—somewhere close to where the village is now. What I haven't yet found is any information that will allow me to pinpoint where, exactly, the settlement was, but it definitely existed." He let his enthusiasm take flight, knowing it was the surest way to fire theirs. "I know it contained a structure that, to be built, required timber beams and tools. I found a copy of a waybill of sorts, listing all the things you'd expect—nails and mallets and such—as part of an order to a warehouse at Clausentum."

He looked around and saw interest sparking in many eyes. "The carter was instructed to collect the goods and ferry them north, then a few miles west. As far as I can make out, that lands the goods more or less in this village, but exactly where the building was, I can't yet say."

"Do you think that, if we find the place the coins came from, there'll be more?" Mandy asked.

"Well," Callum said, "in three other cases I've heard of, a few coins have led to the discovery of what's commonly called a Roman hoard—a collection of coins, gold and silver ornaments, jewelry, and the like. There have been three such hoards found in England thus far—meaning three the museums and so on know of. Almost certainly, other hoards have been discovered and were broken up and dispersed, but the Barkway Hoard in the north and the Backworth Hoard from Hertfordshire and the Capheaton Treasure from Northumberland are all more or less intact. Of those, the Backworth Hoard is the largest—it contained rings of gold and silver, chains, wheel and crescent pendants, brooches, silver spoons and bowls, as well as denarii—like the coins you found—and brass coins as well."

He glanced at their faces, saw the fire of commitment once more burning steadily in their eyes, and grinned. "The Backworth Hoard was found only last year." He didn't add that he'd had a pivotal role in arranging for the hoard to be donated to the British Museum.

"Right, then." Henry clapped his hands together. "So what do we do now? If there's a hoard buried somewhere about the village, we want to be the ones who find it."

The others echoed the sentiment.

Callum looked at Henry, then glanced at the others. "Perseverance, remember? The first question to ask is whether you've thoroughly exhausted all possibilities along the avenue you set out to explore."

He returned his gaze to Henry's face and, from Henry's furrowed brow, deduced that the local squire was thinking hard.

Then Henry grimaced, glanced at the others, and said, "Three of the outlying cottages we visited yesterday were empty. The men living in those cottages are"—Henry waggled his hand—"itinerants after a fashion in that they travel about the surrounding areas for work. We've eliminated everyone else who might have placed the coins in the jars, but not those three men."

Callum nodded encouragingly. "That's the way to think—we have to leave no stone unturned along each path of exploration."

"Well," Henry said, "one of those three men might be the source of the coins, but there's no telling when they'll return to their cottages. All have family elsewhere and might not be back until sometime in the New Year."

There were grimaces all around. Callum drew in a breath and held it while he digested that news, then said, "Let's label that a dead end at this point. Remember it, but it seems we can't push further on that tack at present, so let's turn to our next avenue."

"Which is?" Jamie asked.

Callum smiled at the lad. "If we can't identify who put the coins in the jar, we're left to explore the more direct avenue—where did the coins come from that someone in the village picked them up and put them in the jar?"

Now that he'd convinced himself there was a real chance of a hoard in the vicinity, he wasn't going to give up; he let his determination seep into both his expression and his tone. "It's most likely the coins were found fairly recently—who keeps silver coins in their pockets for long? That means they were unearthed via some recent disturbance of the ground. Some excavation. It might be something as simple as a fox or badger or even a dog digging. It might have been due to some natural event—like a landslip or sinkhole or a boulder coming loose and rolling away, exposing the earth underneath. We can also postulate that the site of this disturbance must be fairly accessible—for instance, close to and visible from one of the paths through the woods."

"Like that fallen tree we were looking at when you first met us?" Lottie asked.

Callum grinned at her. "Exactly like that. The site is unlikely to be deep in the woods, because someone stumbled across the coins by accident, and in this weather, not many people go hiking deep in the woods, off the paths."

The entire crew were nodding, their gazes distant as they imagined what they would be searching for.

"My suggestion," Callum said, "is that you walk the local paths and the lanes as well. In a group, because many pairs of eyes are better than a few in this sort of search. Scan the ground on either side—remember, you're looking for something that was visible to someone else. See if anything catches your eye and draws you to look more closely." He paused, then with quiet certainty, stated, "Somewhere around this village, there's a place where the ground has been relatively recently disturbed— see if you can find it."

The three younger children laughed.

"It's a treasure hunt—a real one!" George said.

They were all smiling now, renewed enthusiasm flowing through them.

"The weather's not that bad," Wiley pointed out. "It's been gray and wintry, but it hasn't snowed for days."

"Perfect for rambling through the woods." Henry clapped his friend on the shoulder, and everyone turned toward the church door. Henry glanced at the others. "We'll start walking the paths tomorrow afternoon, after church. Let's meet on the green immediately after luncheon and go from there."

Murmurs of agreement came from all sides.

Callum was bringing up the rear. "While you lot are scouring the countryside, I'll continue searching the history books. I've several yet to go. With any luck, I'll find some reference that will pinpoint the site of whatever structure some Roman built here."

∾

The next day dawned fine, with a gray sky and a weak winter sun inter-mittently striking through pearly clouds. The service at the church was well attended, and after a satisfying luncheon, Melissa, Mandy, Jamie, George, and Lottie repaired to the village green; they were waiting impa-tiently when Henry and his four friends came striding down the lane.

"Sorry we're late," Henry called. "Cousin Ermintrude wanted to know every last little detail that Harris told us about Roman hoards."

"I think she fancies finding it herself." Thomas blew on his hands. "I saw her talking to the Hall gardener as we came out."

"Well, if she and he turn up anything about the Hall, I'll fall on her neck," Henry said. "As it is"—he waved the assembled group up the rise —"let's pick up the path at the corner of the lake and go around the lake and on past the rear of the Grange and Allard's End for a start."

In a loose group, they climbed the rise and started down the long slope to the lakeshore. The ground there was icy in patches where the sun hadn't reached; they picked their way, with the occasional half-smothered shriek or yell as their boots slid and slipped.

Melissa nearly fell, but Dagenham gripped her elbow and steadied her. Blushing, she thanked him; he waited until she was walking again and no further patches of ice loomed ahead before, patently reluctantly, releasing her.

As usual, she and he ambled at the rear of the group. Eventually, he thrust his hands into his greatcoat pockets and murmured, "How do you rate our chances of finding anything? Any disturbance or excavation— any possible place from which the coins might have been unearthed?"

She slanted a glance at him, then looked forward. For several yards, she made no reply, then she offered, "I think finding the source of the coins is a long shot, no matter what we do or how we approach our search." She returned her gaze to his face. "But surely, this is one of those instances in life where one has to weigh things up and act accordingly, and despite the low chances of success, the potential gains are great, and all for little expenditure on our part." She arched her brows, then smiled wryly. "Besides, the search gives us something to do—a reason to walk through the woods and enjoy the afternoon outdoors."

His lips curved as well, and he tipped his head. "There is that."

They rounded the northern point of the lake and picked up the path that skirted the western shore. After crossing the narrow plank bridge over the stream that filled the lake, in twos and threes, they wandered slowly southward along the path, scanning the trees and bushes on either side—the long upward slope to the crest on their right and the short downward slope to the water on their left—searching for any sign of disturbance.

They investigated several downed trees and the hollows beneath them, but found nothing to indicate recent digging.

On reaching the southern end of the lake, they toiled up the path that led to the spine of the ridge and continued more or less directly south, toward the rear boundary of the Dutton Grange estate. Carefully surveying the increasingly dense woodland to either side, they forged steadily on, ultimately reaching the dilapidated holding known as Allard's End—deserted except, in this season, for Johnny Took and the village's flock of geese.

The group left the path to check with Johnny, who they found in the old orchard behind the ruins of Allard's cottage. The geese were settled on a thick blanket of dead leaves, indolently munching the fallen fruit.

In response to their inquiries, Johnny reported, "Me and all the other village boys've been keeping our eyes peeled, but we spoke after church, and none of us have spotted any sort of digging at all. Not on any of the farms—and we asked our das and the farmhands, too. No one's noticed anything."

Jamie and Henry thanked Johnny.

Henry glanced up at the sun, what there was of it. "We've plenty of afternoon left." He glanced at the others. "Shall we go on?"

Despite the lack of any positive findings, everyone was in favor, and the group returned to the path and continued southward.

Ultimately, they walked all the way through the woods to the Southampton-Salisbury road, then backtracked and picked up the easterly path that ran a few hundred yards south of Milsom Farm.

"The Milsom boys will have checked the farm's fields," Henry said, "but this path is some way from their boundary."

"And"—George Wiley pointed to hoofmarks—"it looks like riders come this way."

Henry nodded. "People on foot and on horseback occasionally use this path instead of going via the main lanes."

The group paid due attention to the dense woodland on either side of the path, occasionally stepping off it to peer into the undergrowth, but found nothing to excite their interest.

When the path descended sharply to join the Romsey lane, Dagenham gave Melissa his hand; she took it, and he gripped her fingers and supported her as she picked her way down the rocky slope. Dagenham's gesture was patently instinctive, an action taken without thought; he'd offered his hand or grasped her elbow several times during the afternoon, whenever the path grew difficult to navigate. However, this time, he didn't release Melissa's hand but continued to clasp it, gently yet firmly, while they followed the others along the path. Only when, at the rear of the group, they emerged from the woods into the open lane did he—with transparent reluctance—relinquish his hold and draw his fingers from hers.

Melissa didn't look his way, and he didn't look at her.

Both pretended to listen as the rest of the group argued over how best to continue the search, but the light was waning, and eventually, it was agreed they would follow the Romsey lane to where the village lane joined it, then take the village lane back to the manor and Fulsom Hall.

The group set off again, still visually scouring the verges to either side. By the time they turned in to the village lane, disappointment had started to rise again.

"It's disheartening." Roger Carnaby spoke for them all.

Henry huffed. "They always say that nothing worthwhile in life comes easily—let's hope this is one of those times when the worthwhile eventually appears."

"Hear, hear," Thomas and George Wiley concurred.

"We've only searched to the south today," Jamie said. "We can't give up yet."

They reached the end of the manor drive and halted, and Dagenham said, "What say we meet tomorrow morning on the green and take the paths to the north?"

The suggestion was met with ready if not enthusiastic support.

Dagenham glanced at Melissa and Mandy. "Shall we say ten o'clock?"

With the time agreed, the group parted, with the five from the manor heading up the drive, leaving the young gentlemen to walk on to the Hall.

With her sister and cousins, Melissa reached the first curve in the drive and couldn't resist glancing back.

The five gentlemen had started on their way, but Dagenham's head was turned, and he was looking at her.

Blushing, Melissa faced forward and walked on.

CHAPTER 7

$\mathcal{T}$he morning air was crisp and cool when the group gathered on the village green. As the church clock struck ten times, they set off, once again, to pick up the path at the northern tip of the lake, but this time, they turned their feet northward and, with renewed vigor, applied themselves to diligently searching for any sign of digging or excavation.

"Harris was in the library when we got back to the Hall yesterday." Thomas clambered down to the path after investigating a fallen tree. "He's still deep in the history books, but hinted he was on the trail of some definite place—a house or villa or something of that sort—that he's increasingly certain was built somewhere around the village."

"He's back in the Hall library now," Dagenham added, "ferreting through yet more books."

The others nodded and continued their searching.

A little later, Jamie offered, "Grandmama said she understands Harris knows quite a bit about finding ancient objects, and that if he says there's a good chance of finding a hoard nearby, she would be inclined to believe him."

The five young gentlemen regarded Jamie, then Dagenham said, "Your Grandmama is a downy one—if she thinks that, she's probably right."

Her ladyship's encouragement buoyed the company as they followed the path around the rear of the Hall's grounds, past Tooks Farm, and on.

Eventually, they stepped out of the woods onto the lane that ran between Romsey and West Wellow.

After exchanging dispirited glances yet clearly attempting to hold disappointment at bay, they turned east and walked to the intersection with the lane from East Wellow, then angled back toward the village along the Romsey lane. Deciding that, to be thorough, they should search along the sides of the lane as it ran south past Swindon Hall, Witcherly Farm, and Crossley Farm, they continued along the well-beaten track, checking on either side, until with disaffected sighs, they turned once more in to the southern end of the village lane.

Seeking a distraction from their lack of success, Dagenham glanced at Melissa. "The day after the carol service, I'll be heading north to join the family for Christmas at Carsington—in Derbyshire." He waited until Melissa met his eyes. "You?"

She smiled. "We"— with a wave, she included her sister and cousins —"will all be going to Winslow Abbey, in Northamptonshire. That's Jamie, George, and Lottie's home, and the family always gathers there for Christmas—the abbey's large enough to easily hold us all."

Thomas said, "It sounds as if we'll all be traveling on the same day— I'll be off to Norfolk to my grandfather's house, outside Norwich. Our family gather there."

"Dags will drop me off in the Cotswolds," George Wiley said, "at the parents' house near Chipping Norton. M'family will be celebrating there."

"It seems all of you will have a decent chance of enjoying a white Christmas." Roger nodded at the heavy clouds that heralded yet more snow. "Meanwhile, *I'll* be stuck in London, where the snow is never white."

Thomas grinned and thumped Roger on the shoulder. "Buck up— you'll still have all your family around."

Roger scoffed, but he was smiling.

"How will you get home?" George asked. "You didn't bring your curricle, did you?"

"No, but I'll leave with Thomas—he has to go through London, anyway, so he'll let me off there."

They halted and milled at the bottom of the manor's drive.

"What now?" Dagenham looked at Henry and Jamie. "As we've just confirmed, we'll all be leaving a week from tomorrow. We have only seven more days in which to find this hoard."

"Assuming it exists," Roger said.

The others all looked at him, then Jamie said, "I think we have to assume the hoard is real. We have to believe it is, or we won't find it."

"Just so." Henry nodded. "So we need to keep searching, but…where next is the question."

Mandy looked around the circle of faces, then focused on her cousins and Melissa. "It's nearly time for luncheon." She looked at the five gentlemen. "Why don't we take the time while eating to think, then the five of us will come to Fulsom Hall, and we can see if Mr. Harris has found anything useful, and discuss where next we should search?"

That plan found favor with everyone, and the group split and went their separate ways, with Melissa and Dagenham again sharing a lingering look as they parted.

Therese heard her grandchildren come in and walked out from her private parlor to find them shedding coats and scarves in the front hall. She studied their faces. "Still no sign of where those coins might have come from?"

"No," George replied. "But we're not giving up."

Therese smiled. "Of course not." She waved them ahead of her into the dining room, and they sat about the table. She waited while Crimmins served the soup, and slices of Mrs. Haggerty's seeded loaf were passed around. Therese continued to wait while the soup was consumed.

When Crimmins returned to clear the empty plates and serve the main course of a thick rabbit stew, Therese gave up waiting and prompted, "Have your endeavors of the morning led to any further insights into where the source of the coins might lie?"

Jamie grimaced. "Not really."

"We searched all along the paths through the woods and along the lanes around about," Mandy said.

"Yesterday to the west and south," Melissa added, "and today to the north and east."

"But we didn't find any sign of digging." George sighed.

"Yet," Lottie trenchantly added.

Therese hid a grin. "I see. And was Mr. Harris searching with you?"

"No." Mandy shook her head. "He's been buried in the library at the Hall."

"On Saturday, he told us about the other Roman hoards and treasures he knew of." George's eyes lit. "Did you know…"

Therese listened as between them, Jamie and George, assisted by

Lottie, elaborated in detail as to the information Harris-Goodrich had imparted. Given what Therese knew of him, such knowledge wasn't a surprise, but that he'd taken the time to share that knowledge with his young searchers was a mark in his favor. After noting that Mandy and Melissa were also nodding, encouraged and enthused despite their age and the group's signal lack of success, Therese inwardly conceded that Callum Harris Goodrich knew how to fire the interest of his searchers.

In his line of work, that was undoubtedly an advantage.

The children ended their recitation with the news that they intended to head to Fulsom Hall for a meeting, to learn if Mr. Harris had gleaned any clues from his search through the history books and, subsequently, to decide how best to proceed.

Therese arched her brows and, her tone even, inquired, "Is Miss Webster assisting with the search?"

The boys shook their heads. "She knows we're searching and that Mr. Harris is helping," Jamie reported.

"We haven't seen her," George said. "Not over the past days."

"I see." Although Therese kept her tone uninflected, from the corner of her eye, she saw Lottie, Melissa, and Mandy staring at her, then the girls exchanged a three-way glance, and Therese saw Lottie's lips form the words, "Miss Webster and who?"

Melissa's brows arched, and she looked at Mandy.

Therese couldn't tell what passed between the sisters, but she suspected it was along the lines of "Mr. Harris? Well, it must be."

As, apparently, the girls hadn't seen Miss Webster with Harris-Goodrich other than in passing, and had been too absorbed with their own activities during the skating party to have noticed anyone else, Therese wasn't surprised that her granddaughters hadn't picked up the signs of burgeoning romance. However, now they'd been alerted, she felt confident she could trust them to supply whatever encouragement fell to their hands.

At the end of the meal, she followed the five into the front hall. "I'll be helping Mrs. Haggerty and Mrs. Crimmins and everyone else in the kitchen for the rest of the day. We're starting on the plum puddings." Therese smiled. "I'm in charge of slipping the silver coins into each pudding."

The children cheered, then, after shrugging into their coats and winding thick scarves about their throats, they waved and set off for Fulsom Hall.

The five were admitted to the Hall by Mountjoy, the butler. He smiled at their cheery greetings. "Sir Henry and his friends and Mr. Harris have just retreated to the library." Mountjoy's eyes twinkled. "Mrs. Woolsey is with them."

He led the way to the library, which lay down a corridor to one side of the front hall.

As she and Mandy followed Jamie, George, and Lottie, who were trailing Mountjoy, Melissa tipped her head close to Mandy's and murmured, "Mrs. Woolsey is a distant cousin of Henry's. She's a trifle…" Melissa paused, lost for words.

Lottie, who had heard, glanced back and, sotto voce, supplied, "Fluttery. She flutters."

Melissa nodded. "That's not a bad way to put it."

Thus forewarned, Mandy smiled and curtsied along with Melissa when, on being announced by Mountjoy to the company in the library, she and her sister and cousins were set upon by a butterfly-like elderly lady, clad in filmy draperies, who swooped upon them, exclaiming and welcoming and making comments in a stream of disjointed statements.

Mandy took her cue from the others in responding only to the comments that seemed relevant.

Henry rescued them. "Excellent! You're here." He ushered the five toward a grouping of chairs set before the large fireplace. "We've told Mr. Harris of our lack of success in searching along the paths and lanes." Glancing back at his elderly cousin, Henry smiled fondly and said, "We'll be going out again soon, Cousin Ermintrude."

"Very good, dear boy." Mrs. Woolsey raised her head and looked over the children toward Henry's four friends and Mr. Harris, who were gathered about the fire. "Do be sure to keep me informed of any advances, gentlemen!"

"We will, Mrs. Woolsey!" Henry's friends dutifully chorused.

Mr. Harris looked bemused—and faintly amused.

"I'll leave you to your endeavors, then." Mrs. Woolsey whirled in a swirl of draperies and made for the door that Mountjoy helpfully held open. At the last, without looking back, she waved over her head. "Good luck!"

Henry nodded to Mountjoy, who departed in his mistress's wake and shut the door. "Phew!" Henry looked at the manor group and grinned. "That was a near-run thing. Cousin Ermintrude got wind of our continuing efforts and was determined to assist Mr. Harris, but it seems she's forgotten."

Mandy frowned. "Does she often do that?"

"Forget?" Henry nodded. "Frequently, from one minute to the next. But she's a dear old thing—quite harmless."

They'd reached the chairs, and the gentlemen, who were all on their feet, waited until Mandy, Melissa, and Lottie sat, then either claimed chairs themselves or propped against the mantelpiece.

"Judging from your reports"—Harris spoke from the armchair he'd claimed—"finding evidence of the excavation that unearthed our three coins is not going to be straightforward. I commend your thoroughness to date and share your frustration."

"Have you learned anything from the history books?" Melissa asked.

Harris glanced around the circle. "I've uncovered enough to feel increasingly certain that the chances of discovering the ruins of some sort of Roman building close to the village are very real." He leaned forward and, with excitement plainly riding him, clasped his hands between his knees and skewered them all with a confident look. "I've confirmed that there was a Roman road between Clausentum—that's to the north of our Southampton—to Sorviodunum, which we call Old Sarum, near Salisbury. That road is probably the forerunner of the present Southampton-Salisbury road, and given the ridge on which the church now stands and the relative distance between Clausentum and Old Sarum, there's a good possibility that there was some sort of staging post here. It's the perfect spot for it—just the right landscape the Romans would look for.

"In addition"—his voice gained in strength, in fervor—"I've found multiple references to a merchant's compound, containing a villa and, most likely, storehouses, somewhere in this area. It's possible there was more than one—the references could be pointing to the compounds of different merchants." Leaning back, he raised both hands. "From what I've found so far, I can't definitively say, but the more evidence I uncover of settlements in this area, the more likely it is that those coins came from a local hoard."

"Have you been able to get any idea of where, exactly, these compounds might have been situated?" Henry asked. "Any landmarks or streams or things like that?"

"Thus far, no." Harris looked frustrated. "A few mentions of the amenities of the place—good water supply and plentiful timber and game, that sort of thing—but no clear description of any major feature. Nothing at all to point us in a specific direction." He grimaced. "Then again, we are talking of a time over fourteen hundred years ago—the landscape will have changed."

He sighed and glanced at the pile of tomes stacked on the massive library table that dominated the room. "I've nearly reached the end of the texts you have here—I've three more to comb through." Harris raked a hand through his hair. "If I don't find anything in those…" He met the others' gazes. "Frankly, I'll be stumped as to how to proceed. Mounting a thorough archeological search over such a wide area…" He shook his head. "That's not going to work. We keep coming back to needing to learn where the coins were found. Missing that…at the moment, I can't even guess where we should look next."

A short silence ensued, then Dagenham looked at the pile of books. "Can we help go through the books? Perhaps that would get through them faster."

Harris smiled wearily. "How good's your Latin?"

Dagenham pulled a face. "Not good at all." He glanced at his friends, but faintly horrified, the other four young men shook their heads.

Harris's smile faded. "It won't take me longer than this afternoon to go through the last three texts. Once I have…" He paused, then went on, "I know it seems as if we're about to reach the end of our search with nothing to show for it, but my advice is: Don't lose hope. Quite often, it's moments like these that push explorers to try something else, something they have, until that point, discounted, and *that*, unexpectedly, leads to a major discovery."

The others exchanged looks, then Henry slapped his hands on his knees and sat up straight. "I need something to do—something I don't have to think about." He looked at the others and grinned. "Anyone for a game of croquet? It'll take our minds off our knotty problem for an hour or so, then when Harris has finished going through the books, we can get together again and see what our minds, being somewhat refreshed, can come up with."

Harris nodded encouragingly. "That's an excellent idea."

Henry, his four friends, and Mandy and Melissa agreed. They quickly organized teams, and Harris waved them away. "Leave me in peace. I'll come and find you when I've got to the end of the last book."

Jamie, George, and Lottie trailed their seniors from the library, but rather than follow on to the games room to help retrieve the croquet hoops and mallets, they dallied in the front hall.

Melissa noticed them hanging back and paused to direct an inquiring glance their way. "Are you going to join in?"

Jamie, George, and Lottie shared a look, then Jamie said, "We'll go and see if Johnny and Georgina Tooks are at the farm. We'll be back in an hour or so to help plan what comes next."

"All right." Melissa turned to follow the others. "We'll see you then. Don't be late."

The three younger children watched Melissa vanish down the corridor, then exchanged another glance. Jamie tipped his head toward the front door. "Come on."

They let themselves out onto the front porch.

"Won't Johnny be off with the geese, all the way over at Allard's End?" Lottie asked.

Jamie grinned. "Very likely, and I think we ought to go in that direction, anyway."

"Why?" George asked.

"Remember Mr. Harris said we needed to be thorough in following through each avenue of our search?" When George and Lottie solemnly nodded, Jamie went on, "And just now, he said that doing something you haven't thought of before might lead to a vital discovery. Well, there are paths we haven't yet searched along."

George's face lit with comprehension. "The minor path between here and the green—and the continuation that goes from the other side of the green, around the back of the vicarage and the church to the stables of Dutton Grange."

"Exactly." Jamie looked at his siblings. "We need to be thorough, and we have time now. Let's go and search along there."

Lottie and George grinned and chorused, "Yes—let's!"

Jamie led the way down the steps and around the house to where the minor path, which they'd just remembered, opened from the rear of the hall's shrubbery.

They hadn't gone far before Lottie observed, "I don't think many people use this path."

It was overgrown in places, and there was even the odd sapling that had started to grow on the path itself. George pointed out, "Most of the Hall staff and others like the Tookses use the main path—the one that leads to the lake. There's likely not much call for anyone to use this path."

"That might be all the more reason for us to search along here," Jamie observed. "Not many other people would have come this way, but someone might have."

"Like one of the men the others haven't yet spoken to," Lottie said.

Jamie and George nodded. Jamie led the way, George at his heels, with Lottie happily bringing up the rear.

They forged steadily on, carefully scanning the ground to either side for any signs of disturbance. The path wended through lightly wooded terrain, but eventually emerged into the open, where it skirted the meadow behind Mountjoy's Store.

Halfway around the curved edge of the meadow, Jamie stopped and stared at the rear of the store. "I wonder if there's some excavation in the meadow."

George halted alongside and scanned the winter-brown expanse. "There doesn't seem to be any paths through it, and the grasses are growing evenly over the whole field."

Lottie's brow wrinkled. "Wouldn't someone have needed a reason to dig there—and if someone had, wouldn't one of the Mr. Mountjoys know?"

Jamie nodded decisively. "And they would have told us if there'd been any digging there." He pointed to the dormer windows, edged with gingham curtains, which were clearly the Mountjoys' personal domain and overlooked the meadow. "They would know if anyone had been digging for any reason."

That decided, they walked on.

Eventually, they reached the village green, paused to exchange a disappointed look, then, chins firming, forged ahead. They crossed the green at an angle, climbing the rise to reach the second of the lesser-used paths. The opening lay just over the crest; on reaching it, they trudged down the path, which cut through denser woodland, some way back from the vicarage.

At one point, Jamie and George leapt and jumped, peering through the trees to the left of the path.

"I can't even see the rear wall of the vicarage garden," George reported.

The increasingly thick undergrowth on both sides of the path forced them to slow. They pushed aside low branches and peered around bushes and trunks.

"The trees are thicker and older around here," Jamie said.

George paused, peering through the trees, toward the village. "I can just see the top of the church tower."

Jamie and Lottie came to peer up and out, too, then the three continued on.

They were still in dense woodland, well back behind the church, when Jamie halted, squinting into the area between the path and the church. "What's that?"

He didn't wait for an answer but stepped off the path, weaving between low bushes to a spot ten or so feet away.

George followed. "What is it?"

Lottie had been searching on the other side of the path. She straightened and looked at her brothers.

Jamie bent from the waist, peering downward. "It's a hole—a deep one. I think it might be an old well."

George reached his brother and stared down into the yawning blackness. "Could be." He stubbed the toe of his boot against a low stone. "It hasn't much of an edging—just a line of stones."

Lottie crossed the path and headed for her brothers.

Both boys dropped to their knees and, leaning forward, reached down to run their fingertips over the hole's walls. "It's not even lined," Jamie said. "Just rock and earth."

Lottie reached George's side, looked, then continued around the hole. "It's quite big."

Frowning, Jamie sat back on his haunches. "But it's not as if anyone would have been dredging anything out of it."

"And," George said, also easing back, "why would anyone hide anything in a well?"

Jamie glanced at Lottie, just as she edged closer to the hole and leaned forward to peer down. "Lottie! Be careful!"

"Oh!" Lottie's foot slipped on a leaf-covered stone, which shifted—then the ground under her crumbled, and she slid, feet first, into the hole.

"*Lottie!*" Both boys scrambled to their feet. White faced, they stared into the hole.

The sound of splashing reached them.

"Lottie! Are you all right?" Jamie struggled against the panic that gripped him.

A second passed, then the beginnings of a wail broke off on a sniffle. A second later, Lottie's voice floated up from the depths of the hole. "I hurt my ankle." Another sniffle. "It's dark and muddy down here." Another sniff, and on a rising note, she wailed, "I don't like it!"

"Wait!" Jamie put all the command he could muster into his voice. "We'll get you out."

George turned a strained face his way. "How?" George glanced around. "We'll need a rope. And the sides are slippery."

Jamie's thoughts were racing. "I'm fastest—I'll go and fetch help. You stay here and talk to Lottie."

George nodded and didn't argue.

"Lottie?" Jamie called. "I'm going for help. George will stay with you."

A hiccup came from below, then a wavering "All right."

Jamie didn't wait for more. He pushed back to the path, then halted. "Which way?"

Dutton Grange was closest, but it was midafternoon—Jamie had no idea if any of the menfolk would be immediately available. And if they weren't?

He thought of the vicarage only to jettison the idea. The reverend would try to help, but they would need someone more physically able. Jamie doubted Lottie could climb out of the well on her own.

By the same reasoning, the manor—which was farther away—wasn't the best destination. Simms and Crimmins were able-bodied enough, but not nimble. Not the sort to climb down a well.

"The Hall." Lips setting, Jamie didn't waste any more time thinking. He set off at a run, dodging branches as he pelted back the way they'd come. Fulsom Hall wasn't the closest house, but it was the nearest guaranteed source of the right sort of help.

And Jamie could run very fast.

He burst onto the green, streaked down and across the rise, and plunged into the path on the other side. It was as long as the path that led from the north end of the lake to the Hall's grounds, but the path along the meadow's edge was more even—better for running flat-out along.

Mere minutes later, Jamie shot out of the Hall shrubbery and raced to the house. He didn't pause to knock but, panting, opened the door and charged into the front hall and on toward the library. "Mr. Harris!"

Callum was deep in a promising description of what he thought was the merchant's villa that a reference he'd found earlier had alluded to; it took him a second to register that the hail for "Mr. Harris" was meant for him. He looked up as the library door burst open, and Jamie staggered in, a hand pressed to his side.

"Mr. Harris!" the boy gasped. "You have to come. Lottie's fallen down an old well."

Instantly, Callum pushed to his feet. "Where? Exactly."

Jamie was breathing hard, but regaining his composure. "In the woods behind the church. There are two lesser-used paths—we were searching along them."

Mountjoy and Henry and the others, who apparently had been heading inside, had heard the commotion and followed Jamie into the library in time to hear his reply.

Melissa rushed to her cousin. "Jamie—what's happened?" Mandy was at Melissa's shoulder.

Callum saved him from having to answer. "Lottie's fallen into an old well." Callum halted before Jamie and held the boy's gaze. "How deep is she?"

Jamie blinked. "I don't know. We can hear her well enough, but we couldn't see her, and she said it was muddy." He paused, then added, "It's very dark down there."

Callum nodded and looked at Mountjoy and Henry. "We need ropes and lanterns." He thought, then added, "And we'll need two strong, heavy men to act as anchors if needed."

Mountjoy glanced at Henry, who, pale, said, "Fetch ropes and lanterns, and tell Billings and James we need them." To Callum, Henry added, "Billings and James are the strongest and heaviest of our men."

Callum scanned the company, then nodded. "We'll do."

He turned to Jamie, saw the anxiety in the boy's face, and clapped a hand on his shoulder. "Let's go." Callum looked at Henry. "Can you wait and follow with the ropes, lanterns, and the men as fast as you can?"

His expression grim, Henry replied, "Of course."

Callum released Jamie and waved him to the door. "Lead on."

The boy had stamina; Callum found himself running in Jamie's wake. Dagenham, Kilby, and Wiley, having left Carnaby to follow with Henry, thundered behind, and the two young ladies were on their heels as they all followed Jamie along the narrow, unkempt path.

They crossed the village green, angling up the rise to race on down an even narrower path that cut through dense woodland.

A hundred yards farther on, Jamie slowed, then pointed off the path and diverted into the trees.

Following Jamie, Callum heard George call, "They're here, Lottie!" An instant later, George added, "Mr. Harris and the others have come to get you out."

As Callum fetched up before the mouth of the old well, he heard a faint sob. Taking care not to disturb the ring of foundation stones circling the edge—all that was left of any raised sides the well might originally have had—he eased to his knees a foot away, leaned forward, and peered down. Blackness yawned below. "Lottie? Are you hurt?"

She sniffed, then said, "I think I've sprained my ankle. It hurts."

"If that's all that hurts," he returned in a bracing tone, "then you're a very lucky girl. I'll be down in a few minutes to help you climb out—we're just waiting for the others to bring ropes and lanterns." He glanced toward the path, but the rest of the crew were just arriving; there was no sign of Henry and the ropes and lanterns yet. He turned back to the hole. "Is it wet down there?"

"It's muddy and slimy, where I am." A pause, then Lottie said, "There's water on the other side of the hole. I fell into a bit of it, but I scrambled out."

"All right—stay where you are. Better on the mud than in the water." Especially if the water was deep. Callum glanced over his shoulder as the others, who had fallen behind on the last stretch but had finally reached them, drew near. He held out a hand, signaling them to stay back. "The edges are crumbling—that's why Lottie fell in." He grimaced and surveyed the site. "It's dangerous leaving a well like this, without a properly constructed lid." The thought gave him pause, then he leaned forward and called, "Lottie—are there any broken timbers around you?"

After a second, she called up, "It's so dark, I can't really see, but there is some wood here—broken bits."

Callum grimaced. In a quiet voice, one he hoped Lottie wouldn't hear, he murmured, "It sounds as if there was a lid on this, but it broke. There might be a dead animal down there with her."

Melissa and Mandy met his eyes. After a second, Mandy whispered, "Let's hope she doesn't find any bones."

Callum fervently hoped so; he didn't fancy having to climb out with a hysterical little girl.

Heavy footsteps heralded the approach of the men with the ropes and lanterns. Callum thought to ask, "Lottie, we can't see you because you're in the dark. But can you see us?"

When she didn't reply, he rephrased, "If you look up, what can you see?"

"I'm looking," Lottie said, "but all I can see is black, with a little bit of light to one side."

Callum grimaced. He looked at the recent arrivals—at Henry and the two heavy men he'd brought with him, both of whom carried long, thick ropes wound over their shoulders. Callum reached for the ropes. "The well—if it is a well—isn't a clear straight shaft. We need a lantern."

Henry and Roger each carried a shuttered lantern; Roger was closest and offered his.

Callum rose and took it, swiftly tied the end of one of the ropes to the handle, then paused. After a second of thinking, he waved Melissa and Mandy to a position several feet back from the lip of the well, to his left. "Take this rope." He passed over the coiled length now attached to the lantern. "Dagenham?" When the viscount, who was long and lean, stepped to Melissa's side, Callum waved at him to take hold of the rope and step to the hole's edge.

He did, instinctively taking up the slack between him and where the rope was attached to the lantern in Callum's hands.

Callum nodded. "Good. I'm going to release the lantern over the well." To Dagenham, he said, "I want you to try to keep it from swinging too much, then when it steadies, play out the rope and lower it gradually —foot by foot." To the two girls, he said, "I want you to feed the rope to Dagenham, but slowly and evenly. If he loses his grip, I don't want the lantern falling like a stone."

The girls nodded. Callum looked at Dagenham. "Ready?"

Dagenham nodded, and Callum unshuttered the lantern, then leaned forward as far as he dared and released it. It swung wildly, but Dagenham reached out as far as he could, keeping the lantern away from the rocky walls. Pendulum-like, it steadied; once it was hanging straight down, Dagenham glanced at Callum, a question in his eyes, and Callum nodded. "Lower it."

Everyone craned their necks and watched as the lantern descended, illuminating crumbling rocky walls. Twenty feet down, and Dagenham murmured to the girls to give him more rope. After a pause, the lantern descended farther, and those close enough to the edge saw why Lottie couldn't see them. A huge whorl of tree roots had grown through the wall and, subsequently, had trapped earth and leaves. Over the years, the mass had grown, blocking more than half the shaft.

By chance, they'd sent the lantern down almost opposite the clump; it continued past and dipped still farther.

"I can see the lantern!" Lottie shouted.

"Good," Callum replied. "Don't try to touch it." He held up a hand to Dagenham. "Stop."

Dagenham did; the lantern was now about two feet below the blockage, but the intrusion prevented them from seeing what lay below.

"Lottie," Callum called, "how much higher than you is the lantern? Don't touch it, but if you wanted to, could you reach a finger to it?"

After a moment came, "*Nearly.* Jamie could reach it, if he was here."

Callum released the breath he'd been holding; he suspected the rooty mass had broken Lottie's fall, and she'd tumbled off it and fallen farther —but how much farther had been the question in his mind. If she was less than ten feet below the mass, the ropes would reach. "Good enough," he called. "I'll be down in a few minutes to fetch you."

"You're going down?" Jamie asked.

Callum nodded. He shrugged out of his greatcoat, tossed it aside, and reached for another rope. "I've done this sort of climbing before."

Quickly, he instructed the two older men—Billings and James—in how to manage his weight as he descended the shaft. Then Callum turned to Jamie and George, backed by Henry, Kilburn, Carnaby, and Wiley. "I'm going to take a second rope with me and tie it around Lottie. I'm hoping there's space enough to bring her up alongside me. We'll see. But the most important thing about pulling her up is not to jerk or pull too quickly. Just slow, steady, hand over hand—and listen for my orders. I'm going to try to teach her to walk up the wall as you pull—that way, there's less chance she'll bang into rocks and get hurt."

They nodded their understanding, and Callum arranged for Kilburn, the heaviest, to act as anchorman, with the others all assisting; given Lottie's slight weight, only one was actually needed to play out the rope, but "helping" meant they all felt they were contributing.

Callum glanced back down the hole, then waved at Dagenham and the two girls. "Slowly, without jerking the lantern, shift around to your left. I don't want to foul the lantern rope as I go down."

Under his direction, the trio edged around until the rope holding the lantern passed down one side of the intruding rooty mass.

Callum finished knotting his rope over his suit coat and around his waist and hips in a workmanlike harness, then he picked up the end of the rope for Lottie and tucked it into his pocket. Grasping his rope, he balanced his weight on the balls of his feet and backed toward the edge of the well. "I'm going to start down now, Lottie. Keep against the side and don't be surprised if you hear rocks falling. If any do, look down and shrink back against the side of the well. All right?"

After a second, she called back, "I'll try."

Callum looked at Billings and James, anchoring Callum via his rope, which was slung around the solid bole of a tree. "Ready?"

When they nodded, Callum leaned back, letting the rope, tree, and men support his weight as he tipped nearly horizontal, then he stepped back, over the well's lip, pressing the soles of his boots flat against the well's rocky, uneven wall.

"Steady as she goes," Callum said and, step by careful step, walked backward down the well shaft. It seemed that everyone but him held their breath, but this wasn't new to him.

He was experienced enough to go slowly, to understand the futility of hurrying, especially with a little girl below.

When he neared the intruding mass, he slowed even more. "I'm almost down, Lottie. Won't be long now."

He had to press his hips and shoulders close to the wall to ease past the blocking clump and descend farther—until finally, he could see what lay below, illuminated by the lantern that now hung to the side, level with his head.

Callum glanced around, met Lottie's eager eyes, and managed a reassuring smile, but they weren't out of the woods—in multiple ways—yet.

CHAPTER 8

*L*ottie's little face lit. "You're here!"

Callum felt the rope holding him give, forcing him to take two steps farther down the well—toward the dark, still water several feet below his boots. "Hold on my rope!" he yelled up to Billings and James.

Once Callum was sure they'd stopped playing out the rope, he edged his feet around the wall so that he could more easily face Lottie. He smiled in heartening fashion. "Well, this is an adventure."

He couldn't stand, because Lottie was perched on the only spot available. She'd landed half in the water—in the pool he would wager was at least several feet deep. Possibly much deeper. If the marks on her coat were any guide, she'd scrambled and dragged herself up, onto the clump of earth she probably thought was solid beneath her feet. In fact, it was a second intrusion of roots, encased in trapped earth and forest detritus.

If Callum tried to even brace against the shelf, it might give way and drop Lottie into the black, icy water. He didn't know if she could swim, and he didn't want to ask—and didn't want to find out the hard way, either.

"Now…" He assessed and considered as he drew down the second rope, looping it in his hands. Although Lottie was showing no outward sign of being chilled, her coat was soaked halfway up her chest, and Callum suspected the clothes below it were equally wet. He needed to get her above ground and into a warm bath as soon as possible, but at the moment, he couldn't even reach her.

He'd shifted so his back was nearly to the rocky wall, and Lottie stood on her potentially unstable perch almost directly opposite. His rope ran down close to the wall—at an angle, but clear of the mass above. If he tried to shift toward Lottie or even lean across to her, his rope would rub against the clumped mass now above their heads. He couldn't afford to dislodge the clump and have it fall on Lottie; she'd been through enough already.

"You're holding up well," he told her. "Now, I'm going to toss you this rope. Do you think you can catch it?"

She nodded eagerly and held out her hands; Callum realized her teeth were beginning to chatter, and she was trying to hide it.

He played out the rope. "It doesn't matter if you miss it the first time. We can try again until you grab it. All right?"

She nodded again, this time impatiently.

He tossed the rope across.

It took three tries, but eventually, she clutched the end of the rope to her chest.

"Now," Callum said, "I'm going to teach you how to fashion a rope harness—just like mine." He proceeded to talk her through the process; although her fingers started fumbling, they were nimble enough to manage the knots. He got Lottie to pull back hard against his tugs, tightening the knots until he was satisfied they would hold well enough for the first stage of getting her out.

"Right." He nodded encouragingly at her. "That's good enough for now. Once I have you over here with me, I'll tighten those knots a bit more." He held up a finger, signaling she was to wait, then tipped his head and shouted, "Billings, James. I'm going to carry Lottie to begin with, until we're past the overhang. Be prepared to take the extra weight."

"Aye, sir," Billings called down. "Ready when you are."

Callum looked at Lottie and grinned. "Do you ever fling yourself at your brothers? Like they might if they were playing ball and wanted to tackle another boy?"

She nodded. "Sometimes."

"Good. I'm going to come a bit closer, and when I say, I want you to fling yourself at me. Don't worry—I'll catch you." He showed her the extension of her rope harness, which he'd looped through the ropes across his chest. "You're attached to me, anyway, but it will help if you can leap across. All right?"

She nodded again, and Callum looked up and, mindful of damaging the mass above, edged around the wall as far as he dared. Then he steadied and looked at Lottie. "Billings, James, get ready."

Then he nodded at Lottie. "Now—jump!"

She flung herself at him; he grabbed her coat and yanked her to him, feeling her arms wrap around his chest like a monkey's. They bobbed on the rope, but it pulled taut, and they steadied.

"Well done!" He shifted her until he was carrying her against his chest. Obligingly, she altered her hold, wrapping her arms about his neck and gripping the sides of his waist with her knees.

He looked down and grinned into her eyes. "Perfect."

Slowly, he pivoted, then edged around the well until their ropes rose straight, clear of the root mass. "Right. Now we're going to start up—past this lump above."

Callum called to the crew, and under his directions, they fell into the rhythm of pulling him and Lottie up, hand over hand. Slowly, they moved upward. It was a squeeze to get past the root ball without squashing Lottie against the wall, but he managed it. As they emerged from the shadow of the overhang, he heard cheers from above—and felt the tension gripping Lottie ease a fraction. "Nearly there," he murmured, although that was a lie.

He jettisoned the idea of having Lottie walk up the side under her own steam; she was shaking and chilled and simply too exhausted by her ordeal.

He tipped his head up and called to the others, "Let's keep going like this. Pull on both ropes at the same pace, slowly and steadily." He gave them a beat, and they held to it, allowing him to walk step by step up the side of the well, while Lottie clung to him like a limpet.

A dead weight of teeth-chattering limpet, but at least she was safe.

Callum murmured to her, telling her of their progress as he labored up the shaft. He was accustomed to supporting his own weight on such climbs, but having to support Lottie's as well was an added strain; the muscles of his thighs and back were burning by the time he neared the lip of the well.

And then, thank God, he walked up and over the edge, and they were safe and sound on solid ground.

Melissa and Mandy rushed to take Lottie from him, leaving Dagenham to haul up the lantern.

Callum relinquished Lottie as Jamie and George rushed up, concern etched in their faces.

"Lottie?" Melissa had wrapped the younger girl in her arms. Anxiety laced her voice as she asked, "Lottie—you're shivering dreadfully. Can you open your eyes?"

A second later, Mandy asked, "Can you hear us?"

Callum inwardly cursed; he finished stripping off his rope harness, then fell to unfastening the one about Lottie, who was stiff and unmoving. He glanced at Henry. "She's chilled and going into shock. Which is the nearest house?"

Everyone paled.

"Dutton Grange," Henry replied. "M'sister's house."

Callum finished loosening the rope around Lottie. He grabbed his greatcoat and enveloped her in it. "Give her to me," he said to the other children. "My body's hottest at the moment, after that climb."

They helped him finish bundling Lottie, then he lifted her and cradled her against his chest.

"This way." Henry was already striding back to the path.

Callum followed, and the others fell in behind. When his feet hit the path, he caught Henry's eye. "She needs to be placed into a hot bath as soon as possible." Callum nodded ahead. "Run!"

Henry didn't wait for more; he took off as if the hounds of hell were snapping at his heels. Callum ran as fast as he dared after Henry, and the others kept up.

Dagenham drew alongside. "If you're in any danger of dropping her, I can take her for a while."

Callum nodded. "Let's see how far this house is. I'm all right for now."

Dagenham didn't push but kept close; Callum appreciated the silent support.

The path ended beside a stable yard. Callum didn't slow but made for the house ahead.

"That way." Dagenham waved to the left. "Up on the terrace and through those French doors. They're waiting for you."

Callum saw Henry and another, older gentleman standing inside, poised to open a pair of French doors. Callum took the steps up to the terrace two at a time, and the doors swung inward, and he carried Lottie, silent and still, through.

Blessed warmth enveloped them, nearly a shock of its own after the icy chill of outside. Until that moment, Callum hadn't registered how low the temperature had fallen—hadn't even noticed the encroachment of evening and the dimming of the light.

The others piled into the room in his wake, then Henry shut the doors.

The older gentleman—by his bearing, a military man—had a face one side of which was a horrid mass of scars. He, however, had eyes only for Lottie. "Christian Longfellow," he said to Callum and nodded at Lottie. "How is she?"

"Chilled, more or less to the bone, but if she's warmed quickly, she shouldn't take any lasting ill." Ignoring the scars, as it seemed everyone else was doing, Callum glanced toward the door he assumed led to the rest of the house. "But she needs to be got out of these clothes immediately. She fell into water, and they're sodden."

"Of course." Longfellow urged Callum to the door. "Come—my wife is preparing a hot bath. I'll show you up."

His heart thumping, Callum climbed the stairs behind Longfellow, with Mandy and Melissa at his heels. Longfellow led them to a bedchamber, and together with Longfellow's wife, Lottie's cousins directed Callum to lay Lottie on the bed and took charge. A copper bathtub wreathed in steam stood by the hearth, along with several more pails, also steaming. Callum and Longfellow retreated, leaving the three women, supported by two maids, stripping Lottie of her wet clothes.

Standing in the corridor, staring at the closed bedchamber door, Callum suddenly felt useless.

Longfellow's hand landed on his shoulder. "Come with me—you need warming up, too."

A brandy before a raging fire was Longfellow's prescription. Callum's unexpected host led him to a long library where the others had already gathered about a fire Henry and a large manservant were building into a roaring blaze.

"Sit." Longfellow all but pushed Callum into an armchair angled to the warmth.

In what seemed mere seconds, Longfellow returned and pressed a cut-crystal tumbler holding a large measure of brandy into Callum's hand. "Drink," Longfellow ordered.

Callum gripped and obeyed. The fiery liquid slid down his throat, into his stomach…and what felt like an icy knot inside started to thaw and melt.

He dragged in a shuddering breath and took another sip of the revivifying spirit. With his wits slowly re-engaging, he looked around—and his gaze collided with Honor's. She sat beside the large library table where, clearly, she'd been working. With relief seeping through him—simply and unabashedly happy to see her—Callum smiled, and she smiled back.

"So"—Longfellow turned from pouring himself a drink—"what, exactly, happened?"

Unable to marshal his thoughts sufficiently well to explain anything to anyone, Callum left the story to the others to relate, and apparently realizing his state, Henry and the other gentlemen proceeded to tell Longfellow all that had occurred.

Gradually warming up courtesy of the fire and the brandy, Callum was content to sit, sip, and surreptitiously feast his eyes on Honor.

For her part, she appeared engrossed by the tale Henry and the others wove; as long as Callum could stare at her unimpeded, he didn't mind.

It was only when she—and Longfellow, too—turned their gazes on Callum, and he realized they were regarding him with something approaching awe, that he registered that Henry and the others had painted him in the colors of a hero. Callum fought a blush, quashed an impulse to squirm, and instead, lightly frowned. "They're exaggerating. The rescue wasn't that difficult—I've led an adventurous life and climbed into holes like that before."

"That," Henry said, "was obvious. But without you knowing what to do and being able to organize us all, we'd never have got Lottie out of that well—not so quickly and not without hurting her and possibly some of us as well."

Thinking to redirect their attention, Callum glanced at Longfellow, who was standing to one side of the hearth. "Speaking of that well, leaving a place like that open—no enclosure, no lid, just a gaping hole in the ground—is the epitome of carelessness." He arched a brow at Henry. "On whose land is the well?"

Henry screwed up his face in thought, then ventured, "I'm pretty sure it's on church land."

Longfellow was frowning, too. "Where, exactly, is it?"

After Henry and the other gentlemen described the well and its location in some detail, Longfellow shook his head. "I've never heard of a well there." He looked at Callum and nodded. "But I take your point.

Regardless of whose land it's on, I'll send a team of men out tomorrow to ensure it's made safe."

Callum inclined his head as the door opened, and Melissa looked in. She spotted Callum and came in, carrying his greatcoat over one arm. "Lottie's recovering," Melissa reported to the room at large. "She's warm again and talking and seems all right." She halted before Callum and offered him his greatcoat. "One of the maids brushed it clean. Thank you for lending it to Lottie to keep her warm."

Callum took the coat and laid it over the chair's arm. "Just as long as she's better."

Melissa smiled. "She's a bit crotchety about not being allowed down yet and so not knowing what's happening." She looked at the others. "I'm off to tell Grandmama and fetch some dry clothes for Lottie. Jamie? George? I think you'd better come, too, so Grandmama can see you're safe."

The boys rose readily.

Henry set down his glass. "I'll come, too." He smiled at Melissa. "Her ladyship is bound to want details."

Callum wasn't surprised to see Dagenham leave the room with Melissa and the others; it didn't seem anyone else was, either.

Callum relaxed in the chair; the warmth, the brandy, and the inevitable aftermath of action were making him drowsy. It seemed only a minute later when he heard voices in the front hall, then Lady Osbaldestone swept into the library. Longfellow entered in her wake.

Callum blinked fully awake and glanced around. Evidently, his host had left the library at some point, along with most of the others. Only Honor remained; she'd returned to the books on the library desk, but had angled her chair so she had Callum in her line of sight.

Lady Osbaldestone halted in the center of the room, her incisive black gaze on Callum. But her lips, he noted, were not quite straight, and her features seemed softer than he recalled as she said, "I understand I have you to thank for my granddaughter's rescue, sir."

Callum struggled to his feet and found his voice. "It was a team effort —we all played a part."

"I've been reliably informed that your contribution was vital to the rescue."

He shrugged noncommittally. "I knew what to do."

"So I've heard." Her tone conveyed, to him at least, that she knew just why he'd known what to do. "Regardless," she went on, "I believe I owe you the greatest debt." Regally, she inclined her head to him. "On behalf of myself and my family, sir, I thank you."

He had no option but to accept that with a half bow. He was saved from further discussions of his actions by Longfellow's wife, who walked in, saw him, and smiled.

She advanced, holding out her hand. "We haven't been introduced, Mr. Harris. I'm Eugenia Longfellow, and I'm very pleased to meet you, sir."

Callum grasped her fingers and bowed over them. "I thank you for your and your husband's hospitality, Lady Longfellow."

"Oh, posh!" Her ladyship waved his comment aside. "It was the least we could do when you were so heroically instrumental in saving little Lottie." She turned to Lady Osbaldestone. "Mandy and Melissa are helping Lottie dress—they'll be down shortly. She's very much improved. I doubt she'll take any lasting harm from her adventure."

"Thank you, my dear Eugenia," Lady Osbaldestone replied. "I've brought the gig and will drive her home when she's ready."

"Now!" Lady Longfellow returned her attention to Callum. "Henry and the others have told me that you've been studying the books in the Hall library, searching for clues regarding Roman settlements in the area."

Callum nodded. "I've found several references, but nothing that points to a specific location."

Lady Longfellow spread her arms, indicating the bookshelves lining the library's walls. "As much as I love the Hall"—she shot a laughing glance at her husband—"the library here is significantly more extensive, especially when it comes to matters of local history." She caught her husband's eyes, a faint question in hers, and smiling, he nodded. Her ladyship returned her gaze to Callum and went on, "As I gather Lottie and the boys were searching for our putative Roman hoard, and subsequently, your rescue of Lottie has brought you here, Lord Longfellow and I are happy to offer you free run of this library as well."

Callum's investigative heart leapt at the prospect, but he glanced at Honor, sitting at the library table and listening to every word. "I wouldn't want to disturb Miss Webster."

"Nonsense," Honor responded, smiling. "I'm accustomed to working in the Bodleian with students constantly around me. Besides"—she looked at the books and papers before her and wrinkled her nose—"all I'm doing is listing references."

Callum understood that drudgery. Still, he hesitated, but he really wanted to—needed to—pursue the location of the merchant's compound. And he wasn't at all averse to spending more time around Honor, even if they were both mired in the past. He caught her gaze. "If you're sure...?" When she nodded, he looked at Lady Longfellow and Lord Longfellow and smiled. "Thank you. If I can locate the site of the Roman merchant's compound that I'm now sure was somewhere near, our search for the source of the coins will go much faster."

"Excellent!" Lady Longfellow beamed.

She, Callum, and his lordship arranged for Callum to commence his search through the Grange library the following day. From the corner of his eye, Callum saw Honor take note, even as she tidied her papers away.

He glanced at the windows; although the curtains had been drawn, through a gap he confirmed it was full dark outside.

A commotion drew Lady Osbaldestone and the Longfellows to the door, then onward; Callum followed, with Honor trailing behind him, clutching a folder containing the professor's papers. They reached the front hall to discover Lottie had come down and was the center of a rowdy group. Relief shone in every smile and rang in the laughter.

Lottie was smiling happily. Then she noticed Callum and pushed past those surrounding her and marched determinedly up to him. She halted before him, looked up into his face, and smiling sweetly, said, "Thank you for rescuing me, Mr. Harris." Then she lowered her voice and added, "You were right—it was an adventure."

Callum felt his face split in a spontaneous, conspiratorial grin, but he was the adult here. He crouched, bringing his face level with Lottie's. "I'm glad you're all right, but next time you approach a deep hole—"

"I'll stop farther back from the edge." Sobering, Lottie nodded. "I won't forget."

Callum smiled and rose. Reaching out, he lightly ruffled Lottie's curls. "I'm sure you won't—and that's the hallmark of a wise explorer, learning from one's mistakes."

Therese was marshaling her brood. She called Lottie to her, and with a shy goodbye to Callum, Honor, and the Longfellows, Lottie hurried to take Therese's outstretched hand. With a farewell wave to the Longfellows, with the rest of her brood gathered close, Therese led the way out of the front door, across the porch, and down the steps to where Simms was waiting with the gig.

"Off you go." Therese waved the other four on, and they ducked their heads against the wind and hurried down the drive, making for the warmth of the manor.

Simms assisted Therese to the gig's seat, then lifted Lottie up to snuggle close beside her. Simms then heaved himself up, flicked the reins, and set the mare plodding around the forecourt and down the winding drive.

Therese hugged Lottie close and felt the little girl's arms reach around her. After a moment of reflection, of giving thanks for the warm little body in her arms, Therese bent her head and whispered in Lottie's ear, "I know you didn't mean to fall into the well, and while I wouldn't wish to encourage such accidents, intentional or otherwise, I have to commend you on the outcome."

When Lottie, her eyes wide in question, looked into Therese's face, Therese smiled and went on, "You've inadvertently achieved something of a matchmaking coup. I've been wondering how to get Mr. Harris and Miss Webster together—to have them spend time together, preferably alone—and you've brought that about. They'll be working side by side in the Grange library for at least the next few days." She paused, then murmured, "The trick to successful matchmaking is to engineer situations without it being at all apparent that you had any active hand in bringing said situation about."

Therese straightened and, smiling fondly, raised a hand and smoothed Lottie's bobbing curls back from her face. "You truly are my granddaughter, my dear—nothing could be clearer."

Lottie beamed. She held her grandmother's gaze for several heartbeats, then snuggled closer as Simms turned the mare in to the lane, then up the manor drive.

Back at Dutton Grange, Henry reminded Callum that Mrs. Woolsey had invited him to dine that evening, and after taking their leave of the Longfellows, in triumph, Henry and his friends bore Callum off to Fulsom Hall.

Callum duly presented himself at Dutton Grange the following morning and, by midmorning, was seated at the library table surrounded by several small mountains of tomes, in one of which he hoped to find the crucial information he sought.

Honor wasn't there when he arrived, and as the clock ticked away the hours, she didn't appear.

Callum reminded himself that he wasn't there to meet with her but to locate an ancient Roman site and knuckled down to the task.

Mrs. Wright, the Grange's housekeeper, interrupted him with a plate of sandwiches and a tankard of her home-brewed ale. "I know what you gentlemen are like," she informed him. "You lose yourselves in those books, and then you'll be starving and looking for sustenance in midafternoon, just when we've all settled with our feet up."

Unable to deny the charge, Callum accepted her offerings with due meekness and genuine thanks. He paused to eat, but as soon as he'd finished the sandwiches, tankard in hand, he returned to flicking pages.

The clocks had just struck three o'clock when the door opened, and Honor came in. She paused on the threshold and met his eyes. "Will I disturb you?"

Yes—and please do. Callum held back the words and, with his most charming smile, waved her in. "I doubt it, but to be frank, it would be a welcome diversion."

She came to the table and set down the journals and papers she was carrying at the far end. "No luck?"

Returning his gaze to the history he was laboriously reading, he shook his head. "Lots of hints and bits and pieces—throwaway references and the like. I've found three sources that mention, in one way or another, a merchant's compound that was located in this area. Two other accounts refer to a villa, and until I prove otherwise, I'm assuming that all the mentions refer to the same site. But as to exactly where the villa or compound was located...*that* critical fact I have yet to sight."

While he'd spoken, Honor had arranged her books on the tabletop. She sat and, down the length of the table, caught his eye. "How are the others faring with the search?"

He grimaced. "Not so well. The excitement of Lottie and the well aside, they've been concentrating on finding any excavation—any digging or disturbance of the soil—that might have resulted in the unearthing of the coins."

"Hmm. There wouldn't be any tilling of the fields in this season."

"No. And they haven't discovered any holes for new fencing or anything of that sort, either." Mentally revisiting the others' efforts,

Callum mused, "It's difficult to imagine how someone local might have come upon those three coins other than by picking them up. We've discounted any local receiving the coins from strangers or while traveling farther afield. Everything points to the coins being picked up locally—as has happened elsewhere often enough—but generally such finds have come from farmers or the like picking up something in their recently plowed field or from around some similar excavation." He shook his head. "But the others have found no sign of any excavation, so the source of the coins remains a mystery."

Honor studied the books piled around him. "Are you looking for any particular sort of account?"

Callum uttered a short laugh and drew his hands down his face. Lowering them, he said, "What I wouldn't give for a good census at this point." He surveyed the texts arrayed before him and grimaced. "I suspect the dearth of detail is largely due to the settlement here being entirely civilian and not connected with the legions at all, so it doesn't appear in any military reports, and for various reasons, those are the accounts historians have always paid most attention to." He glanced at the small pile of books he'd already been through. "As far as I can make out, the settlement here was a staging post of sorts, located just north of the route linking Clausentum, near Southampton, with Sorviodunum, which is Old Sarum. However, that road wasn't considered a major route for movement of the legions—apparently, they traveled via Venta Belgarum—our Winchester—and Calleva, which is Silchester. So while our local staging post was known, not much attention was paid to it. It didn't rate inclusion in military dispatches, so..." He shrugged. "I'm finding mentions, but few specific details."

He drew the book he was perusing closer and, after propping up the tome in front of him, slumped back in his chair. "I'll keep searching, because there's always a chance some helpful scribe decided to keep a detailed diary of his travels, but to be perfectly honest, I don't hold much hope." His gaze on the book's text, he paused, then added, "That said, the hallmark of a true scholar is that we never, ever, give up."

He heard Honor smother a laugh and looked up. Finding her regarding him with smiling eyes and a hand raised to hide her no-doubt-curved lips, he arched his brows in arrogant and demanding fashion.

She lowered her hand and let a soft laugh escape. "You have no idea how much like my uncle you sound."

Callum stilled; everything inside him froze. His eyes locked with hers, he struggled to find the right expression for his face. Eventually, he managed vague blankness, relieved by a slight shrug. "I fear I'm definitely not the scholar he is."

And wasn't that the absolute truth?

She tilted her head, plainly made curious by his odd reaction. "Perhaps not, but you definitely have a scholar's habits."

He dipped his head in acceptance and focused on the book before him.

After a second, Honor lowered her gaze to her papers, and silence settled over the room.

An inability to concentrate on a book to the exclusion of everything about him was not, normally, an affliction from which Callum suffered. But the plodding descriptions of Roman life in conquered Britain failed to keep his mind, let alone his senses, from tracking every move Honor made.

From her actions, he deduced she was wrestling with ordering footnotes and references for the professor's treatise, an occupation with which Callum was familiar.

So familiar that, just by glancing at her movements—from paper, to book, to paper, to list—he could tell that she was going about the finicky yet boring task in a way guaranteed to make said task even more difficult than it needed to be.

A frown had settled on her brow; he was aware of a building impulse to smooth it away by showing her a better approach, but he bit his tongue and forced his eyes to the Latin text before him.

He had a more pressing issue to resolve, namely, what he should do about Lady Osbaldestone's ultimatum. She'd given him a deadline—now six days away—to reveal his true name to Honor, but that assumed that he had some reason for doing so. That he had some expectation of their acquaintance continuing beyond the following Monday.

Did he?

Forcing himself to face and accept the fact that yes, he did, indeed, wish to pursue an acquaintance—and more—with Miss Honor Webster took him nearly half an hour of staring fixedly at the same Latin text. Luckily, mired in her own difficulties, Honor didn't notice.

But he had six days; he didn't need to rush into any potentially difficult revelations. He had time enough to think about what he needed to say and how best to explain himself—and to wait for a suitable opening.

He tried to imagine how Honor might react. The most rudimentary attempt at putting himself in her shoes brought home the fact that with every day he let slide past—with every instance such as the present one, where they were alone and yet he failed to speak—he was digging the hole of his deception deeper.

He shifted, then glanced at Honor.

Her frown had deepened, almost to a scowl.

He looked back at the tome before him, then shut it and drew the next forward.

Regardless of the inherent danger of allowing yet another day to pass, he felt certain that today—now—was not the time to speak.

Honor struggled to juggle her uncle's footnotes into some semblance of order. The first half of his treatise draft—still unfinished—helped her only so far, then she had to contend with his rough notes, which he hadn't put in any order. She was almost ready to tear out her hair.

And she had to keep silent. She would have moaned and groaned and grumbled, except that she was hyperaware of Callum Harris, seated at the other end of the table and occasionally glancing her way.

The curious thing was that, when he did, she sensed his gaze was assessing, but assessing in what way, measuring what about her, she couldn't for the life of her tell.

She wanted to know, which in itself was strange. Normally, she barely registered the effect she had on gentlemen—much less any effect of them on her. In that respect, Callum Harris was quite different—indeed, he was unique.

It was a battle to keep her mind focused on ancient Vikings and not respond to Callum's fleeting glances by looking up and meeting his eyes.

Just as it was a fight not to blush whenever she realized he was looking her way.

She gritted her teeth and forced her wayward wits back to ordering her uncle's references—marginally preferable to organizing his footnotes.

Mrs. Wright, the housekeeper, provided a welcome diversion; she brought in a tea tray and poured them cups of tea, then remained to chat about what they were doing and encourage them to eat slices of her plum cake.

Honor savored a bite of the rich cake, then examined the slice she was consuming. "Are these the same plums that prompted Lady Osbaldestone to embark on supplying plum puddings for the whole village?"

"Aye, miss. That they are. We had such a crop this year as never has been seen before—if it wasn't for her ladyship's notion of plum puddings, we'd never have been able to use them all, which, as they're especially sweet and juicy this time, would have been a shocking waste."

"It must be quite an undertaking," Callum said from the other end of the table. "To make plum puddings for the whole village."

"That, it will be." Mrs. Wright nodded sagely. "But her ladyship's Haggerty has a recipe I'd kill for, and there's no doubt but that she and Mrs. Crimmins are up to the task."

Tea consumed and cake devoured, Callum sat back and grinned. "I'm trying to imagine a plum pudding factory in the manor's kitchen."

Mrs. Wright chuckled and gathered their empty teacups. "Aye—it'll be a sight to see. We sent all our pudding basins over the lane. First Christmas since the master came home that I won't be filling any myself."

Honor considered the cook-housekeeper. "Will you miss it? Making a Christmas pudding?"

About to heft the reloaded tray, Mrs. Wright paused, then said, "Aye, I will, that." She lifted the tray and turned to the door. "That said, I'll be happy to serve Haggerty's plum pudding—I can't wait to try it m'self."

With a nod for them both, Mrs. Wright left, and after sharing a smiling glance, Callum and Honor returned to their respective tasks.

Callum finished searching through two more books, then Honor glanced up at the mantelpiece clock, gave vent to a frustrated sound, and started to gather her papers.

Alerted to the time—after five o'clock—Callum glanced out of the windows, confirming that dusk had come and gone, and it was nearly full dark. He looked at Honor. "Are you heading back to your cottage?"

She nodded. "Mrs. Hatchett—the cook-housekeeper from the vicarage —has been cooking for us as well, but Uncle Hildebrand won't stop to eat unless I'm there to force the issue."

Callum only just bit back the words *He always was one to skip meals.*

He reordered the pile of texts he'd yet to read, then rose. "I'll walk with you down the drive."

She threw him a brief smile, and together, they quit the room. Hendricks, the Longfellows' majordomo, met them in the front hall and assisted them into their overcoats, then bowed them from the house.

They set off across the forecourt, with Honor clutching a cardboard folder containing the professor's papers to her chest. With his hands sunk in his pockets, Callum matched his stride to hers as she walked briskly down the winding drive.

The skeletal trees cast shifting shadows over the gravel, their bare branches creaking ominously in the wind. "I hate that sound," Honor confided. "It's so...haunting."

Callum cast her a teasing glance. "I'll save you from the bogeyman."

She rolled her eyes, but her lips had curved.

They reached the lane and halted. Honor turned to him and nodded. "No doubt I'll see you next time I'm in the library." She tapped the folder. "I'm not even halfway through."

Callum looked past her down the lane. It curved to the right; the cottage to which she was heading was out of sight around the bend, and the way to it was drenched in shadows.

He waved her on. "I'll walk with you until you can at least see the cottage."

She hesitated, but he stepped out, and she turned and fell in beside him. "Where are you heading? I don't want to take you out of your way."

Through the gloom, he sent her a self-deprecatory smile. "I'll drop in at the Arms for some of their pie before hying to my cottage. I don't have anyone to cook for me, although given I'm rarely there, it would be wasted effort, I fear."

Her steps faltered. "So I am taking you out of your way."

"It's only a few yards." Callum waved her on, and with an almost-silent huff, she resumed walking alongside him.

They rounded the bend, and the cottage came into sight.

Callum forced his feet to halt. "There you are." He nodded at the cottage and smiled at her. "I can see you to the door from here."

She shook her head at him. "Thank you. No doubt I'll see you in the next few days." She paused, scanning his face through the darkness, then tipped her head to him. "Good night."

He echoed the farewell, then stood and watched as she walked on. She reached the gate, opened it, and went up the path to the door.

Callum lingered just long enough to see her open the door, then swung around and walked away into the darkness, letting the shadows veil him from anyone inside the cottage.

Every impulse he possessed had insisted he walk Honor all the way to her door, but he couldn't risk the professor seeing him.

Not yet. Not before he'd located the hoard.

∾

After shutting the door behind her, Honor set the folder on the small side table, unbuttoned her coat, shrugged it off, and hung the heavy garment on the hook behind the door. For an instant, she paused and let her mind range over the events of her afternoon, ultimately focusing on the sensations and stirrings Callum Harris's glances had provoked. Primed by that magical interlude on the ice, was she reading too much into his attentiveness? Or was there something truly there—something, some emotional connection, growing between them?

After a moment of staring into space, she shook herself and whispered, "I have no clue. And no time to daydream and wonder." With that reminder of her pressing duties, she went through to the cottage's kitchen. The pot Mrs. Hatchett had left on the stove emitted a delicious aroma, but not even such an enticing smell had managed to rouse her uncle.

Smiling fondly, she walked through the archway into the small sitting room he'd commandeered as his study. "Come along, Uncle Hildebrand. It's time to eat."

"Heh? What?" Her uncle looked up at her and blinked several times as if to bring her into focus. Then he glanced at the windows, which now looked out into darkness. "Damn it." He slumped, frustration in his face. "I've only just started making progress. Where did the day go?"

"The same place yesterday went," Honor dryly replied. "And you've let the fire go out again."

Her uncle turned to stare at the fireplace. "So I have."

He sounded so surprised, Honor had to battle an affectionate grin. "Why don't you get it going again, while I lay the table?"

Hildebrand Webster looked at the papers strewn over the small desk behind which he sat and heaved a heavy sigh. "I suppose I'd better." He rose and rumbled, "I'm not at all sure I'll have this done in time."

Honor walked back to the kitchen, but called over her shoulder, "You always grumble—but you always manage. And this time, as the society is honoring you, you really don't have a choice."

CHAPTER 9

*T*he next morning, Callum was back in the Dutton Grange library, carefully perusing yet another tome dealing with the Roman occupation of the area, when Jamie, George, and Lottie burst in.

"There you are!" Jamie skidded to a halt at the end of the table.

"When we couldn't find you on the green, Henry told us you were here," George said.

By then, Lottie had reached Callum; she caught his hand in both of hers and tugged. "But you have to come to the pageant."

Callum pushed away from the table. "Pageant?" He looked from Lottie to her brothers.

"The village pageant," Jamie explained. "It's one of Little Moseley's Christmas events."

"Everyone in the village comes," George assured him. "You can never tell what might happen."

"It's important to be there to find out." Lottie tugged again.

With a last glance at the boring text, Callum allowed himself to be drawn to his feet and towed out of the library.

Jamie opened the front door, explaining Hendricks's absence with "Most people will already be there."

"And the rest will soon follow," George added.

Callum lifted his greatcoat from the rack, shrugged into it, then walked with the trio out into a day that, in keeping with the days before, remained unrelievedly threatening. There'd been a decent snowfall the night before, and low clouds still hovered, but none had yet attained the puffy, steel-gray state that would signal further falls. Blessedly, the wind had eased, leaving a mere wisp of icy air intermittently brushing over any exposed skin. With the scent of winter wrapping about them, Callum strode beside the children down the drive, touched by the realization that, not finding him on the green where, apparently, the village was gathering, they'd come to fetch him.

They reached the lane and came face-to-face with Honor, carrying the folder containing the professor's papers.

She smiled at Callum and the children. "Are you going somewhere?"

"To the pageant!" the youthful trio chorused and promptly informed her that she absolutely had to attend, too.

Honor looked at the folder.

Callum held out a hand. "Let me run that up to the library for you. It won't take me a minute."

She hesitated, but the children were looking encouraging and impatient, so she relinquished the folder.

Callum loped back to the house, set the folder on the library table, and ran back again; he had long legs—as he'd foretold, the task hadn't taken him long. And the folder being in the Grange library ensured Honor would return there later, after the pageant had run its course.

He rejoined the others in time to hear Honor stand firm over disturbing her uncle. "He's working hard to finish the paper he's writing —he has to have it completed by the end of the year—and events like the pageant are not the sort of entertainments he enjoys. If we haul him out, he'll fret and fume and scowl the whole time."

Truer words were never spoken.

When the children looked unconvinced, Callum said, "Now you've successfully corralled me and Miss Webster, you'll have to act as our guides. How much time do we have until the pageant starts?"

As he'd anticipated, the children didn't have watches and so weren't sure. They forgot about the professor and urged Callum and Honor to hurry toward the village green.

"The village pageant," Jamie explained, "is really a re-enactment of the Nativity, with boys and girls from the village playing the various roles."

"But with real animals." George looked up at Callum and Honor, and his grin couldn't have been wider. "Duggins, the donkey—the one that carries Mary to the stable—is a little unpredictable."

"Sometimes, he behaves," Lottie translated, "but sometimes, he doesn't."

"And then there are the sheep." Jamie glanced at George. "I wonder if they'll bolt again this year."

George looked at Callum and Honor and explained, "At the end of the play, the sheep always want to rush into the crowd."

"They have ever since we've been coming here, to Little Moseley and the pageant," Lottie said.

"Although last year," Jamie admitted, "none of the sheep got very far."

It was plain that the children considered the unpredictable pageant a highlight of Christmas in Little Moseley. As they reached the white expanse of the village green and saw the crowd thronging the snowy sward, Callum murmured to Honor, "It appears the pageant is a universal favorite."

Everyone he'd encountered in the village seemed to be there, along with many others he hadn't yet met. Although the villagers all knew each other and the event was clearly for locals, everyone who saw them smiled, and those who knew them hailed them in welcome.

Callum and Honor were soon smiling and nodding to right and left.

Jamie, George, and Lottie towed and herded them along; the trio clearly had some specific destination in mind.

Sure enough, after tacking and weaving up a slight, in-parts-slippery incline, they joined Henry and his four friends, along with Melissa and Mandy, all of whom were standing with their backs to the stone wall at the side of the vicarage garden and had saved places for the three children and Honor and Callum.

After guiding his small band into position, Jamie proudly declared, "This is the best vantage point."

Although she was leaning this way and that to see between shoulders and heads, Lottie stated categorically, "From here, you can see everything."

Callum exchanged a smiling glance with Honor, then looked down at Lottie, standing before him. After a second, he bent and whispered in her ear, "If you like, when it starts, I'll lift you up to my shoulder. You'll see even more from there."

She turned wide eyes on him, then hesitated and said, "Mama says I'm a bit heavy now."

He fought to keep a straight face as he rose. "After our adventure in the well, I'm fairly sure I can manage. We'll see."

Her smile bloomed, and she nodded and returned to tracking what was going forward on the green.

Farther along the wall, Dagenham, standing beside Melissa, dipped his head to hers. "I wonder if Duggins will behave himself. I heard someone say that this year's Mary was rather sturdy and wasn't happy about having to ride a donkey."

"I can't imagine Duggins will notice one way or the other," Melissa replied. "From all I've heard, he's more likely to decide to be difficult simply because he can. And I can't say I blame our Mary, whoever she is. Anyone having to ride Duggins, even over such a short distance, is surely tempting fate."

Dagenham chuckled. "I heard Longfellow say that Duggins has always been an ornery beast."

Melissa lowered her voice. "Apparently, this year, they've decided to add goats. That might also be…interesting."

"Indeed." Dagenham grinned and looked out over the excited crowd. "I have to say that in terms of village Christmas events, the Little Moseley pageant is a perennial success. It's clearly a fixture for everyone round about and draws people together, which is the whole purpose of Christmas events."

Melissa nodded. She leaned to her left and stretched up on her toes, the better to peer in the direction from which the parading Mary, Joseph, and donkey would come; her foot slipped on a snow-slicked rock, and she gasped and started to tumble.

Hard hands clamped about her shoulders; they drew her back and steadied her. "Careful," Dagenham murmured.

A frisson of sensation shot down Melissa's arms from where his hands gripped so firmly; sensation of another stripe slid down her spine, fueled by his tone and the warmth of his breath as it teased the tendrils of hair by her ear.

Her shoulder brushed his chest. They were close enough for her to sense the steely strength of him—the warmth of his hard body—as he all but braced her against him.

She dragged in a breath, then couldn't release it. She managed a small nod and settled, planting her feet; only then did his hands fall away.

She was blushing, but while shifting to put her back to the wall, she slanted him a grateful glance. "Thank you."

His eyes met hers, and for just a second, despite being part of a large crowd, they seemed to fall into each other's eyes, and there was no one else on the planet but them.

A heartbeat passed, then slowly, solemnly, he inclined his head. "It was entirely my pleasure."

Still feeling the lingering heat of his hands imprinted on her skin, Melissa fought down her blush and faced forward once more.

Mandy, on Dagenham's other side, tapped his arm. "Can you see what's happening?"

Dagenham obediently looked and reported, "All seems ready at the stable." He swung his gaze the other way. "And Mary's just being helped aboard Duggins."

Expectation rippled through the crowd, and people craned their necks, looking toward the mustering area on the lower slope of the rise screening the lake.

Along with Honor, Callum followed the others' gazes. Then he traced the winding avenue being quickly cleared by the three younger members of the Whitesheaf family; employing the same good-humored tactics they used to manage their customers in the Arms, the trio were creating a path through the crowd, linking the knot of impatient, costumed children and the supposed stable—a makeshift construction, much like a large fairground booth, that had been erected on the green, closer to the lane, with the stable's rear opposite the Arms' front façade.

Callum had felt Honor's gaze touch his face, then slide away. He hesitated, then glanced at her and saw she'd followed his gaze to the stable. "The men were putting that up this morning, when I walked past," he said. "I didn't realize this was what it was for."

She threw him a smiling glance. "I've seen Nativity plays before, but always in a church. I've never seen anything like this. Have you?"

He shook his head. "Perhaps it's a regional Christmas rite."

On reaching the stable, the Whitesheafs had joined what Callum realized was the regular church choir, who stood in ranks to one side of the booth—the side opposite a collection of animals. He peered into the stable. "I can see a manger and a calf, sheep, goats, and... Are those ducks?"

"Geese, I think." Honor added, "Apparently, one of the farmers manages a flock of geese that supplies birds for the village's Christmas tables."

"It's interesting seeing what different villages about the country do," Callum said.

Honor grinned. "My uncle insists that community celebrations are critical to passing on traditions, which impart valuable lessons about how a particular society functions."

Callum wryly nodded. "A historian's view, but nevertheless true."

"Look!" Honor pointed to their left. "The procession's starting."

All eyes focused on Mary, perched rather precariously atop the gray-brown donkey now trotting along the path. Joseph, in flowing sheets and a blue robe with a low turban wound about his head, was battling to keep the donkey from breaking into a run.

Callum leaned down as Lottie looked up hopefully. He smiled and reached for her waist. "Let's see how strong I am." He hefted her easily and settled her on his left shoulder.

Lottie smothered a squeal of delight and wrapped one arm about Callum's head.

Assured she was stable, he returned his gaze to the Holy Couple, to see Mary, teeth gritted and with the doll that represented Baby Jesus slung in a shawl across her chest, gripping the donkey's mane in white-knuckled fists as she jounced on the beast's bony back.

Joseph was almost running alongside.

At that moment, Mr. Moody raised his baton, then swept it down, and the choir commenced what sounded like a Christmas serenade.

The donkey's ears went back, and he stopped short, front legs stiff with hooves digging into the snowy ground, all but tipping Mary over his head. She shrieked and hung on as Joseph was jerked to a halt as the rope tether unexpectedly pulled taut. Joseph's headgear was too loose and slid down his face.

The crowd held its breath.

The choir—unaware of the drama—sang on.

Disaster loomed as the principal characters in the re-enactment teetered on the brink of hysteria or tears. Or both.

Then Lord Longfellow, who'd been following the donkey, loomed at the beast's shoulder and tugged on the tether. "Come on, Duggins. Let's go."

To the watching crowd, Longfellow appeared to merely wave his arm, indicating the path ahead, but Lottie's eyes were sharp. She clutched Callum's head more tightly and reported, "Lord Longfellow has a carrot."

Callum chuckled. "His lordship is obviously one who likes to be prepared for all eventualities."

"Duggins is his donkey." Henry grinned. "M'sister says the grouchy beast will often only deign to follow Longfellow and refuses to behave for anyone else."

Joseph righted his turban, Mary visibly hauled in a breath and wriggled into a more secure position atop Duggins, and the procession continued without further incident. The choir completed their introductory piece just as the Holy Couple reached their destination. The pair deserted Duggins as rapidly as they could and took refuge within the stable, and Reverend Colebatch's voice rose and carried over the gathering as he read what Callum assumed was a specially scripted account of the Nativity tale.

Shepherds duly arrived, leading more calves, several gamboling lambs, and two bumptious kids.

The three Magi were called forth and came striding along the path, bearing gifts that appeared to be church lamps and censers, all of which emitted wafts of incense, readily discernible in the crisp, cold air.

From her elevated perch, Lottie kept up a whispered reportage, directing the others' eyes to this curious happening, then that.

Ultimately, Reverend Colebatch called on the Heavenly Host, and three young girls, draped in flowing white sheets with small feathered wings attached to their backs, skipped along the path, eventually joining the group gathered in the stable about the manger, welcoming the Holy Babe to the world.

Mr. Moody stepped forward, raised his baton, and the choir launched into a triumphal chorus.

When the joyful voices faded, the crowd, their faces lit with much the same emotion, waited, patient and silent. Then Reverend Colebatch walked forward, halted before the stable, and into the expectant silence intoned a special benediction, bringing the pageant to a close.

Leaning his head close to Melissa's, Dagenham whispered, "The singing wasn't as effective as ours last year—that silence at the end wasn't as shivery and tight." He met her eyes as she glanced at him. "But still, the singing was a nice touch. Compared to the first pageant I witnessed two years ago, this, with the singing, was definitely more engaging."

Melissa lowered her gaze to his lips, then drew in a breath and nodded. "More memorable," she whispered, rather breathlessly, back.

Meanwhile, Lottie had had Callum set her down, and her sharp ears had caught Dagenham's comment and Melissa's reply. She eyed the pair innocently. "I think the pageant changes a little every year."

Jamie nodded. "This year's wasn't *exactly* the same as last time."

George added, "I think Reverend Colebatch must adjust things to fit in all the children who want to take part. We haven't seen the Heavenly Host before."

Dagenham smiled and, together with Melissa, scanned the activity around the stable as proud parents converged and villagers offered their congratulations to all the children involved. Then Dagenham choked on a laugh. Blindly, he reached for Melissa's arm, but instead of encountering her sleeve, his hand found hers—stilled for a second—then his fingers gripped, and she gripped back as he pointed to the side of the stable. "Look! The sheep are making a break for it, and the goats are chivvying them along."

The sudden bleating and baaing was greeted with hoots, laughter, and not a few cheers as various children set off in pursuit of the sheep, lambs, goats, and kids. Duggins and the calves looked stoically on.

"Come on!" Jamie said. "We're missing the fun!" He, George, and Lottie pelted down the slope and flung themselves into the game of "catch the animals."

Most of the crowd had grown up on farms; the adults allowed the chase to continue just so far, then stepped in and assisted the assembled children to secure the runaway beasts.

Once that was done and calm again descended on the green, the women collected their children and beasts and started moving away, while the men set to, breaking down the stable and gathering all the paraphernalia of the day.

Callum glanced at the clouds massing over the wooded hills. "It looks like that snow is rolling our way."

Henry squinted at the clouds. "I doubt it'll reach us until evening—at least not to snow." He waved at the green, with the snowy blanket now trampled and far from pristine. "But by morning, I predict all this will be untouched and gleaming again."

Callum looked at Honor and smiled. "That was definitely entertaining. I'm going to help dismantle the stable. The more hands, the faster the task will go."

She smiled encouragingly. "I'll come, too—I can help gather the pennants."

Henry, his friends, and Melissa and Mandy followed Callum and Honor down the slope. Soon, they were all lending a hand, either with breaking down the wooden framework of the stable or, for the ladies, gathering and packing into baskets the fabrics that had formed the sides and front swags of the stable tableau, the guy ropes that had anchored the structure, and the red and green pennants some enterprising soul had looped about the roof.

"The pennants are also new," Melissa informed Mandy and Honor.

"They did add a splash of Christmas color," Honor said.

Working with Dagenham, Callum had just loaded the last of the long framing timbers into Farmer Tooks's dray and was walking back to join the others when he spotted Professor Webster stumping slowly through the snow toward the spot where the remaining crowd had congregated. Webster was patently searching for Honor; he looked rather lost.

Now isn't the time.

Not while they were surrounded by others and Honor was present as well. Callum lengthened his stride, then broke into a jog; there were enough people between him and Webster and Webster and Honor to make the action safe enough. He fetched up beside Honor and, uncaring of who saw it, grasped her hand and squeezed, bringing her swinging to face him and immediately gaining her complete attention.

He adopted his most relaxed and charming smile. "I've just remembered something—I need to get back to the library."

Her answering smile was understanding. "Of course."

He hesitated for a second, and so did she, then her smile deepened, and she turned her hand in his and lightly squeezed his fingers. "It's the middle of the day—I'll be fine walking back to the cottage. I'll see you next time I get to the library."

Remembering her folder on the library table, he nodded. "Until then."

He forced himself to release her hand without giving in to the impulse to raise it to his lips. He stepped away and saluted her, then turned and, his back to the remaining crowd, walked swiftly up the slope toward the rear corner of the vicarage garden wall.

The light was poor and, if anything, was worsening with the approaching storm. Even if Webster—whose eyesight was fading with the years—glimpsed Callum's retreating back, it was unlikely Webster would realize it was him.

Callum paused at the corner of the wall; he'd noticed a shortcut that gave access to the churchyard, from which another path led to the Grange. Screened by the wall, he risked a glance back.

Webster had found Honor and was speaking to her, judging by his gestures, with some urgency. Neither Webster nor Honor was looking

Callum's way, yet he felt a pointed stare boring into him. He scanned the increasingly empty expanse of the green. Beyond where the stable had been, his gaze locked on Lady Osbaldestone, who appeared to be waiting for her grandchildren to say their goodbyes to the village boys and girls. Her ladyship's eyes were trained on Callum.

He didn't need to guess to know what message her challenging stare was intended to convey. He had to tell Honor the truth, and soon.

He considered that prospect and, after a moment, nodded, once, to her ladyship, then turned and walked away.

Therese watched Callum vanish around the rear of the vicarage garden, no doubt on his way back to Dutton Grange.

She shifted her gaze to Honor and watched that young lady take her uncle's arm and lead him toward the lane and their cottage.

Therese had witnessed Callum and Honor's brief exchange before he'd beaten a hasty retreat. She hoped his nod meant what she wanted it to mean.

Before she could dwell further on the matter, her younger grandchildren came racing up.

"Grandmama!" Jamie's eyes were alight. "Can we go sledding?"

George pointed up the rise that lay between the green and the lake. "The others say the downward slope is nicely covered—perfect for sledding."

Lottie grasped Therese's hand. "Please, Grandmama—we'll be good."

"We promise not to go anywhere near the lake." Jamie fixed her with a pleading look, matched by George and Lottie.

Therese glanced up as Melissa and Mandy—accompanied by Dagenham, Henry, and the other young gentlemen—came up. She arched a brow at the group. "Are you intending to go sledding as well?"

They assured her they hoped to make an afternoon of it.

Therese returned her gaze to the younger three, who hadn't abated their hopeful looks one jot; it took effort not to laugh. "Very well." The cheering nearly deafened her, and she held up a staying hand. "There should be several sleds in the manor stable—you may ask Simms to fetch them out. But only after luncheon. Mrs. Haggerty's been cooking plum puddings all morning, but has made time to prepare a tasty meal, so we must do it justice." Therese looked at Henry and his four friends. "That includes you, gentlemen. I will be delighted if you will consent to assist us in consuming Mrs. Haggerty's offerings."

"Oh—good-oh!" Henry said.

The others—all of whom had partaken of Mrs. Haggerty's cooking in the past—beamed their acceptance.

Therese smiled at her grandchildren, then waved the group on. "Come —it's time we returned to the manor."

As she fell in beside Therese, Lottie sang, "Because the sooner we finish eating, the sooner we'll be able to sled!"

Therese laughed and walked on.

Callum spent the following day in the Dutton Grange library with his nose buried in books.

The village had been almost snowed in by the storm that had struck the previous evening. Callum was grateful for the roaring fire in the large fireplace at his back; Hendricks came in now and then to feed and encourage it back to a blaze.

Despite his apparent industry, Callum was making slow progress. Too often, his mind would stray, and he'd find himself dwelling on the difficulties of confessing all to Honor.

Regardless, he steeled himself and waited for her to appear. When the clock ticked on, and Mrs. Wright appeared with sandwiches and then returned to remove the empty plate, and Honor had still not arrived, he wasn't sure whether to feel relieved or disappointed...

Perhaps he'd been wrong—overeager—in imagining there was anything between them, in thinking that she was as attracted to him as he was to her. Perhaps, contrary to what Lady Osbaldestone believed, Honor didn't think of him in any personal way.

Presumably, even Lady Osbaldestone was wrong occasionally. Perhaps this was one of those times.

If Honor didn't care for him—if there was no chance of him having a future with her—then there was no reason for him to confess anything, was there?

Callum considered that conclusion for several long minutes while, behind him, the newly stoked fire popped and flared.

Everything, he realized, depended on the answer to one question: Did he truly wish to pursue Honor Webster? Regardless of what she might think of him or feel for him, that was the critical—the defining—issue.

He was a trained scientist; it was second nature to evaluate even such personal matters in a logical fashion. He focused on elucidating what he wanted his life to be like and the qualities he therefore required in a wife. Neither question was one he'd pondered before, but now...

It was impossible to avoid the conclusion that, for a gentleman-scholar-explorer such as he, Honor would make a superlative helpmate. She already understood many of the pressures that shaped his life. She'd already been exposed to the field in which he worked.

He knew she'd already amassed insights into the arena of his endeavors, one few ladies ever entered.

On a personal plane, she engaged him as no other lady ever had. She and he shared likes, dislikes—shared a common view on many subjects—and she understood his fascination with ancient objects and customs.

She was the wife he hadn't even got to thinking about.

Yet now...he doubted he would ever find a better candidate to fill the role.

Add that to the way he felt about her and the way she made him feel —for instance, when she smiled at him spontaneously and that smile lit her eyes...

Viewed objectively, the only fly in the ointment regarding him and Honor was her relationship to Webster and his own past with the professor.

That was the one hurdle...

He blinked as his mind served up the notion that, in fact, Honor's relationship to Webster might not be a negative but a positive in disguise.

Callum sat straighter and let the book he'd propped before him fall flat on the table, disregarded. "If Webster and I were to reconcile..."

That had been his hope in going to Oxford; he'd intended to try, yet again, to speak with Webster and fully explain his approach regarding what Webster stigmatized as "selling" artifacts. Yes, he negotiated a sale, but only as a middleman; he never claimed ownership of the artifacts in question. Indeed, he didn't think of them as his in any way; he saw himself as a temporary caretaker, one who shouldered the responsibility of seeing any artifact that came into his hands appropriately housed and displayed for all the populace to view and learn from.

If he could repair his relationship with Webster, then marrying Webster's niece would be... "Nice."

Surely one day soon, he would succeed in opening Webster's eyes to the reality that Callum's path was the way of the future in their field.

And when he did...

His thoughts went around and around, spinning out into imagining a life with Honor, one in which he and Webster had made their peace and, possibly, were working side by side again.

If he was asked to describe his most-desired future, that would be it.

But what should be his first step? His first step toward such a future.

Should he try, again, to speak with Webster?

If he did and, as had occurred several times in the past, Webster refused to listen, what then?

Should he, instead, speak first with Honor? Once he'd confessed to the connection between him and Webster, how would she see him? He had no idea what Webster might have told her about him—no notion of in what colors Webster might have painted his erstwhile student and acolyte, Callum Goodrich.

Given he had no real certainty over how Honor saw him—him, the man, Callum Harris as she thought he was—then telling her that he was, in fact, Callum Goodrich held significant risk.

He sat for long minutes, staring unseeing at the book before him, before accepting that, as of that moment, he couldn't make up his mind what to do.

How to proceed.

He shook himself—tried to shake away his confounding dilemma—and with a conscious effort, refocused on the book before him and the question he was researching.

Given all the references he'd found, he was now willing to state that there had been a merchant's compound, very likely including a substantial villa, in the immediate area.

Together with the discovery of the three Roman coins, that meant there was a very real possibility of buried treasure—of Roman artifacts buried in the vicinity—just waiting to be found. A hoard that, almost certainly, would prove entirely worthy of all efforts to unearth it.

Callum sat back and stared at the books before him. Distantly, he heard the strains of the organ and the voices of the choristers singing in the church, the sounds of the carol practice whipped toward the Grange on the icy wind that rattled the shutters.

The choristers were applying themselves, with dedication, for the greater good.

He could do no less.

Callum dragged the next book into place before him, opened it, and settled to the task of scanning the entries and reading every single reference he could find to the local Roman compound.

CHAPTER 10

*C*allum kept at his self-appointed task, doggedly working through all the tomes in the Grange library that referred to the Roman occupation of the area in any way whatsoever. He was losing hope of finding any clue to the exact location of the merchant's compound, let alone the villa built within it, but he accepted that if he didn't comb through every last book, he would always wonder if he'd stopped too soon and missed the vital passage.

He now knew a great deal more about the merchant; Silvesterius Magnus had been an importer-exporter, bringing in wine, oils, salt, other condiments, and fabrics via ships coming into the protected harbor near Clausentum and, subsequently, distributing the goods to all the major Roman towns in the region.

On the other side of the ledger, Silvesterius Magnus had exported Welsh silver, wool sourced from the midlands to the southwest, and curiously, various herbs peculiar to England and Wales.

Callum had found enough detail to have pieced together a picture of the merchant as a wily and solidly successful man. That some of his household treasures might lie buried somewhere around Little Moseley remained an intriguing possibility; everything Callum had learned had only increased the potency of the treasure's allure.

He paused to straighten his spine. Stretching his arms above his head, he wondered how the others—his crew of searchers—were faring. He'd met them that morning while walking to the Grange; they'd told him they intended to drive around the surrounding lanes, looking for any signs of digging or disturbance of the soil, and they would stop and ask at all the nearby farms as well, in case any of the farmhands had noticed anything out in the fields.

Callum lowered his arms and looked at the dwindling pile of books he'd yet to examine. "I sincerely hope they're having better luck than I am."

Jaw firming, he drew the next book to him, opened it, and started to read.

The minutes ticked by. The clock had just chimed ten times when the door opened, and Honor came in, clutching her folder to her chest.

Callum smiled and started to rise.

Smiling in return, she waved him back to his chair. "Good morning." She hesitated, then asked, "Are you sure I won't bother you?"

Resuming his seat, he grinned. "You started working here first—it is I who should ask if I will bother you."

She colored slightly and shook her head. "You won't."

Callum considered her light blush. Was she lying? He watched as she set the folder containing the professor's papers and her notes on the other end of the table. When he'd returned to the Grange after the pageant, the folder had been on the table where he'd left it, but contrary to his hopes, Honor hadn't returned to work on the references and footnotes during the afternoon; he'd been left to slog through the books without distraction. But she must have come to the library after he'd left—perhaps to work through the evening—because the folder had been gone when he'd arrived yesterday morning.

Knowing how pedantic Webster was about his footnotes and references—and his propensity to keep changing them until he'd set the final period to his paper, and even after that—Callum wasn't surprised to see a frown lay siege to Honor's brow as she settled in the chair opposite and focused on the various lists and notes she'd spread before her.

He returned his attention to the book he was scanning and left her to her laborious task.

He whittled the stack of books yet to be perused to one last tome. He breathed in and, drawing the book to him, glanced down the table.

Honor's brow was now deeply furrowed, and the set of her lips and chin proclaimed her frustration.

Callum studied her tense movements and deduced that she was attempting to order the professor's currently unordered references.

Callum had sat precisely where she now was, staring at a slew of random citations and wondering how to tame them. He knew the solution—the best and easiest way forward.

But if he spoke...

He hesitated, and engrossed in her struggle, she heaved a sigh, dropped the pencil she'd been using, propped her elbows on the table, and closing her eyes, massaged her temples.

"There is a relatively easy way of listing such references." The words were out before caution could claw them back. When Honor's eyes flew open and met his, Callum let his lips twist in a self-deprecatory grimace and admitted, "I've sat where you are myself." He searched Honor's eyes and saw hope blossom. "Would you like me to show you?"

She straightened and waved at the lists. "Please. Any suggestion of how to deal with this would be welcome." She paused, then said, "I've never had to order references for such a major work. Ordinary papers or lectures usually have only a handful of citations, and of course, usually the work is already fully written and in its final state." As Callum rounded the table and drew up a chair beside hers, with her eyes on the lists, she shook her head. "In this case, quite aside from the sheer breadth of the work—and the correspondingly long list of references—Uncle Hildebrand is still working on his treatise. I'm sure he'll add even more references, and that will throw out all my lists."

"Indeed." Callum studied the lists, then rearranged them. "Which is why, for major works such as this, it's better all around to opt for a different way of noting references. Rather than using a numbered list— which as you say, will continually change until the very last minute and is unwieldy to adjust—it's advisable to list references alphabetically."

He picked up her pencil and amended the notations for the various references on one of the pages of the draft treatise, then showed Honor. "You note the references in the body of the treatise like that, then list the references alphabetically at the end. That way, when a late reference is added, you're simply amending one entry in the body of the work and adding an entry to the reference list."

She took the sheet and studied it. Her frown had lightened, but remained. Eventually, she met his eyes. "I'm not sure my uncle will accept references listed in such a way."

Callum held her gaze. Then before caution could talk him out of it, he said, "Trust me—he won't even notice."

She blinked, twice, then, her frown deepening, she searched his face. "How can you know that?"

Surreptitiously, he dragged in a tense breath and, without shifting his gaze, confessed, "Because my full name is Callum Harris...Goodrich."

Her eyes flared wide, and she sat back in the chair. "What?" One hand gripping the chair's wooden arm, she leaned away from him as her gaze raked his face. Her expression—one of shock and confusion—made it plain she'd recognized the name.

His lungs constricted, and he rushed to say, "I don't know what your uncle has told you, but he's never allowed me to explain what I do, so whatever he has said is wrong—misinformed."

"Indeed?" Her tone was cool.

Callum could see her retreating, see her putting up walls between them. Mentally gritting his teeth, he forced himself to face the issue that lay between them and address it—clearly, calmly, and directly. "Has he told you why I left my position as his assistant?"

After a second more of staring, she blinked. "I thought..." She paused, and her gaze grew distant, as if she was recalling some incident, then she refocused on him. "I was given to understand that he'd dismissed you."

Slowly, deliberately, Callum shook his head. "I daresay he would have, after our argument, but I left—resigned my post—before he could." He paused, then, lowering his gaze, quietly added, "So that's the first inaccuracy in his account."

Honor stared at the man who, even now, her senses told her she could trust. But...her uncle turned literally apoplectic at the mere mention of his erstwhile acolyte-cum-assistant. "Betrayer" was the most complimentary adjective her uncle had used for Callum Goodrich.

His lids rose, and he met her eyes again. His blue gaze remained steady and unwavering.

Her impulsive side prodded, and she settled in the chair. "Perhaps," she challenged, "you should tell me your version of what happened between you and allow me to judge whose account is more believable."

He studied her for an instant, then, somewhat to her surprise, nodded. "We fell out over a personal find—a bronze figurine, dating back to the Dark Ages and with connections to Stonehenge." He paused, then said, "But to start at the beginning, I was your uncle's assistant for more than two years. During that time, I accompanied him on several expeditions and digs, but the finds from those were either relatively minor or had already been claimed and disposal arranged by others, and we were invited merely to provide provenance. Through those excursions, I learned the accepted way of dealing with discovered antiquities—or at least the manner of dealing with them espoused by college academics such as your uncle."

Honor suddenly found herself the recipient of a piercing look, then Callum asked, "Have you ever been with him in the field?"

She shook her head. "I know something about how academics such as my uncle go about finding antiquities—what such expeditions entail—but I know little about what happens to the antiquities afterward."

"Nevertheless, you'll have noticed the competitiveness between the various academic institutions involved in the study of antiquities—each institution, each college, wants to be able to say they have this ancient bowl or sword or statue."

"*That*, I have seen."

His lips tightened. "To a large extent, that compulsion is what lies at the heart of what transpired between me and Webster—the source of our falling-out. Anything he finds, he claims for the college—for Brentmore. What that means is that the antiquity, whatever it is, disappears into the college's vaults and is only made available to professors and students of the college for study. Others can gain access only at the master's whim, and gaining such permission is a rare occurrence. That process of acquisition and sequestration is how each college specializing in ancient history builds its reputation and its antiquarian assets."

He paused, then went on, "Webster and I share an interest in the same periods of history—that's why I became his student, then his assistant. During one term break, I took leave from my position—a holiday—to pursue a rumor of a site on Salisbury Plain, not far from Stonehenge. There are always rumors about this or that, but I thought this one worth investigating. It was my first solo excursion—it hardly warranted the term 'expedition'—and I funded it purely from my own savings." His lips twisted wryly. "The costs weren't large—it was just me and a shovel."

She watched as his expression altered, enthusiasm seeping in along with his memories.

"The long and the short of it was that I unearthed an early bronze figurine. The style suggested it was very old, and the location was close enough to Stonehenge to support an association." He paused, then, enthusiasm fading, he firmed his chin and went on, "I took the figurine back to Oxford and showed your uncle. He was as excited as I. Of course, he assumed I would hand it to the college—to Brentmore—for the college's greater glory. However, I'd stopped in London on my way back and talked to several curators I by then knew at the British Museum—and back in Oxford, I also spoke with those at the Ashmolean. Some were contemporaries of mine, and through them, I'd learned that one outcome of the colleges' policies of keeping all finds to themselves was that the museums were starved of exhibits. In many instances, even though the curators heard of finds through academic channels, they were unable— effectively barred—from even setting eyes on the treasures the colleges had claimed."

Honor saw a new, stronger, harder flame ignite in Callum's eyes.

"I felt that was wrong." His tone had grown more definite, more incisive. "If the role of academics is to search out, find, and accumulate knowledge, then the reason for doing so and for acquiring artifacts in furtherance of that surely should be to share our knowledge—and those artifacts—with the wider public, not to sequester all away for our own use, for our own edification alone." He caught her gaze; she felt as if he was willing her to understand. "I didn't want the figurine I'd found to disappear into the vaults of Brentmore College, never to be seen by anyone but the college's own professors and students."

He paused, then said, "In law, the figurine was mine to do with as I pleased—so I had to make a decision, a decision that was mine to make." Boldly, he asked, "Can you understand my position?"

She could, but none of what he had said aligned well with what her uncle had given as the principal cause of the rift between them. Regardless, she nodded. "I can understand the ideas, the motives, that drove you, but what did you actually do?"

That was the nub of her uncle's complaints—the wellspring of his rabid fury against Callum Goodrich.

His lips twisted in a bleak smile. "I talked to my friends, the curators, and learned that, even though they wanted to acquire the figurine for their museums, they couldn't afford the outlay to display it—not on the floors open to the public. Displaying objects means cases and time and care, and that means money from their budgets, money they don't have." He paused, then went on, "My family is an old one, long-established within the ton. Given my interests, I knew of several lords with money to burn who were keen to acquire antiquities for their collections, so I approached them."

Callum's features hardened. "If I had wanted to, I could have sold the figurine to one of them and pocketed a small fortune."

Honor nodded. "So you did." She made it a statement and didn't try to keep the disdain from her voice; her uncle had informed her—several times—that Callum Goodrich had, indeed, sold that find and all others he'd subsequently stumbled upon to wealthy collectors for his own gain. That was the crux of her uncle's accusations; in his eyes, his protégé had betrayed his cause.

"No." Callum's eyes locked with hers, the single-word reply absolute and resonating with simple honesty. "I sold the figurine to a collector, *but* I didn't pocket the fortune, and the curators at the British Museum got everything they wished for—the figurine and the money to display it."

Confused, she frowned. "I don't understand."

He huffed and muttered, "Nor does Webster." After a second, he went on, "I didn't simply sell the figurine. Instead, I recognized that most collectors—not all, I grant you, but most—want the world to know of their collection. Those collectors aren't interested in hiding their acquisitions away, keeping the pieces solely for themselves to enjoy—most such collectors are admirers of the art of artifacts, rather than being scholars. Many of the aristocratic collectors are keen to build their fame in their chosen fields —to have their names publicly associated with specific artifacts. In short, such collectors want to accrue status—public status—through their funding of expeditions and the public display of the fruits of those endeavors. They want to be seen to be great benefactors in their chosen fields."

She continued to frown, but nodded at him to go on; she knew enough of human nature and the wealthy to accept his argument thus far.

He drew breath, then said, "So with the figurine, I arranged a contract of sale—one between me and the most appropriate collector, who happened to be Lord Devon—and as part of that contract, his lordship agreed to gift the figurine to the British Museum, while I agreed to give eighty percent of the sale price to the museum to cover the costs of displaying the figurine appropriately in their public halls." He paused, then said, "Everyone got what they wanted. The figurine is in a case in the museum for everyone to see, and it bears a plaque honoring Lord Devon's gift to the nation. I, in turn, retained twenty percent of the money Devon paid—that kept me going and financed my next expedition."

Honor stared at Callum as she sorted through the implications of all he'd said.

He tilted his head and, his gaze steady on her face, added, "Some-times, the artifact is given as a gift, as was the case with the figurine, and sometimes it's given as a permanent loan from the collector's estate, but either way, the artifact goes permanently on public display. Over the past four years, I've made quite a successful life as a finder of artifacts—and the museums of the country have benefited greatly from my activities."

Everything he'd told her could be checked and verified. She held his gaze. "I assume that, were I to ask the curators at the Ashmolean, they would sing your praises."

A grin tweaked his lips. "They would—before attempting to extract from you news of what I'm currently pursuing." He paused, then with a faintly affectionate look, confided, "I never tell them what trail I'm following—they tend to get overexcited."

Her mind racing, she drew in a breath, then said, "I have several questions."

He inclined his head, inviting her to ask them.

"First, why does my uncle believe the worst of you?" She narrowed her eyes at him. "Why haven't you explained what you do to him—exactly as you have to me…"

Her words trailed off as she realized the answer, even before Callum's features grew rigid, and he said, "I've tried. On several occasions. But the first time, over the figurine, as soon as I mentioned the word 'sold,' he erupted, and ever since, the instant he sets eyes on me, he slams the door in my face."

She bit her lip. She was well acquainted with her uncle's propensity for leaping to conclusions and, as Callum had put it, erupting. Hildebrand Webster had lived too long alone, working largely alone; he'd never been forced to learn how to control his temper.

"I tried to explain in a letter," Callum said, "but it was returned unopened." He stared at her for a second, then went on, "As a matter of fact, hoping—again—to explain matters to him was what brought me here. I was on my way home for Christmas and stopped in at Oxford to speak to the Ashmolean curators about the current state of their displays —what period of artifacts they feel they're currently most in need of. I recently obtained a Grecian vase for the British Museum, and I try to more or less equally assist both museums to grow their respective collections."

He paused, then continued, "Before I left Oxford, I thought to try again to clear the air—it was nearly Christmas, after all. Nearly the end of another year. I called at Webster's house in the faint hope that he might—by now—have calmed enough to hear me out. To listen to the complete explanation of what I do—how I operate—but he and you had already left."

"You followed us here?"

He met her gaze and, after a second, admitted, "Mrs. Hinkley told me he'd left in a rush, and she had the address. Little Moseley. I knew the only reason he would up and leave like that, especially in this season, was that he'd learned of some potential find."

She tipped her head. "That answers my second question—how it was you turned up here." She studied his eyes; his expression remained steady, open, without guile. "My third question is: What now?"

Confusion darkened his eyes, and she elaborated, "If you—aided by the others—succeed in finding the source of the three Roman coins, this hoard you've been seeking, what then? Will you claim it and"—she waved a hand—"make one of your arrangements with a collector and a museum?"

He studied her, then admitted, "That would be my intention, *but* as the professor is here and was instrumental in leading me to Little Moseley, then I would hope to…reach some accommodation."

She frowned. "Accommodation?"

He sighed. "Legally, if I find the hoard and it's on Crown land, it will be mine to do with as I wish. If Webster finds it first, it will be his. But regardless of who lays hands on it first, I would hope he would be amenable to discussing some reasonable division of the find."

"So some to go to Brentmore and some to be sold to…?"

"Some collector who will gift the items to…" He paused, considering, then said, "For Roman coins or artifacts, I would prefer to direct the find to the Ashmolean."

Honor studied him. Everything he'd said sounded oh-so-plausible. Indeed, it all sounded honorable and…forward-thinking, something she knew her uncle wasn't. Yet…

After a second, finding no delicate way of framing it, she said, "You deliberately duped me by giving me a false name."

His features tightened. "I didn't set out with the intention to deceive anyone, but by the time we met in Mountjoy's Store, I'd already encountered the children. Knowing Webster was in the village, I told the three that I was Harris, and from them, I learned about the coins and that you were Webster's niece and that he was stuck in the cottage, writing. No one with experience was overseeing the search, and there seemed no other way for me to remain in the village and direct the search other than by concealing my identity. And finding the source of the coins—establishing a new site of Roman occupation—is important in many ways, and arguably more important to me, given the stage of my career, than to Webster." He paused, then, his gaze steady on her eyes, continued, "Initially, I could see no reason not to hide who I was. I wasn't hurting anyone by doing so."

She searched his eyes, his face, trying to read what lay behind his words, especially the last two sentences; they implied that something had changed. She thought back over all their exchanges. "Just now"—she waved at her lists—"you deliberately engineered a situation that led me to ask a question that brought on your...confession." She held his gaze. "Why?" When he didn't immediately reply, she added, "You didn't have to tell me who you really are."

For a long moment, she sensed he wrestled with some revelation, then he sighed, closed his eyes briefly, opened them, and said, "There are two parts to my answer. First, since I met you in Mountjoy's, the situation between us has changed—at least from my perspective. I've come to know you, and even though our association has been brief, I've learned enough to realize that you are the sort of lady whose thoughts and opinions I value." He paused as if replaying his words, then continued, "In short, I've come to value you—too highly to go on deceiving you."

She blinked, then stared at him, scrutinizing his handsome face.

What did he mean by valuing her, let alone that the situation between them had changed? Changed how? In what way?

In turn, he searched her face, then, once again, briefly closed his eyes —as if seeking strength. When he opened his eyes again and fixed them determinedly on her face, she sensed that whatever he was about to tell her was the part of his confession that bothered him most.

"I also want to tell you—because I definitely don't want you to learn of it later from someone else and imagine it means more than it does— that Lady Osbaldestone recognized me. She knew I was a Goodrich and worked out the family connections—that my mother's family were the Harrises. Her ladyship realized I was Callum Harris Goodrich, and somehow, she learned of my association with your uncle—of his enmity toward me."

She couldn't keep her surprise from her face. "During dinner at the

Colebatches, Reverend Colebatch asked after you, and as usual, Uncle Hildebrand all but exploded."

Callum grimaced. "So he's still exercised to that degree?"

"Unfortunately." After a second of considering that, she refocused on the man before her. "Was that what you wanted to tell me about her ladyship?"

He shook his head. "That was just the beginning. She...extracted my story from me, much as I've told you today. Then she made me promise that I would tell you the truth—who I was—by Monday evening, before she leaves Little Moseley on Tuesday morning."

His gaze searched Honor's face, her eyes, while she tried to keep her thoughts concealed. She could make sense of Lady Osbaldestone giving him the ultimatum she had...but only by admitting a truth she'd largely hidden from herself.

She'd done her level best to ignore how Callum made her feel, yet now...

He'd done as Lady Osbaldestone had asked and confessed all to her. He hadn't needed to do that, not unless...

She stared at him—as he patently waited for her to respond to his revelations. His confession.

As he waited for her verdict.

When she didn't immediately say anything, he swallowed and, his tone less confident, said, "I hope you can see your way to forgiving me for my deception, and that we...can put the issue behind us and go forward from here." He looked oddly uncertain, an expression that didn't sit well on him, then quietly said, "Your regard is important to me, and I don't want to lose it."

And there, lurking in the soft mid-blue of his eyes, was the answer to why he'd seized the chance of being alone with her in the library to engineer the right moment for his confession.

He wanted to put things right between them, so they could go on...

Where?

Regardless, did she want to go forward with him?

Slowly, her mind fed words to her tongue. "You've told me much I hadn't previously known. You've given me a lot to think about." Her tone was largely uninflected, affording him no clue as to the direction of her thoughts, much less her inclinations.

In truth, in that moment, she couldn't predict either herself.

She looked away from him, then sat up and, moving slowly and deliberately, gathered her lists and the papers she'd been working through and slid them into the folder.

Then she pushed back the chair and stood, bringing him to his feet beside her.

She looked up, met his eyes—and realized he'd dropped every last shield; she felt as if she could see into his soul.

And what she saw there…

She hauled in a breath and wrenched her gaze away. There were so many emotions whizzing through her, if she tried to concentrate on any one of them, she'd feel dizzy.

Being deceived was never encouraging, but the deception hadn't hurt her. As for the sense of betrayal her uncle felt, that wasn't her emotion to own, and it seemed to be largely of her uncle's own making.

But as for all the rest…

So much hinged on trust. Could she still trust Callum—as, from the first, her instincts had insisted she could?

She honestly didn't know, and she couldn't think clearly, sensibly, with him there, within arm's reach.

Drawing in a slow breath, battening down her senses—so very aware he was close—she picked up the folder, raised her head, and looked him in the eye. "Don't ask, because I can't answer. Not yet."

She saw his lips tighten, but after a fraught second of searching her eyes, he inclined his head.

She didn't wait for more; clutching the folder, she turned and made for the door. With a hand on the doorknob, she halted, then, without glancing back, said, "Thank you for your help with the references. I now know what I should do."

She heard his rumbled "My pleasure," but didn't respond. She gripped the knob, opened the door, whisked through it, and closed it behind her.

Callum stood rooted to the library floor and stared at the door—then expelled the breath trapped in his lungs. He raised his hands and raked them through his hair, then let his arms fall and gazed at the floor.

Shock of a sort held him immobile. Until the moment she'd refused to let him ask if she accepted his explanation, he hadn't realized just *how much* things between them had changed.

He hadn't, until that instant, realized how much Honor now meant to him—how much losing her would hurt.

He stared at the parquet floor as the realization sank into his brain that the true treasure Little Moseley had to offer him wasn't the one he'd been

hoping to find—along with the fact that Honor was a treasure among treasures, one utterly beyond price.

After Honor had left him, Callum hadn't been able to summon the interest
to plow through the last remaining tome. Consequently, he returned to the
task the following day.

He spent all morning painstakingly combing through the work. There
was a reason he'd left that book to the very last; it wasn't written in Latin
but in a bastardized form of Old English. He would have infinitely
preferred Latin; it would have made the book easier to decipher.

While he worked, his ears strained for any hint of Honor arriving. He
hadn't sighted her in the lane or about the village; he didn't have any idea
how she would choose to view him, to deal with him in the wake of his
confession, but he wanted to find out.

Wanted to know if he had any chance of following the path that,
above all others, he now wished to pursue.

But Honor didn't come.

Nor, Callum noted, did the professor. If Honor had told her uncle that
Callum was there, Webster would have come looking for him; of that,
Callum had no doubt.

So Honor had kept his presence to herself, leaving Callum to wonder
what that meant—what that said of how she now regarded him.

Time and again, he had to drag his mind from dwelling on the options
and refocus it on the words before him.

He'd just reached the last page—with nothing new to show for it—
and dejectedly closed the heavy tome when Mrs. Wright came bustling in
with a plate of sandwiches and a mug of ale and, as had become her habit,
stayed to chat. Over the past days, he'd found her unexpected interest
helpful in terms of sorting through his findings. Today, in recounting to
her what he'd found—as well as what he hadn't, namely a specific location of Silvesterius Magnus's villa—he realized that, his frustration aside,
his search hadn't been entirely without result and that it behooved him as
a scholar to make a record of what he'd gleaned.

Once Mrs. Wright had left, taking the empty plate and mug with her,
Callum hunted in a sideboard and located paper and pen and set about
making a formal record of all he'd discovered in the tomes of the
combined libraries of Fulsom Hall and Dutton Grange.

He didn't have that many facts to lay out, but the act of setting each down in logical order focused his mind. When he reached the end and reread what he'd written, a notion stirred; he considered it, then left it to stew in his brain while he made two copies of his report—one for Dutton Grange, one for Henry at Fulsom Hall—so he could take the original with him when he left the village.

If he was to reach Guisborough by Christmas Eve, he would have to set out by Wednesday morning at the latest.

The thought of leaving without locating the source of the coins left a sour taste in his mouth. If he returned in January, would Honor and Webster still be there?

Once Webster submitted his treatise, due by the end of the year, would he devote himself to the hunt in Little Moseley or return to Oxford?

All were questions to which Callum didn't know the answers.

He finished and blotted the third copy of his findings. He set two aside, then stared at the original and allowed the vague notion from earlier to resurface in his brain.

After a moment, he slumped back in the chair and stared across the room.

The Romans had habitually sited their settlements to make best use of the landscape. Callum recalled seeing on the map on the wall of Mountjoy's Store a largish stream—possibly large enough to be a river—that ran roughly west to east across the map less than a mile north of the village. If he was remembering the region's topography correctly, the stream would join with others and, eventually, would reach the sea not far from where Clausentum had been.

Eyes narrowing, he considered what that might mean in terms of the siting of Silvesterius Magnus's compound. "He would have wanted it not too far from the Clausentum-Sorviodunum road, but the ability to transport goods via river would have been an advantage a merchant like Silvesterius wouldn't have ignored." Callum sat up and tapped the edge of his report on the tabletop. "That could well mean that the lane that currently runs north beside the village might originally have been a track for Silvesterius and his people to access the river." Callum knew the crew of searchers had scanned the lane's surrounds. "But they were looking for digging close to the lane. Perhaps we need to extend the search on either side of the lane."

They had two more days to make headway. After that, the crew would disperse, and he would have to leave soon after.

They had time for one last-ditch effort.

He rose and fell to pacing, mentally organizing a viable search of the area most likely, at one time, to have played host to Silvesterius's compound. He needed to speak with the crew.

On the thought, he heard the faint strains of singing, borne on the wind. He glanced at the clock. It was nearly four-thirty, which meant the crew were in the church, practicing.

On a surge of determination, Callum folded the original and one copy of his report and tucked them into his coat pocket, left the second copy prominently displayed on the library table, quickly returned the last books to the shelves, then headed for the door.

After seeking out and thanking Longfellow and Lady Longfellow for the use of their library, conveying his few findings and that he'd left a detailed report of what he'd uncovered on the library table, Callum quit the Grange and strode rapidly down the drive.

Dusk had fallen, and night was closing in. The wind was cold, chilled as it whipped over the snow lingering in drifts along the sides of the drive and beneath the trees. They hadn't had fresh snow for several days, which in terms of searching the ground was helpful, but the premonition of snow being on the way—almost a scent of it—shivered in the air.

Callum reached the lane, paced along, then turned beneath the lych-gate and quickly climbed to the church. With every step, the sound of the choir grew louder. Light spilled through the church's diamond-paned windows, painting golden splotches on the snow-dusted ground.

The main door opened noiselessly. Callum slipped inside, then paused to take stock. The choir—which included all those Callum regarded as his crew—were ranged on the altar steps, with Moody, before them, conducting enthusiastically, and Mrs. Moody at the organ to one side.

To Callum's ears, the choir had improved considerably since he'd first heard them; they sang with obvious confidence, and their voices blended in glorious harmony.

Silently, Callum walked forward and slipped into the rear pew. The lamplight didn't reach that far, and he remained cloaked in shadows.

He didn't think of himself as a religious man, but the sound of the carols, the familiar words of joy and hope and love, sank into him and buoyed him. Lifted his soul.

He and his searchers weren't beaten yet. They still had a chance to locate the villa and unearth the artifacts he felt sure were there, waiting to be found.

The choir was singing "This Endris Night" when Callum felt the air stir and realized the church door had opened, then shut. He glanced that way and saw Honor standing in the dimly lit foyer, her gaze locked on him.

He watched as she hesitated, plainly debating, then, chin rising a notch, she came forward through the shadows and slipped into the pew from the other end. She glided closer, then gathered her skirts and sat with a bare foot of space between them.

Callum's heart leapt, then thudded. He didn't know what to do—whether to speak or... He looked at the choir.

"I was on my way to the Grange library to speak with you and spotted you ahead of me in the lane, coming this way, so I followed." Honor kept her gaze fixed forward, although she barely registered the choir lined up before the altar; her focus wasn't on them. Unable to resist, she glanced sidelong at the gentleman beside her, let her eyes fleetingly trace his profile—the patrician nose, the strong brow, and squared, determined chin.

She directed her gaze toward the altar and, her voice low enough so that, given the sound of the choir and the occasional bark of Mr. Moody's instructions, no one else would hear, continued, "I've spent a great deal of time thinking about all you told me. While I appreciate your stance and what prompts you to espouse it—indeed, speaking personally, I applaud your vision and commitment—I also understand my uncle's feelings, misinformed though those undoubtedly are."

She paused, debating how frank she could be, then she recalled this man had worked alongside her uncle for years. "Yes, Uncle Hildebrand is overquick to judge and can be rigidly stubborn once he's taken a notion into his head. I know how irascible and difficult to reason with he can be, especially when discussing a subject on which he has already made up his mind." She knew what she wanted to say—had spent half the night rehearsing her words—yet actually uttering them in coherent fashion wasn't proving as easy as she'd hoped. She drew in a tense breath and, clasping her hands more tightly in her lap, went on, "All of that is to say that I can understand why you opted to conceal your full name from me—and from all the others." She slid a glance his way and found him watching her. "You wanted to avoid one of Uncle Hildebrand's eruptions, which would have severely compromised your ability to search for the source of the Roman coins."

Callum couldn't deny the assertion—didn't attempt to—but his mind had locked on what, to him, was the more important implication. He caught and held her gaze. "You believe me," he whispered.

She blinked, then met his gaze and quietly stated, "I believe *in* you. In your purpose and what you are striving to achieve."

Callum hoped for—wanted—much more. But if he wished for it, he would have to reach for it, ask for it, fight for it if necessary...

Between them, he offered her his hand, palm up. "Do you think you could come to believe in *us*?"

The organ swelled and voices soared while she studied his eyes. Then she reached out and laid her fingers in his and simply said, "I'm willing to try."

Callum closed his fingers around hers. He couldn't restrain his smile —and her own smile bloomed in reply.

She shifted her gaze forward. "Don't get cocky. You still have shoals to negotiate."

"I know." But now, he had her hand in his. He smiled even more broadly and followed her gaze.

The choir was giving their all in singing "Joy to the World." As the uplifting strains swelled around him, propelled by genuine and enthusiastic belief, he felt his heart respond, taking flight.

Still facing forward, he raised Honor's hand to his lips and lightly kissed her knuckles. "Thank you," he murmured and knew he was speaking not just to her but to the power that dwelled in the church, that gave such joyous power to the carols.

He felt Honor lightly squeeze his fingers in reply, and he lowered her hand and held it cradled between his own.

Apparently, "Joy to the World" was the final carol the choir had to practice. At its conclusion, Mr. Moody beamed upon his choristers, commended them all on their devotion, and acknowledged this practice had been the last before their Monday evening performance.

"We'll look to see you all a half hour before the start," the choirmaster informed his troops.

"Don't be late!" Mrs. Moody called from where she was tidying the music scattered around the organ. "We'll meet in the vestry for a warm-up."

The members of the special choir—all bright faces and huge smiles—

assured the Moodys they would be there in good time, then hauled on coats, tossed scarves about their necks, and came hurrying up the aisle.

The manor five spotted Callum and Honor and made a beeline for them. Reluctantly, Callum released Honor's fingers, and she withdrew her hand as the youngsters, with their older cousins and Henry and his friends in tow, gathered around, kneeling in the pew in front and standing in the aisle and in the space behind the rear pew.

"Have you found something?" Lottie's bright blue eyes were trained on Callum's face; she'd already flashed Honor a wide smile.

Before Callum could reply, Henry rather glumly said, "We haven't turned up a thing."

"Not for want of trying." Kilburn thrust his hands into his coat pockets.

"We've searched—we've asked," Dagenham said. "But not one hint of a clue have we found."

"*Yet,*" Callum insisted, determined to share the perhaps irrational yet quite definite hope that had, over the last hour, steadily built inside him. He swept his gaze around the circle of faces. "The undeniable fact is that those coins came from somewhere, and one thing we have established through all your hard work is that those coins are unlikely to have come from far afield—ergo, they came from somewhere near the village."

"But where?" Jamie's tone reflected the plaintive frustration in the others' expressions.

Callum nodded—serious, yet not downcast. "Yes, we've yet to locate the source, but I have learned something more."

The sudden flare of interest from the group was palpable. Callum hid a smile; this unexpected crew of his were as driven to succeed as he.

"What?" George settled on the pew in front of Callum, his expression now intent.

Seeing the same demand on every face, Callum explained his theory that the lane that ran north beside the village might have been a track for the merchant to access the stream. "If Silvesterius Magnus sited his compound roughly midway between the stream and the Salisbury-Southampton road, that would place it more or less level with the village and, I would suggest, most likely within a hundred yards or so of the lane."

Henry's gaze had grown distant. "So Witcherly Farm, Crossley Farm, and the manor grounds, and all the woods between."

Callum nodded. "I think Swindon Hall is too far north."

Henry frowned. "There's a lot of untouched woodland south of Crossley Farm—although, presumably, we'd only be looking at the area from the farm's southern boundary to level with the rear of the cottages along there." He arched a brow at Callum. "If we want to keep closer to midway between the road and the stream?"

Callum nodded again. "We've only got two days before the majority of us will have to leave, so—"

"Actually," Mandy broke in, "we'll only have one day." She glanced at the others. "Don't forget Grandmama has invited you all to lunch tomorrow after church."

"And afterward," Melissa added, "we're all to lend a hand in hauling in the yule log."

"We can't forget that!" Lottie declared.

Melissa looked at Callum. "Grandmama asked us, if we saw you, to invite you as well." She waved at the others. "It's really just us—the younger people—and the professor and Miss Webster."

George grinned. "Those who will enjoy the food and the fun of hauling in the yule log."

"I...see." Callum glanced sidelong at Honor.

Leaning forward, she said to Melissa and Mandy, "Please tell your grandmother that, while I accept with delight, my uncle must decline—he's too far behind in his writing to attend, but he thanks her ladyship for the invitation."

Melissa and Mandy nodded, and when the pair looked at Callum, awaiting his response, he smiled. "I'm honored to be included and gladly accept."

"Well!" George Wiley said. "That means we have only one day left—Monday—in which to locate this compound."

Callum refused to be—couldn't find it in himself to be—glum. "Buck up!" He looked around at the others and smiled, encouraging and understanding at once. "From experience, I can tell you that, quite often in such searching, as they say, the night is darkest before the dawn. Just when you think matters are hopeless, that's when something will happen—something you didn't expect and would never have thought of—which leads you to the item you seek."

In the momentary silence as the group digested that, heavy footsteps could be heard approaching the church door.

"I suppose," Dagenham said, "it's one of those character-building things—that we have to hold to our determination until the very end."

Henry nodded. "Until we succeed."

At the edge of his vision, Callum saw the church door open. A familiar shape was silhouetted against the gloom outside.

"Honor?" Webster peered into the church.

Honor shot Callum a look and rose. "I'm coming," she called. She directed a swift smile at the others. "I'll see you all here tomorrow." Then she walked out of the pew and around to the door, where the professor had, thank heaven, remained.

Callum slouched a little lower in the pew as the others chatted over and around him. He saw no benefit in confronting his erstwhile mentor in public, although, obviously, as he wanted to pursue a future with Honor, the time for that confrontation was fast approaching.

As far as possible, he would do it on his terms—namely, the more private the better. He might be determined to make Webster understand that he wasn't the blackguard the professor had, in his mind, painted him, but he doubted forcing the man to acknowledge his error in public was a viable way forward—not on multiple counts.

Despite all that had passed between them, he owed Webster for his teachings, his encouragement, his support for many years. Given a choice, Callum would prefer to spare the man any unnecessary abrading of his feelings.

Tipping his head, Callum peered between two greatcoated bodies at the door. Honor had met Webster and urged him to turn back; she'd pulled the door closed, but the wind had blown it open again, and Callum could see Honor and Webster walking arm in arm down the path.

Callum's gaze fixed on Webster's broad back. He needed to set his mind to how best to build the necessary bridges—or more accurately, how to repair the bridges that had once been there. Until he had them shored up and functional again, he wouldn't be able to move forward along the path he now knew beyond question he wished to tread.

Callum looked toward the altar, then gathered himself and rose. Smiling vaguely, he joined the others, and together, they left the church.

CHAPTER 11

*T*herese looked around her dining table and smiled to herself. It did her good to occasionally surround herself with those of the younger generations; they widened her horizons and forced her to consider matters from different perspectives.

The main course had been served, and silence had engulfed the table. She seized the opportunity provided by everyone else's absorption with Mrs. Haggerty's roast capons to cast a glance up the table. Callum Goodrich occupied the chair there, with Honor Webster on his right. Therese hadn't been the least surprised that the professor—who had buried himself in the cottage, writing his treatise, even to the extent of not attending Sunday service—had declined her invitation; indeed, given she'd invited Callum as well, she'd rather counted on the professor's refusal.

It wasn't her place to force professor and ex-assistant together; it was up to them to reconcile however they may. Her interest lay in fostering the romance between Callum and Honor. She felt perfectly certain Callum's parents and, even more, Honor's, were they to be apprised of Therese's intentions, would thank her; however one measured such things, a marriage between the pair would be an excellent match.

Therese cut a glance at Dagenham, whom she'd directed to the chair on her right. She'd subsequently waved Melissa to the chair on the viscount's other side, and in between mouthfuls, the pair were conversing in low tones. Indeed, in tones that, to Therese's educated ear, spoke of a level of ease, of mutual acceptance, that was striking. And telling. To her mind, there was no benefit in attempting to keep Dagenham and Melissa apart or, contrarily, to explicitly encourage them; one of the hallmarks of an experienced matchmaker was knowing when it was necessary to step back and allow Fate to play her part.

Mandy sat on Therese's left, with Henry beyond her. Therese was aware that, in between bantering with Henry, Mandy often focused on her sister and Dagenham. Meanwhile, to Therese's continuing delight, Lottie, seated in the middle of the table, was dividing her wide-eyed glances equally between Callum and Honor and Melissa and Dagenham.

Therese looked around the table again and decided she'd given the company sufficient time to take the edge from their appetites. "I fear," she said, directing the comment to the table at large, "that I have fallen behind in my understanding of your endeavors regarding the source of our three Roman coins." She arched her brows, inviting their response. "How goes your search?"

Led by Jamie and Henry, but with each and every one bar Honor making some contribution, the group described their efforts in searching for who had placed the coins in the jar, and when that had turned up nothing, their subsequent search for any excavation that might have unearthed the coins.

Therese nodded in understanding. "I'm impressed," she informed them all. "You seem to have been remarkably thorough."

"Much good has it done us." Henry grimaced. "We've found no one who recalls the coins, and no sign of any digging."

"Thus far," George put in. He looked up the table and met Therese's eyes. "Mr. Harris has thought of where else we should search."

"Indeed?" Therese looked at Callum and arched her brows.

He dabbed his lips with his napkin, then, while the Crimminses cleared the plates and ferried in a sherry trifle, explained his notion of their Roman merchant's compound being most likely sited to one side or the other of the lane running north along the edge of the village. "Somewhere along there, roughly level with…" He paused, then continued, "The manor, in fact, would be equidistant from the Salisbury-Southampton road—which was already there at the time—and the river."

"I see." Therese served the last of the trifle, then looked again at Callum. "And what evidence is there that this compound existed?" She asked out of interest and also to encourage Callum to display his erudition before the appreciative audience consuming her trifle on his right.

When Callum concluded his mercifully brief, if thorough, listing of all the information on the compound he'd found in the books recording the village's history, Therese inclined her head. "Excellent. So as matters now stand, how do you propose to proceed with your search?"

Callum looked at Henry and Jamie; Therese wasn't surprised when the three led the company in formulating a plan for quartering the land on either side of the lane on the morrow.

"If we start immediately after breakfast," Henry concluded, "we should be able to thoroughly search that area."

They duly arranged to meet at the manor after breakfast on the following morning.

Therese hid her delight when Callum turned to Honor and asked, "If you can spare the time, would you like to join us? You've spent a lot of your stay in the village indoors."

Honor met his gaze and returned, "As have you. But point taken." She glanced at the others, all of whom looked at her encouragingly, and smiled. "If I can manage it, I'll join you all here tomorrow morning."

"Good-oh!" Henry said. "The more eyes on the ground, the better."

Callum simply beamed.

Then George Wiley—who, along with Roger Carnaby, tended to be quieter than the rest of the often-boisterous company—shifted in his chair, then looked at Jamie and Henry. "Hearing you revisit our earlier searches... As I recall, we found three of the outlying cottages empty. You said they belonged to men who moved around the area for work. We never went back to see if those men had returned and ask if they remembered the coins."

"That's right!" Jamie looked at Henry. "Those three men were the only ones in the village we never asked."

Henry's jaw set determinedly, and he nodded. "Right, then." He glanced around at his friends. "Perhaps, after we've helped bring in the yule log, we could drive out that way—there'll be enough of the day left."

All agreed. As Jamie said, they would leave no stone unturned.

Inevitably, the talk turned to the looming departure of Therese and her five grandchildren and Henry's four friends from the village, scheduled for the morning after the carol service, and a thread of concern crept into the voices; the clock was ticking on their search, and none of them liked the idea of leaving without succeeding in their quest to discover the source of the three old coins.

Therese noted the look exchanged between Melissa and Dagenham;

the quest wasn't the only endeavor their departure threatened to prematurely end.

In between the talking, the trifle had vanished. Therese looked up as Crimmins entered.

"My lady," Crimmins announced, "Pyne, the woodcutter, has arrived and is ready to lead you and your guests to the log he's chosen as the manor's yule log."

Therese smiled. "Excellent!" She looked around the table at a circle of expectant faces. "Bringing in the yule log is an old tradition that is too often neglected in this modern age. It was always intended as a group activity, and to me, it seemed appropriate that this particular group should come together to bring in the manor's log for this year." She rose and waved them to their feet. "Shall we?"

They sprang up with alacrity. The next minutes went in donning coats, scarves, and gloves. Carrying heavy ropes looped over his broad shoulders, Simms joined the melee in the front hall, as did Mrs. Crimmins, Mrs. Haggerty, Therese's dresser, Orneby, and the manor's maids, Tilly and Dulcie. Everyone was rugged up for a tramp through the woods.

"Just as well," Therese observed, "that there's been no more snow."

"Aye." Simms nodded. "Should be easy enough to drag a log along the damp ground."

Crimmins had volunteered to remain behind and prepare the fireplace in the front hall to receive the yule log; when everyone was ready, he opened the front door, and they filed out to join Pyne, a grizzled man of middle years, who had awaited them on the porch.

"Good afternoon, Pyne." Therese nodded regally.

Pyne dipped his head. "My lady. I've found a log that'll do the manor proud." He cast twinkling eyes over the assembled crowd. "And I see you've plenty of willing hands to help us bring her in."

Jamie, George, and Lottie were acquainted with Pyne, whom they'd met several times while rambling through the woods. Lottie tugged Pyne's sleeve. "Whereabouts is our log, Mr. Pyne?"

"Well, Miss Lottie, if you'll all come with me, I'll lead you to her." To Therese, Pyne said, "She's deep in the manor woods up north of the house."

Therese waved expansively. "Lead on."

Pyne tipped her a salute and set off around the house, and Jamie, George, and Lottie went with him. Henry, who also knew Pyne, followed close behind with Dagenham and Melissa, and Mandy, Kilburn, Wiley, and Carnaby trailed after them. The latter group were followed by Therese, Honor, and Callum—who quickly discovered that, although Therese normally wielded a cane and today had brought a shooting stick, she was sprightly enough to clamber about the woods without needing assistance. Simms and the rest of the manor's household brought up the rear, chatting to themselves as the group struck into the woods directly behind the manor's kitchen garden.

Pyne led the group steadily up a gentle rise, then they ambled beneath bare branches and detoured around old firs.

There were no pathways through the manor woods; it was an old wood, and the tall, wide-boled trees grew sufficiently far apart to allow easy passage. A thick blanket of dead leaves covered the ground, dappled here and there with clumps of lingering snow. Occasional thickets had grown up, dense enough to afford wildlife refuge, but none were large enough to impede the group's progress as they followed Pyne deeper into the wintry scene.

"How are things going in East Wellow, Pyne?" Henry called. "Is your rector still that peevish-looking fellow?"

"Oh, aye," Pyne replied. "But truth to tell, you're more likely to find me at St. Ignatius's, listening to Reverend Colebatch, than attending the East Wellow church. You've a bigger and happier congregation here."

George, walking beside Jamie, frowned.

Jamie noticed; he jogged his brother with his elbow and arched his brows.

George hesitated, then looked at Pyne. "Pyne, do you ever stop in at the Arms—or at Mountjoy's Store?"

Pyne glanced back at his company—now rather strung out—then halted and looked at George. "Aye, young sir. That I do—often enough." In glancing again at the others, still making their way toward him, Pyne missed the look of surprised awareness his reply evoked on the faces of those who'd heard him. His gaze on the laggards, Pyne continued, "Mountjoy's carries many more things than our little shop in East Wellow, and the beer at the Arms is better than what one gets at the Wellow tavern."

Henry could barely contain himself. "I say, Pyne, you don't happen to remember having any odd old coins, do you?"

Pyne shifted his gaze to Henry's face, and a puzzled frown overtook his expression. "Old coins?"

Eagerly, Jamie said, "They might not have appeared odd or old, but did you put any coins into the jar that was on the bar counter at the Arms? Or perhaps into the jar on the Mountjoys' counter?"

"The jars that collected silver pennies for the plum puddings," Lottie put in.

Pyne studied the children, then slowly nodded. "Aye. I put a few coins —three, it was—into the jar at the Arms one evening. The villagers about here give me a lot of steady work, and I picked up the pennies from down this way, so in keeping with the season and all, it seemed right those coins stayed in the village and went into the plum puddings."

The others had come up in time to hear Pyne's statement.

While most caught their breath in almost-fearful excitement, Callum asked, "Where did you find the coins?"

When Pyne blinked at him, Callum rephrased. "Do you remember where you picked them up?"

"Aye—more or less." Pyne glanced at the others. "Why?"

Henry, Jamie, and Callum told him, while the excitement built and gripped everyone in the group.

"We've been searching *everywhere* and asking *everyone*," Henry said. "But we only asked those who are part of the village, and no one's been able to tell us anything."

Pyne looked amazed. He glanced from one to the other. "Roman coins, heh? Well, I never." He focused on Callum. "I didn't take much notice of the coins themselves—I just thought they were pennies some soul had lost from their pocket."

"So where was it?" Jamie jigged up and down. "Can you take us to where you picked up the coins?"

"Aye." Pyne looked about, clearly getting his bearings. "It was on the day I came up here, looking for the right log for her ladyship—the one I'm taking you all to fetch now. I started into the woods from the corner where the lanes meet"—Pyne tipped his head to the southeast—"and I tramped up behind the cottage down there, then on and up through the manor woods, making a circuit of the manor's grounds, see?"

Everyone nodded, the children all but quivering with eagerness.

Pyne pointed to the southeast. "I picked up those coins over that way."

Callum battled to contain his excitement. His tone even, he said, "Let's go and see." He exchanged a wide-eyed look with Honor, one brimming with hope.

She smiled and fell in beside him as Pyne led the company in the direction in which he'd pointed.

The children hurried at Pyne's heels, and Henry wasn't far behind them. The rest trooped in a loose line in the vanguard's wake. They dodged around trees, angling down a gradual slope, then Pyne walked into a relatively flattish clearing.

As he stepped past the bole of a massive ancient oak and into the clearer, more-level space, Callum scanned the area, and his breath hitched. He stopped dead and whispered to Honor, "Look around. The old trees—they form a very large ring. Younger trees have seeded and grown inside the space, but there are no old trees inside the ring..." He swung around, gauging the topography. "Good Lord," he murmured. "This spot is perfect."

Pyne was kicking at the blanket of leaves a little way from the center of the clearing. "It was about here that I picked up those coins." He gestured. "They were just lying, scattered among the leaves."

Callum heard and walked over. He halted where Henry and the children were already scouting around the spot Pyne had indicated. "This place," Callum declared, "is exactly where Silvesterius Magnus's compound should be."

When the others looked at him, Callum pointed through the trees to the east. "We're about a hundred yards from the northbound lane—the one Silvesterius would have used to cart goods to the river to send to Clausentum and the coast." He swung and pointed south. "And we're not all that far from the Clausentum-Sorviodunum road—it's roughly the same distance as the river is from here."

He could no longer keep the excitement from his voice.

The children and Henry stared at him, then looked at the ground they'd been searching.

"There are no holes here." Lottie scuffed her shoe through the leaves. "No digging or anything like that."

Callum glanced around. The rest of their party had gathered in a knot about Lady Osbaldestone on one side of the clearing. Callum did a swift head count, then nodded. "Right, then." He looked at the children, their cousins, Henry, and his friends. "The chances are excellent that the source of the coins is somewhere near. The area we're standing in was probably the central clear space in the merchant's compound, which means all the buildings were likely built around its edge, extending between the larger trees into the gaps where the wood has since encroached. Those are the areas we need to search."

He waved the others up. "We need to spread out and circle this space." He pointed to the edges of the clearing. "We're looking for any sort of excavation that's resulted in earth being turned—an animal burrow, anything like that. Squirrels and even birds move coins, although usually not far." He drew a tense breath and stated, "What we're searching for has to be somewhere close."

Everyone fell to with a will. Even Lady Osbaldestone, closely accompanied by her dresser, Orneby, forged into the section of undergrowth to which Callum directed the pair.

In short order, the entire perimeter of the ancient clearing was being closely searched.

Jamie, George, and Lottie claimed one of the larger sectors, between two huge old trees. There, the growth of brush was dense. The three pushed past a minor thicket and nearly tumbled into a huge hole left by the roots of a massive tree that had fallen outward from the clearing's edge.

Lottie clutched George's sleeve and pointed—below the clump of the tree's gnarled roots. "Look! There! See it glinting?"

George bent and squinted, then shot Lottie a grin. "It's another coin!"

Jamie put his hands to his lips, forming a trumpet, and yelled, "*Here! We've found more coins!*"

Then Jamie followed Lottie and George as they slithered and slipped down the crumbling side of the hole to fetch up before the massive ball of roots.

The others came crashing toward them. "Where are you?" Henry called.

"Past the thicket," George yelled. "But watch out—there's a hole!"

The others took him at his word and edged cautiously past the thicket, then fanned out about the rim of the hole, peering into the depression in which the three children were enthusiastically scrabbling.

Then Jamie cupped his hands, and Lottie and George dropped the coins they'd found into his palms, then while the younger pair went back to poking and sifting through the loose soil, Jamie stretched upward and held up their find.

Crouching by the hole's edge, Callum reached down, and Jamie poured the coins into Callum's palm.

Callum straightened, and the others pressed close, watching as he brushed the coins free of dirt, then held one up. "Another denarius." He poked at the seven coins remaining in his palm. "More denarii and another siliqua. Good Lord!" The exclamation was one of awe.

Then Lottie stood and waved something over her head. "There's goldy things here, too!"

Along with the others, Callum looked down and focused on what Lottie now held in her chubby fingers. "Dear heaven—that's a cloak pin." He looked at Honor, then, grinning hugely, glanced at the faces all around. "This is real. We've found a hoard!"

The children cheered, and so did everyone else. Laughter, exclamations, and questions rang out.

On his way through the manor gardens, Simms had picked up a short shovel, which he now offered to Callum. "I thought we might need it to clear the way for the log."

Callum accepted the shovel with thanks and, when the children invitingly shifted aside, dropped down into the cramped hole. After examining the limited site, with the children peering at his elbows and everyone else peering from above, Callum used the shovel to carefully drag up clods of earth from beneath the ball of roots.

The children fell on the clumps, swiftly sifting through the soil and eagerly brandishing the coins and other pieces they found, then handing them up to the others waiting around the hole.

Mandy donated her short cape as a means of collecting and carrying the finds. There was much excited chatter and talk as those waiting around the hole organized a search of the ground around the fallen tree, and Tilly and Dulcie found more coins, and Mrs. Haggerty found part of an ancient buckle.

There were so many of them moving around beneath the trees, all talking and exclaiming and looking at the ground, that no one realized anyone was approaching until Professor Webster came huffing and puffing up a slight incline toward them.

Henry, Dagenham, and Melissa were on that side of the fallen tree.

The professor glanced up, saw them, and waved. "I heard the cheering and all the chatter." He huffed out a breath as he halted before them. "Don't tell me you've found something?"

Henry, Melissa, and Dagenham shifted, allowing the professor to see the ball of roots and the hole beyond and below—just as Callum, until then crouched in the hole, straightened and looked that way.

The professor paled, then choleric color rushed to his cheeks. "You!"

He took an aggressive step forward, to the lip of the hole. "What the *devil* are you doing here?"

Callum studied Webster for a second, then waved at the mini-excavation at his feet. "I'm helping unearth the hoard left by Silvesterius Magnus, a Roman merchant who built his compound here."

The professor goggled, and his angry color deepened, then he saw the small pile of items resting on Mandy's cape, and something akin to horror filled his face. "See here!" He pointed at the treasure. "You can't touch that—I won't have it! You're no better than a damned poacher—selling antiquities for gain! It's appalling. It shouldn't be allowed. The authorities…"

The professor railed on.

His face devoid of expression, Callum stood stock-still and let the angry tirade roll over him.

The others watched, eyes narrowing as the professor angrily denounced Callum. Gradually, Henry and his friends and those from the manor shifted around the hole until the group stood spread at Callum's back, flanking him. It hadn't been the professor who had been helping them search for the hoard for weeks; it hadn't been the professor who had been with them today, when they'd finally found it.

Eventually, Callum noticed the others' silent show of support. He glanced to either side, seeking Honor. He found her standing beside Lady Osbaldestone; her gaze flitted between her uncle and Callum, but her position and her determined expression very clearly declared she was on his side. Her eyes briefly met his before she looked back at her uncle.

The professor followed Callum's gaze and finally noticed his niece. Webster's heated words trailed off, and in the sudden silence, belatedly taking in the tableau and its implications, he frowned. "Honor?"

Therese caught Callum's gaze—caught the appeal in his look. She'd already noted the glance he'd shared with Honor; even before, from Honor's reaction to Webster's tirade, Therese had realized that Callum had satisfied her ultimatum. Honor knew who Callum truly was, knew of his relationship with her uncle, and had chosen to accept his explanation and stand with him. To support him and his way forward.

From the first, Therese had suspected that Honor had a sound head on her shoulders.

Apparently reading the signs of growing resistance toward him, Webster, still choleric, puffed himself up, pointed at the pile on Mandy's cape, and in ringing tones, declared, "I claim this find for Brentmore College."

Callum reacted to that. "Oh no, you don't." He started climbing out of the hole; Simms reached down and gave him a hand. Once standing on the rim, Callum faced the professor. "You've done nothing to assist the search—you weren't even here when the hoard was discovered."

Before Callum could say more, Therese stepped forward. "No, indeed." As it happened, she was equidistant from the professor and Callum as they glared at each other across the hole. She leaned lightly on her shooting stick and fixed first Callum, then the professor, with a warning eye. "But before this discussion proceeds, allow me to point out that the hoard was discovered on Hartington Manor lands and, initially, was discovered by my grandchildren."

She paused to bend an approving look on the three still standing in the hole, then smiled, looked around the circle, and stated, "I believe that makes the hoard mine—or at least in my charge, mine to direct as I see fit." She paused, then, when neither the professor nor Callum sought to contradict her, smoothly continued, "In that light, I am willing to entertain submissions as to what should be done with the Hartington hoard."

Callum and the professor spoke over each other.

Therese held up a hand, and they quieted. She looked down and opened the seat of her shooting stick, sat, settled, then regarded the two men. She gestured to the professor. "Professor Webster first. Explain to me, Professor, why I should hand over this hoard to Brentmore College."

Webster shot a triumphant glare at Callum; clearly, he believed his case superior on every count. Curling his fingers around his lapels and taking up a stance—no doubt the same stance he used when lecturing— Webster tipped back his head and made what Therese mentally labeled the scholar's pitch. "With a hoard of such potential historical significance, it's crucial that the find be given into the hands of those recognized and erudite scholars who will best appreciate it, who will study it appropriately, establish and record its significance, and ensure that it is kept safe." Webster paused as if replaying his words, then nodded, as much to himself as anyone else. "That, in a nutshell, is why Brentmore College is the right place for this treasure."

With that, Webster looked belligerently at Callum, as if daring him to attempt a counterargument.

Therese shifted her attention to Callum and, in a clear voice, directed,

"Now, Mr. Harris-Goodrich, if you please, explain to me your proposal, and why I should agree to it, rather than to Professor Webster's."

Callum stared at Lady Osbaldestone as the full gamut of what the old lady had managed to achieve slammed into his awareness.

He was surrounded by supporters who believed in him; he'd successfully guided the search, and the fruits of their labors lay at his feet. Honor was there, too, and she understood and was willing to stand by him.

And he was facing Webster with a hoard between them.

Callum couldn't imagine any other scenario that would better force Webster to *listen* to Callum's ideas—to pay attention and understand them.

He'd called in at Oxford hoping to speak with Webster and make him understand; in reality, Webster would never have listened to Callum's explanations, certainly not long enough to comprehend the true nature of Callum's approach. The same qualities that had made the professor a dogged and successful archeologist-explorer—his stubbornness, his persistence, his refusal to bow or bend—were hurdles when it came to changing his mind.

Callum kept his gaze trained on Lady Osbaldestone—the redoubtable benefactress he had no idea what he'd done to deserve—while he drew in a steadying breath and rapidly organized his arguments. "To begin with, I concur with the professor's assertion that, for a hoard of this type, to properly establish its significance, it's absolutely vital that the find be made available to the best and brightest scholars for study, for verification and validation. And of course, ensuring the hoard's safety goes without saying." Without looking at the professor, Callum tipped his head the older man's way.

"However," he went on, "I would argue that achieving those things alone is not making the most of any find. Our view of history—the general populace's knowledge of such times—is a central plank in our understanding of ourselves and of other countries, other nations, as well. History itself is important in teaching us how to live, and how do ordinary people learn about history?"

He glanced at the others. "The only place ordinary people would ever see a hoard such as this—or any other historical artifact—is in a museum." He returned his gaze to Lady Osbaldestone. "Should you give this hoard to Brentmore College, no one other than scholars of the college will likely ever see it. Ordinary folk won't even know it exists."

Lady Osbaldestone arched her brows. "And your alternative is?"

Callum drew in a breath. "If you assigned the hoard to me, I would offer it for sale—"

"To whom?" Lady Osbaldestone demanded, overriding the professor's imminent outburst.

Callum paused for effect, then offered, "Lord Lovett or Lord Lynley —possibly both. Both are wealthy enough, and both are avid collectors of Roman antiquities, and I know they are willing to accept the proviso I would attach to the sale, namely, that whoever buys the hoard gifts it immediately to a suitable museum. In this case, I would stipulate the hoard goes to the Ashmolean Museum in Oxford—I know the curators there are seeking more Roman artifacts for their collection."

Webster gave vent to a disgusted snort. "So you'll sell the find and pocket the cash yourself!"

Unruffled, Callum looked at the professor; this was the point Webster had never listened long enough to hear, let alone understand. "I would keep a commission—twenty percent of the final price. That allows me to live and to fund my next expedition to find ancient artifacts—and many of the expeditions I now undertake are at the behest of various museum curators."

Callum returned his gaze to Lady Osbaldestone, then looked at the others about the hole. "The other eighty percent of the money from the sale—the bulk of it—would be split between"—he glanced at Lady Osbaldestone—"in this case, Lady Osbaldestone—"

"And the village of Little Moseley," that grande dame supplied.

Callum inclined his head. "That would be for you to decide. But the eighty percent would be split between you and the institution—in this instance, the Ashmolean—to cover the costs of proper cleaning, restoration if required, and presentation and public display of the hoard."

From the corner of his eye, Callum watched Webster's scowl fade to a puzzled frown.

Callum focused on Lady Osbaldestone; it was time to hammer his point home. "You asked why you should favor my proposal over that of Professor Webster. The answer is that, through my proposal, everyone stands to gain. Me"—he pointed to himself—"in having enough to go on with and fund my next expedition. You and the village through your share of the proceeds of the sale—the money Lovett and Lynley will happily hand over. Lovett and Lynley also benefit because they live to see their names on plaques beside artifacts displayed to the public—thus having their erudite largesse acknowledged. The Ashmolean will benefit both through the enlargement of their catalog and by having the funds to pay their staff involved in the housing, preparation, and display of such artifacts. As for scholars, those from far and wide wishing to study the items in this hoard will be able to do so through the good offices of the museum. And last but not, to my mind, least, the wider public will benefit by being able to view the hoard and learn about the past—boys and girls and parents and others will be able to see the coins and pins and all the other items in the hoard and wonder and imagine how people lived long ago. Their eyes will see, their imaginations will be sparked, and their minds will be broadened."

Webster's scowl had returned, but it now held a pouting quality as he directed it at Callum. "You've changed your tune."

Calmly, his gaze open and direct, Callum met Webster's eyes and shook his head. "No. I haven't changed at all. You simply never gave me a chance to explain—you never waited to hear me out. That's the same pattern I've used for all the items I've handled, commencing with the bronze figurine."

Webster pointed an accusing finger at Callum. "You sold that figurine —don't try to deny it!"

Imperturbably, Callum nodded. "I did, and it's been in the British Museum ever since, with a plaque beside it citing Lord Devon—who paid me for the figurine—as the benefactor who donated the piece."

Webster's mouth worked, as if he wanted to scoff but couldn't find the grounds to do so.

Lady Osbaldestone's voice cut through the tension. "I'm acquainted with Lord Devon, and I've heard his version of the arrangement he made in buying the figurine. Although his lordship refused to name the source of the find, the details he revealed were, indeed, as you, Mr. Goodrich, have described." Lady Osbaldestone sat straighter. "I gather the same sort of arrangement pertained with a certain vase from Pompeii that Lord Wallace snaffled. His lordship was quite chuffed about that, as he informed me on the opening night of a special exhibition of ancient pottery during which the vase was displayed."

Therese watched as Webster blinked and blinked again—as if to clear dust from his eyes. "Indeed," she continued, "I am acquainted with several of the curators at the British Museum, and they have given me to understand that the recent manner of acquiring artifacts via what they term 'aristocratic patronage' has given them new heart. They feel they finally have a chance of amassing sufficient items to give the public a better understanding of how people lived in ancient times." She nodded at Callum. "Like you, the curators and, indeed, their governors believe that to be an important part of their role."

She paused, then shifted her gaze to the professor, who was still frowning, but now in a rather more self-directed way. "Well, Professor Webster?" She felt reasonably certain he wasn't the sort of man who would feel embarrassed by having his mistaken understanding aired before others. When he glanced at her from under his bushy eyebrows, she continued, "Do you wish to advance any reason as to why I shouldn't consign this find to your erstwhile assistant, Mr. Goodrich, to guide into the hands of the Ashmolean Museum?"

Webster compressed his lips and all but glowered at her.

Callum shifted, drawing her attention. "If I might make a suggestion?"

Therese arched her brows, then, curious as to what he might say, inclined her head.

Callum gestured at the mound of items on Mandy's cape. "We've already retrieved quite a lot of coins"—he glanced into the hole and saw that Jamie, George, and Lottie had grown bored and returned to sifting through the soil and had amassed another pile to add to the collection; he smiled at the children—"and it seems there are more. In addition, we have multiple other artifacts, and those are of particular interest to collectors like Lovett and Lynley." Callum raised his gaze and met Therese's eyes. "Perhaps we can split the find? I can't see any reason why we couldn't retain enough to ensure Lovett's and Lynley's backing, while also allowing a sample of both coins and possibly artifacts to be donated from you and the village of Little Moseley directly to Brentmore College, for the study of the scholars there."

Therese managed not to beam too triumphantly; she was delighted with Callum's suggestion—delighted with him for having the insight, sense, and fortitude to step forward and offer his old mentor an olive branch.

Along with everyone else who had listened to the entire exchange with avid interest, she looked at Professor Webster.

Aware of the attention directed his way, the professor considered carefully, then somewhat gruffly said, "It appears I misinterpreted Mr. Goodrich's methods and have misjudged his behavior." He cleared his throat and nodded to Callum. "For that, I apologize, m'boy. I shouldn't have doubted you."

There was a quality in the professor's voice that suggested his contrition was genuine and deeply felt.

Webster raised his head and looked at Therese. "As for the suggestion of dividing the hoard, on behalf of Brentmore College, I would be happy to accept whatever portion your ladyship considers appropriate."

Therese smiled unrestrainedly. "Excellent!"

Callum circled toward the professor and held out his hand—and after the barest of hesitations, the professor grasped it firmly. Therese's hearing was excellent, and she made out the professor's gruff words as he released Callum's hand. "Forgive me, Callum—I was an old fool. I should have known better than to think what I did."

Callum smiled faintly, then shrugged and looked down, into the hole. "Best we put the past behind us." Then he grinned and glanced sidelong at Webster. "I'd say we've got our work cut out for us in getting as much of the Hartington hoard as we can out of the ground before dark."

Webster grunted and looked at the sky. "You're not wrong about that."

In less than a minute, both men were in the hole, and all the others had gathered around; it was quickly agreed that Simms would return to the manor and fetch tools for digging out and ferrying the hoard to safety, while Callum and Webster took turns to dig, and Lottie, Jamie, and George dealt with the looser soil while larger lumps were passed up to willing hands waiting on the rim of the hole for further breaking up and sifting.

Simms returned, and with Callum and the professor supplied with more appropriate tools, the excavation went faster.

For her part, Therese kept her eyes on the sky, but although the clouds thickened as the light slowly waned, and even though the wind dropped and the scent of snow intensified, none fell.

At last, Callum and the professor straightened and handed up the tools they'd been using, then stood in the now much wider hole and peered at the ground.

The professor huffed. "I believe that's it—at least for now."

His gaze on the ground, Callum nodded. "I think we've cleared the cache." He glanced at the roots of the toppled giant. "Whoever buried it placed it at the foot of this tree, thinking to return to it sometime." He turned and looked toward the clearing. "Further excavation to see if we can locate the villa itself will have to wait."

The professor nodded. With Callum's assistance, the older man climbed out of the hole. Callum lifted Lottie out, watched the boys as they scrambled up to the rim, then grasped the hand Simms held down and allowed himself to be hauled out.

Thoroughly satisfied with all that had transpired thus far, Therese looked to the others. "Pyne?"

The woodcutter had been helping as eagerly as anyone. He came forward and bobbed his head to Therese. "Aye." He glanced upward. "If we go now, we should have just enough time to fetch your yule log in."

They went, all of them. They tramped through the woods, following at Pyne's heels, with Simms steering the handcart he'd brought, into the bed of which they'd loaded their treasure. The cart bumped over branches and slid over dead leaves, but it was deep enough—and there were eyes enough on it—to ensure nothing fell out.

Finally, when they were deep in the woods to the north of the house, Pyne halted and pointed. "There she is." A large, thick log lay waiting in a small area cleared of leaves. "Just like I left her." Pyne ran a hand over the bark, then patted the log as if it were sentient. "A perfect log for your purposes, this is. She'll burn strongly but steadily and see you through the night to the dawn."

Therese smiled. Clearly, Pyne was one of those who remembered the old ways. Living as he did, constantly surrounded by and at the whims of Nature, she couldn't say she was surprised.

All the males gathered around the log. Simms unwound the rope he'd carried, and advice on how to harness the log for hauling came from all sides.

Ultimately, however, it was Mrs. Haggerty who showed them the best way to tie the log, leaving two long sections of rope to act as hauling reins; the old cook was another who "knew things."

Once that was done, they set off, walking through the woods and taking turns to drag the log along; even the professor and Therese took a turn. Laughter bubbled, and a sense of achievement buoyed the group's spirits. Simms followed close behind the log, pushing the handcart, and the younger men assisted as they descended the uneven slope that would eventually return them to the manor's grounds.

Therese fell back, the better to consider whether she needed to meddle any further, but Callum and Honor were walking side by side, and their expressions and the way their gazes met and held suggested they, at least, had found the right path forward. The professor and Callum had plainly buried the past, and Webster walked on Honor's other side, but not too close.

The party came to a slippery section, and Callum took Honor's hand and helped her over it, then, instead of releasing her, he tucked her hand into the crook of his arm, and they walked on, closer than ever.

Therese smiled to herself and shifted her attention to the other couple in whom she had an interest. Indeed, an even deeper interest.

Melissa and Dagenham remained with the knot of Henry's friends, yet for all that, the pair might as well have been walking alone. Each had eyes and awareness only for the other, but there was a quality of uncertainty between them now—very much as if each saw something they wanted, but couldn't see how to reach for it.

While the tenor of their whispered exchanges, the way their heads dipped together, spoke of a closeness that—in Therese's experience—meant only one thing, a sense of imminent hopelessness seemed to have afflicted them both.

Therese viewed the pair with more sympathy than she allowed to show; she could read the signs. They'd reached a certain understanding, and with the wealth of decades of experience behind her, Therese could guess what would happen next.

She wasn't entirely surprised when, apparently spontaneously, without glancing at Dagenham, Melissa started to sing her part of "The Holly and the Ivy."

Her clear alto floated through the wood, haunting and sweet.

Dagenham's eyes had locked on her face. When the moment came, he took up the refrain. Between them, they sang all six verses of the song—to the delight of the others, but, Therese wondered, at what cost to themselves.

When the final note died, Mrs. Haggerty nudged Mrs. Crimmins and started to sing a song about the yule log, and as Mrs. Crimmins and Tilly and Dulcie joined in, Therese discovered her staff had fine voices and also knew a thing or two she hadn't about the old ways.

The children were delighted and skipped before the log, and then the company reached the manor's grounds, and in a giddy, laughing rush, Henry and his friends took the ropes and hauled the log around to the front door.

All the men lent a hand maneuvering the log into the house and, under Crimmins's direction, placed it just so on the bed of shavings and twigs Crimmins had laid ready in the hearth in the front hall—the original hearth of the manor's great hall and the largest in the house.

Therese called for ale, cider, and mulled wine, and the group repaired to the drawing room to warm themselves before the fire there. When everyone was sipping, she looked around and, smiling, said, "What a very eventful afternoon we've had. We've found the Hartington hoard, we've dragged in our yule log, the carol service will come tomorrow, and…" She caught her younger grandchildren's eyes and raised her glass. "It's nearly time for Christmas."

Predictably, the three cheered, as did everyone else.

It was, Therese thought, a fitting end to the day.

CHAPTER 12

*I*n the Hartington Manor household, Monday had been designated "Plum Pudding Day."

As Therese and her brood would decamp from the village the following morning, Monday had been chosen as the most appropriate time to distribute to every house and cottage in the village the dozens of puddings the manor's kitchen had produced.

Along with his usual fee and a sizeable tip, in recognition of his assistance in locating the hoard as well as providing the yule log, Pyne had been gifted with a pudding the evening before. But when Monday arrived, the rest of the puddings, wrapped in red and green cloths, stood stacked on every available surface in the manor's kitchen, and despite her fiercely proud expression, Mrs. Haggerty swore she couldn't wait to see the last of them.

The day had dawned chilly, damp, and foreboding, as if more snow was massing in the clouds and would soon fall.

Originally, the household had planned to distribute the puddings at the carol service, but with the search for the hoard concluded, during the celebrations the previous afternoon, they'd arranged for the erstwhile crew of searchers—along with their carriages—to gather at the manor after breakfast to aid in ferrying the puddings to their destinations around the village.

Mrs. Crimmins and Mrs. Haggerty were in charge; they had a list of destinations, and in many cases, given some village families were large, there was more than one pudding assigned to an address.

Jamie, George, and Lottie begged Therese to be allowed to commandeer the manor's gig. Given Jamie was now a responsible ten-year-old and Therese felt confident in his ability to manage the manor's quiet gray mare, she agreed, and after reporting to the generals in the kitchen, the three youngsters were the first to set off, carrying five puddings to be delivered along the lane—one to the vicarage, one to the Moodys, one to old Mrs. Harmer in the cottage by the village green, and two to Mountjoy's Store.

Therese waved the trio off, then welcomed Henry and his friends, who had just driven up in their curricles.

With much laughing and joking, along with Mandy and Melissa, who had waited for the young men, the group tramped into the kitchen and reported for duty. Mrs. Crimmins and Mrs. Haggerty seized the opportunity to send the curricles—driven by Henry, Dagenham, and Thomas Kilburn—first to the more far-flung and out-of-the-way cottages.

As the groups emerged from the kitchen, burdened with plum puddings, Therese smiled and nodded encouragingly and, privately, thought it a pity propriety dictated that Melissa and Dagenham couldn't be allowed to travel the lanes alone. Instead, George Wiley climbed into Dagenham's curricle beside Melissa, and he and she balanced the six puddings with which they'd been entrusted as Dagenham flicked the reins and set his pair pacing out along the drive.

Therese watched them go. There was a certain fragility in the way Melissa and Dagenham were interacting today, enough to leave Therese uneasy. Dissatisfied. But there was little if anything she could do. Sadly, when it came to her granddaughter and the handsome viscount, matters were, in this instance, out of her hands; altering facts was a feat not even she could accomplish.

In contrast, with a laugh and smiles all around, Henry set his curricle bowling down the drive after Dagenham's, with Mandy and Roger Carnaby sharing the seat beside him, then Thomas Kilburn took Simms up with him and set his bays pacing in the other curricles' wakes.

Once the carriages were away, Therese returned inside, shut the front door, and walked to the dining room.

Callum, Professor Webster, and Honor had taken possession of the dining room table, the surface of which Mrs. Crimmins had covered with an old blanket. The professor and Callum had their heads together, poring over the assorted coins. Before they'd left the manor yesterday, the entire crew had assisted with washing and cleaning the coins and all the other items extracted from the site in the woods. Now, Callum and the professor, both wielding jeweler's loupes, were engaged in making a detailed inventory, while Honor sat with a sheet of paper before her and a pen in her hand, noting their findings in a neat script as the pair of scholars—erstwhile mentor and successful graduate—worked their way through the hoard.

Therese stood in the doorway and watched for a moment; the men were so engrossed neither noticed her, but Honor did and sent her a quick smile.

Callum had arrived early that morning, just as Therese and her brood were sitting down to breakfast, and she'd invited him to join them. He'd eaten with the sort of appetite she associated with gentlemen who lived alone, and when the children had asked, he'd explained what needed to be done before any division of the hoard was attempted—namely, that a formal inventory of the find needed to be made.

"The inventory must be beyond question, of course." He'd caught Therese's eye. "Would you be agreeable to myself and the professor collaborating on that?"

She'd arched her brows. "Of course." Then she'd added, "But if I've understood Honor's plaints correctly, the professor needs to devote himself to finishing his treatise."

"As to that"—Callum had pushed a last piece of bacon around his plate—"I have to leave to go north on Wednesday at the latest, and I would prefer to take the inventory—or at least the list of pieces for which you agree to allow me to negotiate a sale—with me. In this season, Lovett and Lynley will be on their estates, and I can drop in and speak with them on my way back, after Christmas."

He'd paused, staring at the bacon, but she'd doubted he'd actually been seeing it, then he'd glanced at her. "I thought that, if the professor would consent to helping me finalize the inventory today, then as I'm aware of all the latest happenings in the area he's addressing in his treatise, in light of our rapprochement, I could work with him in gathering the final references and so on tomorrow, and also return to Oxford immediately after Christmas and work with him and Honor to expedite the completion of the treatise in time."

Therese had hidden a smugly satisfied smile and had graciously inclined her head. "That sounds like an excellent plan. Once you've finished with that piece of bacon, perhaps you should walk to the cottage and lay your proposal before the professor and Honor?"

After reading her approval in her eyes, Callum had relaxed, grinned, and done just that. Consequently, there the three were—the professor, Callum, and Honor—creating a scholarly inventory of the Hartington hoard.

Callum looked up from the piece he was examining and said—dictated—something to Honor. The professor grunted a wordless assent, and Honor duly entered whatever the description was into the inventory.

Finally noticing Therese standing in the doorway, Callum said, "Your ladyship, I've been meaning to ask… Yesterday, you referred to the hoard as the 'Hartington Hoard.' Is that the name you would like formally associated with the find?" He waved at the inventory. "For instance, should we label this the Official Inventory of the Hartington Hoard?"

Therese thought for a second, then nodded. "Yes."

When she said nothing more, Callum studied her, then inquired, "Is there some reason for that, other than Hartington being the manor's name?"

The boy was insightful. Therese smiled and looked down the room at the painting that hung above the mantelpiece. It was a portrait of an older lady with a gentle face and eyes that seemed to smile, even now. Therese tipped her head toward the picture. "I inherited the manor from my aunt, Gloriana Hartington. She was a renowned eccentric in her day. It seems appropriate that any Roman treasure found on the property should bear her name."

Callum grinned. "That's an excellent idea—and it's the sort of connection that will appeal to the collectors and also the museum."

Jamie, George, and Lottie burst into the front hall, and Therese swung to face them.

"We're back!" the trio chorused.

"And we're ready for our next load," George declared.

"We spotted Dagenham's curricle coming along the lane, so they're on their way back, too," Jamie reported.

Lottie grinned up at Therese. "Giving out the puddings is fun—we want to be first out again." And with that, the three barreled on toward the kitchen.

Therese laughed and followed them.

She was assisting the trio to carry five more puddings out to the gig when Dagenham, Melissa, and George Wiley came in, their faces flushed and expressions eager.

"Everyone's been thrilled to receive the puddings," Melissa reported.

The three hurried on to the kitchen to collect their next consignment.

In all, a grand total of forty-seven plum puddings were delivered through the morning and into the early afternoon. The snow continued to threaten, but held off, although the skies were all shades of gray and hung ponderously heavy and low.

Meanwhile, the scholars in the dining room completed their inventory of the hoard. Subsequently, summoned to the dining room, Therese sat with Callum and Professor Webster as they re-examined the inventoried pieces, and with the guidance of the two scholars, Therese decreed which pieces she wished to donate to Brentmore College in her aunt's name and that of the village. With that settled, she delegated Callum to contact those collectors most likely to be interested regarding purchasing the remaining pieces and gifting them to the Ashmolean Museum.

Callum said that all he needed was a fresh copy of the inventory to show the collectors. When the professor looked surprised, Callum almost bashfully admitted, "These days, my reputation is enough to guarantee the authenticity of the find, and your name added to mine on the inventory puts the question beyond doubt." Callum had glanced at the piles of coins, pins, brooches, and other bits and pieces. "And frankly, carrying any of that with me wouldn't be a wise idea."

"No, indeed." Therese duly summoned Crimmins, and with Callum's and the professor's help, they transferred the Hartington hoard in its entirety to Therese's private parlor.

At Callum's and the professor's uncertain looks and glances at the window, Therese smiled and assured them, "Later, we'll place the hoard in the manor's lockbox for safekeeping, but I fancy we'll have a few visitors this afternoon who would like to see it."

Before sitting down with the scholars, Therese had sent Simms to deliver invitations to view the hoard to the Colebatches, the Mountjoys, and the Whitesheafs at the Arms, all of whose assistance had been pivotal in leading to the discovery of the treasure.

Therese regarded the pile of gleaming silver, with the occasional glint of gold. "Before we send any of it on to Brentmore or the Ashmolean, we'll have to arrange a proper viewing for the entire village, but that can wait until later."

The sound of arrivals in the front hall drew them in that direction. Before leaving the room, Therese lifted the parlor door key from the pot in which she hid it and handed it to Crimmins, and he followed her out and locked the parlor door.

In the hall, she found the plum-pudding deliverers had returned—a touch weary and definitely hungry, but happy. They were all there, eagerly exchanging stories of how the recipients of the puddings had reacted.

Therese looked past the youthful crowd and saw Mrs. Crimmins and Mrs. Haggerty ferrying pies, fresh from the oven, into the reclaimed dining room. Therese was about to clap her hands to attract the company's attention, but the aromas wafting from the pies reached the group, and heads turned as noses twitched.

She laughed and called, "Luncheon is served," then when the group looked at her, she waved them to go ahead of her into the room.

Therese settled at the table's head and glanced around. The entire delivery crew were there, plus Callum, Honor, and the professor. Therese watched as, after she'd instructed them not to stand on ceremony—it was after two o'clock, and they'd worked without pause all morning—they attacked Mrs. Haggerty's pies and poured themselves glasses of mulled cider from the pottery pitchers on the table.

She consumed a small slice of pie and waited until they'd all had their fill and relaxed in the chairs, replete and comfortable. Then she tapped her spoon to the side of her glass, and when everyone looked her way, said, "I would like you all to charge your glasses, then gather in the front hall. It's time we set our yule log alight."

"Yes!" cried Jamie, George, and Lottie.

Everyone else grinned and did as Therese had asked.

Holding glasses of the still-warm cider, the company streamed into the front hall, just as Crimmins opened the door to the Colebatches, the Whitesheafs, and the Mountjoys.

The next minutes went in showing the newcomers the hoard, and the plum-pudding deliverers also crowded into the parlor and gathered around; most hadn't previously seen the collection displayed in any organized fashion. Crimmins wove between the guests, making sure everyone held a glass of mulled cider or wine.

Eventually, Therese, aided by Mandy and Melissa—who, to Therese's impressed surprise, instinctively stepped to her side in support—herded everyone back into the front hall. The manor staff, all holding glasses of their own, appeared and joined the crowd.

At the huge old fireplace, Crimmins and Simms made a great show of setting the yule log alight, while everyone else stood around and, smiling and quietly chatting, watched.

Once the log was crackling nicely, Therese raised her glass of mulled wine. "I give you a toast." She waited while everyone readied their glasses, then smiled upon them all and said, "Here's to the season, to the year passed and the year to come, to our yule log, to the Hartington Hoard, to our plum puddings, and most importantly, to the plum trees that started it all!"

The company cheered, loud and long, then drank.

In the consequent momentary silence, Lottie's piping voice rang out. "Look! It's snowing!"

She pointed to the fanlight above the front door, through which fat snowflakes could be seen whirling and swirling.

Therese smiled and caught Lottie's eye. "It appears we'll have a thoroughly white Christmas after all."

Several hours later, split once more into their various households, the members of that happy company trooped through the steadily falling snow, their boots crunching on a crisp white blanket as they toiled up the path to the doors of St. Ignatius on the Hill.

Candlelight welcomed them, spilling, golden and warm, from an interior wreathed in and scented by holly and fir. This year, the Dutton Grange household had volunteered to decorate the church for the carol service, and if the appreciative looks on the faces of the congregation were any indication, everyone thought it a magical idea.

Murmured greetings and smiles abounded as the congregation filed in and filled the pews, with latecomers lining the walls.

The Moodys were on their mettle and soon had their choristers marshaled and ready, arranged in rows on the altar steps. Then the organ gave voice, and Reverend Colebatch led the ceremonial procession into the church and down the aisle, and everyone rose, and the service began.

It was the third such service Therese had attended, and while she'd doubted it was possible to trump last year's effort, the Moodys and their assembled choir proved her wrong.

Voices, strong and sweet, soaring and rumbling, delicate and powerful, filled the church in a glorious paean to the Father, the Son, and the Holy Ghost.

No matter how familiar the carols were, it was the delivery that captured minds and hearts and set souls singing.

Therese watched her grandchildren, saw their innocent passion and joy, and wallowed in the moment.

During the short sermon, she surreptitiously glanced around, taking note of those in the pews on the other side of the aisle.

Callum was sitting next to Honor, with Professor Webster on Honor's other side. Therese had noted all three singing as lustily as any in the crowd; she suspected all three felt sincerely grateful for the changes their sojourn in Little Moseley had wrought.

As she watched, Callum glanced sidelong at Honor, and she, as if feeling his gaze, looked at him, and the pair shared a smile—a gentle, private smile that spoke of connection, of closeness, of evolving emotions. Smugly satisfied, Therese faced forward.

Immediately following the sermon, Melissa and Dagenham stepped out from the choir's ranks and, to the beat of Mr. Moody's baton, raised their voices and sang "The Holly and the Ivy" with such poignancy that Therese—along with every adult female in the church—was forced to find her handkerchief and dab at brimming eyes.

She couldn't recall when a rendition of the carol had so moved her. Tonight's performance was more intense, more potent than the pair's effort yesterday in the wood; that had been almost playful in comparison. More clearly than anyone else in the audience, Therese comprehended the root cause of the emotional tension that infused Melissa's sultry alto and Dagenham's powerful yet rigidly controlled tenor.

The pair stood on the cusp of a decision, one that, even had they been older, more experienced, would have been difficult to make. They were faced with taking a step—one way or the other—and in neither direction was the outcome rosy. They knew it; Therese knew they did—the evocative emotion infusing their voices proved it.

And for once, she couldn't interfere. Not this time—not with this.

She couldn't even hint or steer. This was one decision that had to come entirely from them—from their hearts.

Sometimes, those one loved had to be allowed to work out matters of the heart for themselves, for who could truly speak for another in that sphere?

Therese watched the pair as the last note, laden with feeling and carried in perfect harmony, soared through the church, then the sound crested, ebbed, and faded away. Silence fell, and the pair looked down, drew breath, then without so much as a glance at the other, stepped back and rejoined the choir's ranks.

She stifled a sigh. She would support them in whatever decision they made; she would be there with as much wisdom as they would hear, but she could not save them from the maze of thorns Fate had set in their path.

Whether they found their way through it to the other side and came together again, hand in hand, would be entirely up to them.

The service continued, and if Therese still felt the chill touch of a looming shadow, the rest of the congregation was unaffected, and as the songs of joy swelled and filled every corner of the church, raising spirits and buoying hearts, the expressions of those around her glowed with happiness.

Finally, the last carol was sung, and Reverend Colebatch intoned the benediction, then, beaming, led his congregation up the aisle.

The good reverend paused before the doors, then reached forward and opened them cautiously—not knowing what lay waiting on the other side.

Those closest peered past him and caught their breaths—in wonder, in delight.

The snow had ceased, and the wind had cleared the sky, but no longer blew. The night air was icy and still, and the stars twinkled like bright white diamonds scattered over the ink-black sky. And strewn across the ground, myriad ice crystals glinted and sparkled in the silver moonlight.

It was a magical scene, and the children of the village poured forth in utter, boundless joy. Even the adults, following more circumspectly to gather in groups on the snow-covered lawn, nodding and calling greetings, their breaths fogging in the icy air, couldn't do less than beam.

The transformation seemed a benediction conferred by Nature herself on their little village—as if to acknowledge that yuletide was nigh, and all was well in their corner of the land.

After patting Reverend Colebatch's hand and complimenting him on his sermon, Therese joined the Swindons, Mrs. Woolsey, and Henrietta Colebatch on the front lawn as they exchanged season's greetings with the other village families.

From the corner of her eye, Therese saw Professor Webster leave the church. The professor looked around, then headed her way. Callum and Honor stepped through the doors in the professor's wake, but after taking note of the professor's direction, Callum tugged Honor's sleeve and, when she glanced at him, took her arm and drew her to the side, into the shadow thrown by the church.

Therese smiled and greeted the professor. "Did you enjoy the service?"

With his hands in his greatcoat pockets, Callum halted in the lee of the church, where a splotch of shadow created at least the illusion of privacy, and swung to face Honor.

In her bright-blue pelisse, with her hands tucked in a fur muff, she obligingly halted; relaxed and at ease, a gentle smile on her lips, she looked questioningly up at him.

Clinging to the moment, he smiled back, basking in the glow of her attention. He could only marvel at how, during his days at Little Moseley, everything—every aspect of his life—seemed to have somehow fallen into place. He couldn't help but feel this was a moment he needed to seize.

Honor tipped her head, her smile remaining as her eyes searched his.

He hadn't planned this—hadn't rehearsed any speech or thought of the correct form of words—but a sense of magic hung in the air, and emboldened, he licked suddenly dry lips and said, "I realize you don't yet know me well enough to make any life-defining decisions, that asking you to do so would be presumptuous—and precipitous—but I was wondering if you would be agreeable to allowing me to spend more time with you." Unexpected nerves pricked his spine, and he shifted and hurriedly added, "Just in the normal way, not as part of any search—not as part of anything academic." A sudden thought occurred, and he rushed to reassure her, "And I definitely don't want to displace you as your uncle's assistant."

Her smile deepened. Despite the shadows, he thought her eyes brightened.

He took heart and sighed. "I'm making a muck of this, but while I know and acknowledge that it's too soon for me to make any formal—or even informal—declaration, I know my own mind, and in time, I'm determined to secure your hand...if you think you might come to consider marrying me."

Honor arched her brows, but before she could reply to the implied question, Callum locked his gaze with hers and, more soberly, went on, "I never thought to find a lady like you—one who understands what I do and who could be a helpmate in all aspects of my life—a partner in life and not just in making a home. You have all the talents I could wish for"—his voice lowered and deepened—"and I hope you'll allow me the chance to show you what you already mean to me and how much I want you by my side."

Her heart had skipped, tripped; now, it soared. In his eyes, she could read his sincerity—that he was speaking from the heart.

She could do no less. "If you asked for my hand today, I would gladly give it, *but*"—she tipped her head—"I appreciate your point that, for us, in terms of our acquaintance, these are early days, and I agree with your suggestion and would welcome the chance to get to know you better—and for you to get to know me."

Gazing into his eyes, she felt as if she was sinking into the welcoming blue. "Neither of us is young and silly—we've the years and, I hope, the maturity to feel certain of what we want and need."

We're old enough to know we're falling in love.

She didn't say the words, yet she would have sworn they hovered in the crisp air between them. There was a clarity in the moment, making it impossible not to see and acknowledge that they—he and she—stood on the cusp of a future worth seizing.

She drew a hand from her muff and laid it on his arm. He drew his hand from his pocket and gently clasped her gloved fingers. Emotion welled within her, and she allowed all she felt to show in her eyes as she turned her hand, gripped his fingers, and smiling, said, "Let's take the next month—or even two—to learn all we should know of each other. And then you can offer, and I can accept, and we can go forward from there."

He blinked—she could almost see him replaying her words in his head—then a glorious smile broke across his face, widening to one of unabashed joy. His eyes on hers, he raised her gloved fingers to his lips and kissed them. "That, my dear Honor, is an excellent plan."

Their gazes remained locked. The air between them all but quivered as they stood toe-to-toe in the shadow of the church. Honor read in the blue of Callum's eyes that he wanted to kiss her—and she felt the shove of her own instincts urging her to rise on her toes and press her lips to his—but then his gaze flicked past her. She followed his glance to the ever-widening spread of villagers crowding the lawn, the nearest of whom were now only a yard away.

Honor took in the crowd, then glanced at Callum.

He met her look with one of disgruntled disappointment, and a laugh bubbled in her throat, and she grinned at him. "Come on." She shifted to stand beside him; he retained his hold on her hand and wound her arm in his. She patted his arm. "Let's go and join Uncle Hildebrand—he's over there with Lady Osbaldestone and the Colebatches."

With an irrepressibly smug smile, Callum steered her in Professor Webster's direction.

As they joined the circle anchored by Lady Osbaldestone, her black eyes dwelled assessingly on him and Honor, then her ladyship smiled, caught his eye, and inclined her head approvingly...

Callum managed not to frown. *How could she know...?*

Then again, she was Lady Osbaldestone.

Satisfied that one romance-of-the-season was progressing toward a happy conclusion, Therese turned her attention to her other emotional concern. While exchanging comments and observations with those around her, she searched the crowd for Melissa and Dagenham. After quitting the church with the rest of the choristers, they'd initially remained with the group of Therese's grandchildren and Henry's friends, but now, Therese noted, the pair had drifted away from the others into the less-populated graveyard on the other side of the path.

Melissa halted beside one of the larger, still-upright gravestones, where the shadow cast by a nearby tree provided a measure of privacy, and swung to face Dagenham. He halted before her, his back to the crowd still milling before the church.

Through the dimness, his eyes met hers. Half a minute passed, then, unobtrusively, he reached for her gloved hand, and she surrendered it.

His fingers moved over hers, a subtle caress she felt even through her gloves.

Their gazes held; they both knew this was the moment in which they had to face reality. Last year, this year—all the moments of their mutual past led, inexorably, to this.

When he didn't say anything, she drew in a tight breath, tipped up her chin, and stated, "I'm only fifteen. And now you're on the town..." She shook her head. "I can't ask you to wait for me. That wouldn't be fair."

He stared at her for a long moment, then, his voice deep, countered, "Can I ask you to wait for me?"

She considered that, then inclined her head. "You could try..."

He studied her face, his thumb drawing circles over her knuckles, then his lips twisted, and he whispered, "That wouldn't be fair, either."

She drew in a breath and shifted to stare, unseeing, across the quiet graveyard. "It's as if Fate is toying with us—letting us find each other when I'm still so young." Her tone ached with frustration.

Dagenham's lips fleetingly lifted. "I'm not that old, either."

She met his eyes. "Old enough."

He knew what she meant; at twenty-one, he was old enough to go on the town—indeed, henceforth, he would be expected to be seen in London's ballrooms and drawing rooms and making the rounds of the clubs—and being heir to the Earl of Carsely, he was also of sufficient age to be expected to look about him for a bride.

He could put off that necessary decision for some years, yet from the opening of the upcoming Season until he chose his bride, he would rank as one of the most eligible noblemen in the ton.

His gaze steady on hers, he didn't try to deny any of that—didn't try to argue.

Feeling tense almost beyond bearing, Melissa dipped her head and conceded, "But that's not really the point. Not really relevant—not here and now." She drew in a breath and brittlely stated, "The truth is that there's nothing we can do but agree to let this"—she raised the hand he still held a few inches, then let it fall—"whatever it is, whatever it might mean, go. It's come too early—happened too soon. Neither of us is ready —neither of us is in a position to make anything of it, even if we wished to."

"We wish to." Uttered without hesitation or doubt, the clipped words were absolute.

Her eyes had flown to his; she considered what she could read in the shadowed gray, then tipped her head in acknowledgment. "Perhaps—but we can't."

She swung her gaze to the graveyard once more, trying to marshal the words that had to be said between them. "Neither of us has yet lived long enough to learn what else might be out there—what our futures might hold. You're about to start at the Home Office—you don't know if that will suit or where your path might take you. I…have at least two years yet in the schoolroom—more likely, three. At least. And that's assuming nothing unexpected happens that might interfere with my coming-out." She gathered her will, raised her chin, and forced herself to say, "We can't do anything other than agree to go our separate ways."

His fingers tightened around hers. "We could wait and see…"

She pressed her lips together and briefly closed her eyes. He wasn't making this easy; she hadn't expected him to be so reluctant. Opening her eyes, she drew in a short, tight breath and, still looking at the gravestones, said, "We have to part—we have to agree we each have no claim of any sort on the other—but yes, we can still wait and see..."

She didn't believe their ill-fated romance that hadn't even had a chance to bloom would survive. "If this, between us, is meant to be—"

They'd spoken in unison.

She broke off as he did, her gaze rising to his face.

His eyes captured hers, and he drew in a tense breath and continued, "If *we* are meant to be, then perhaps, in time..."

When he faltered, she supplied, "Perhaps, in time, we will be."

If this is love—and if it lasts.

Neither of them knew; neither could tell.

Neither could make any promise.

The unvoiced words and the acknowledgment of their helplessness were conveyed in the look they shared.

A sudden rush of footsteps crunched through the snow toward them.

"No! Stop!"

"Ooh, don't you dare, Georgie Tooks!"

A bevy of village children raced past, shrieking and darting between the gravestones, a flurry of snowballs flying.

Melissa's and Dagenham's breaths hitched, and they stepped back.

Then they looked at each other, and Dagenham squeezed Melissa's fingers one last time, then let go, and they turned and, with him sliding his hands into his greatcoat pockets and her wrapping hers in the ends of her shawl, walked, side by side, to where the others, still talking and laughing, remained gathered in a knot on the lawn.

"What-ho!" Henry clapped his hands together as Melissa and Dagenham rejoined the group. Henry tipped his head to where Lady Osbaldestone and her circle were starting down the path to the lane. "Looks like it's time we were on our way to our dinner at the manor."

Everyone smiled and agreed, and the company—including Jamie, George, Lottie, and Mandy—headed off along the path. As with Dagenham on one side and Mandy on the other, Melissa walked toward the lychgate, she accepted that there truly was nothing more to be said— and nothing at all that she or Dagenham could do.

No option; no real choice.

They had to place what might have grown between them in the hands of Fate—and wait and see what the years ahead brought.

～

Therese looked around her dining table with a sense of abiding satisfaction bordering on contentment. Dinner at Hartington Manor following the carol service was becoming an established tradition among the gentry in the village. All those she'd invited were there—Horace and Sally Swindon, Christian and Eugenia Longfellow, Ermintrude Woolsey, and Jeremy and Henrietta Colebatch, as well as Henry and his four friends, along with Therese's grandchildren, and last but not least, Professor Webster, Honor Webster, and Callum Goodrich.

On arriving, everyone had taken due note of the yule log, burning steadily in the grate in the front hall. The initial gathering in the drawing room had lasted only long enough for everyone to partake of Mrs. Crimmins's eggnog, before Therese—informed by Crimmins that Mrs. Haggerty, who had slaved all day to prepare what she deemed a suitable feast, was growing anxious over the state of the geese—had waved her guests into the dining room.

She'd duly directed everyone to their places, this year putting Jeremy Colebatch at the head of the table opposite herself. As soon as everyone had sat, Therese had invited Jeremy to say grace, then Crimmins and Orneby had ferried in the first course, a rich game soup that had warmed everyone up.

The company talked, laughed, and exclaimed and—inevitably—started telling stories as they progressed via a remove to the fish course and, subsequently, to the main course, anchored by two succulent roast geese and a roasted haunch of boar.

Therese had spent some hours mulling over her seating arrangement. As she had in years past when entertaining in Little Moseley, she'd ignored correct protocol, which would have placed Dagenham—the most senior peer present—by her side and, instead, sat people in the places she deemed most helpful in assisting her in her aims.

Consequently, most members of the older generations were seated closer to her, with only Sally Swindon and Ermintrude Woolsey flanking Jeremy at the far end of the table. Therese had placed Horace Swindon on her left and Henrietta Colebatch on her right, with the Longfellows next along on either side.

Beyond Eugenia and Christian sat the Websters, across the table from each other, with Callum Goodrich on Honor's other side. Having observed the connection which seemed to be strengthening hour by hour between Honor and Callum, and also the degree of mutual relief flowing between the professor and his erstwhile protégé, Therese had thought that placement sensible and helpful, and as the meal was devoured and comments exchanged across the board, she felt vindicated in that regard.

In the drawing room, she'd stolen a moment to have a quiet word with the professor; it had transpired that he wasn't as blind as she'd feared, and from what she'd gleaned, he viewed a potential marriage between Honor and Callum as something close to a dream come true.

As he should; having Callum working in close association would do the old man good.

On the Goodrich-Webster front, Therese felt thoroughly content. And in respect of the Hartington Hoard, all was decided and would, no doubt, proceed as they'd agreed, and Callum and the professor had spoken of the possibility of returning in summer with a band of students to excavate further in the manor woods, a prospect Therese was quite looking forward to. Aside from all else, the proposed return would allow her to monitor Callum and Honor's progress to the altar; indeed, with any luck, they would be married by then.

Smiling in anticipation, Therese studied the pair, then allowed her gaze to continue down the table.

She'd sat Lottie next to Callum, with Dagenham beyond; despite Lottie's tender years, Therese had every confidence that Lottie would listen and not unnecessarily interfere with the conversations on either side of her—those between Callum and Honor and between Dagenham and Melissa. Moreover, neither gentleman would feel overly pressured to make conversation with a seven-year-old girl, particularly not one giving an exceedingly good imitation of being entirely engrossed with the food on her plate.

Hiding a small smile, Therese glanced across the table; she'd placed Henry opposite Callum, and Mandy opposite Lottie, with Thomas Kilburn beyond—opposite Melissa. As Therese had hoped, despite occasional concerned glances at Melissa, Mandy devoted herself to holding both Henry's and Kilburn's attention to the extent that neither so much as looked at what was transpiring across the board.

The rest of the company—George Wiley, Jamie, Mrs. Woolsey, Reverend Colebatch, Sally Swindon, George, and Roger Carnaby—were ably entertaining themselves about the other end of the table; Therese wasn't sure—couldn't tell—if anyone other than herself, Mandy, and Lottie was aware of the constraint that now existed between Dagenham and Melissa.

They attempted to smile, to keep up appearances, and given the rest of the company's apparent obliviousness, in that, they largely succeeded. They continued to speak to each other, exchanging comments as anyone would expect, but now their tones were subdued and their expressions somber, and when their eyes met, their gazes would lock for but an instant before one or the other—and most often both—would look away.

From the aura of fatalistic sadness that hung over them both, Therese concluded that they'd made their difficult decision and released all claim on each other. She felt a pang over what she suspected they were feeling, yet in her heart, she knew they'd made the right choice and could only commend their courage in doing so.

They were too young to tie themselves down—both too young to make a pledge that would link them for the rest of their lives. Yet Therese was a firm believer in the old adage that if something was truly meant to be, Fate wouldn't forget and, when the time was right, would move her pieces on the board of life, and the inevitable would come to be.

Viewing the pair, all but feeling their youthful heartache, Therese made a mental note to have a word with her daughter Henrietta, Melissa's mother, stressing that Melissa and Dagenham were to be supported in their decision—that it now rested with Fate and not any human agency as to whether, years from now, something came of this nascent connection, and moreover, that nothing would be gained, and worse, all could be lost were any attempt made to influence the outcome.

Therese's gaze shifted to Mandy, and Therese noted the swift glance Melissa's older sister sent Melissa's way. Therese had wondered what had been behind Mandy's insistence on accompanying Melissa to Little Moseley; she'd been concerned about what motives Mandy might have harbored vis-à-vis Melissa and Dagenham. But she needn't have worried.

Although these last weeks had been the first during which Mandy had spent any extended time under Therese's eye, she had to admit to being impressed by the traits that, transparently to Therese, Mandy had displayed. She'd been first and foremost concerned for Melissa, but after meeting Dagenham and seeing Melissa and him together, Mandy had been nothing but supportive. She was, it seemed, naturally caring and protective, and in dealing with the issue of her younger sister's ill-fated romance, Mandy had shown and continued to demonstrate more maturity than Therese had expected from one of her years.

Therese had also noted that Mandy wasn't susceptible to the charms of, for instance, Thomas Kilburn, despite considerable effort on his part. That, too, was all to the good. Mandy appeared to have a sound, level head on her shoulders; Therese added that to the information she intended conveying to Henrietta.

Therese viewed her new insight into Mandy's character as another blessing accruing from the past three weeks.

After taking several minutes to contribute to the conversations nearer at hand, Therese swept her gaze once more around her table and felt contentment well and warm her. To her mind, the outcome of this year's events—the Roman hoard, the evolving romance between Callum and Honor, the long-overdue reconciliation between Callum and the professor —stood as testimony to the inherent magic of Christmastime in Little Moseley.

Her gaze settled on her three younger grandchildren; judging by the animation they'd displayed throughout their stay, barring unforeseen disasters, she suspected that she and her household could look forward to hosting them again next year.

The prospect filled her heart with joyful anticipation; the pleasure and entertainment the three brought to her and her staff—indeed, to the whole village—was a gift quite literally beyond price.

Not long after, with everyone sitting back, replete, and the platters all but empty, Crimmins, Mrs. Crimmins, and Orneby came in to clear the table. The instant they did, Tilly and Dulcie swept in, bearing large jugs of steaming golden custard.

After setting the jugs on the table, the maids stepped back, eyes alight, their gazes going to the door. Then Mrs. Haggerty appeared, bearing a large plum pudding, wreathed in blue brandy-flames, on a silver platter.

Mrs. Crimmins and Orneby followed, bearing two more fiery plum puddings.

The women set the puddings down along the board, then, after the guests had oohed and aahed and the flames had died down, served slices onto plates, which the maids handed around.

The staff stood back against the walls. Therese glimpsed Crimmins and Simms peering in from the hall. With everyone watching, Therese picked up her spoon and gestured to her guests to do the same.

At her signal, the company dug into the luscious pudding, soft and sweet and surprisingly moist. Therese savored her first mouthful and spontaneously closed her eyes in sensory delight. From all about her came sounds suggestive of gustatory swoons.

She opened her eyes, intending to compliment Mrs. Haggerty—who'd been watching anxiously—but Henry spoke first.

"Oh, my Lord! This is heavenly." Henry grabbed his goblet and raised it to Mrs. Haggerty. "I give you the inimitable Mrs. Haggerty and her plum pudding recipe!"

"Hear, hear!" came from everyone at the table as they raised their glasses to the cook, who blushed deeply and executed a rather wobbly curtsy, then without more ado, the staff—all the rest smiling fit to burst—beat a hasty retreat.

The door had barely shut when Lottie let out a squeal. She held up a shiny coin. "I've got a sixpence!"

The others laughed, smiled, and congratulated Lottie, then applied themselves to their plates, and soon, Henry, and then—of all people—Callum found silver pennies in their helpings, while Honor was blessed with a threepence, and Mrs. Colebatch as well, and finally, Mandy found another penny.

"That's correct." Smiling, Therese nodded down the table. "Each pudding had two coins—a penny in each, plus one other silver coin."

"So we've found all the treasure," Jamie said, with just a thread of disappointment in his voice.

Therese noted it, along with the look Callum exchanged with Honor; his eyes plainly stated that, about that table, treasure existed in many forms.

Deeming the sentiment exquisitely en pointe, Therese reached for her glass and raised it. "I have a toast for you all." She waited until everyone had their glasses in hand, then looked at her grandchildren, one by one. "I give you our most precious treasures, wherever they are found."

The "Hear, hear" that followed was powerful and strong, and everyone drank, then returned to the remnants of their puddings, and the celebration—of the season, of Christmas, of love and good cheer—rolled on.

"Thanks," Therese whispered, entirely to herself, "to the magic of Little Moseley."

A magic that drew its power from the strength of a supportive community and the intrinsic good in human souls. Therese smiled and sipped in a private toast, then returned her attention to her plum pudding.

∾

Dear Reader,

This book was a challenge to write, primarily because of Melissa and

Dagenham. As they both acknowledge, they are simply too young to continue the romance that has blossomed between them—as Melissa is still in the schoolroom, it would be unlikely Dagenham would be able to even see her in London. But, of course, in breaking up as they have, they've set the stage for coming together again, albeit ten years in their future. I already know what happens with them and plan to write and release their love story in a few years' time.

I should add that, eventually, Jamie, George, and Lottie will also have their stories told—those fell into my mind while writing this book as well.

I had a lot of fun researching what was known, in 1812, of the Roman occupation of England and unearthing the possibilities of what might be lurking buried around Little Moseley. My interest was in part inspired by having lived alongside the Roman villa at Eynsford in Kent for more than four years, albeit decades ago.

Another point to note is that in 1812, pennies were still silver and not the copper of later decades. Also, although the British Museum, the Ashmolean Museum, and the Bodleian Library are all entirely real, Brentmore College is not, and the tension discussed between academic colleges and museums is purely hypothetical.

I hope you enjoyed following Therese and her grandchildren through another adventure in Little Moseley in the lead up to Christmas.

My next release will be the latest in the Cynster Next Generation novels, *The Inevitable Fall of Christopher Cynster*, scheduled for March 19, 2020.

As ever, I wish you continued happy reading!

Stephanie.

For alerts as new books are released, plus information on upcoming books, exclusive sweepstakes and sneak peeks into upcoming novels, sign up for Stephanie's Private Email Newsletter http://www.stephanielaurens. com/newsletter-signup/

Or if you don't have time to chat and want a quick email alert, sign up and follow me at BookBub https://www.bookbub.com/authors/stephanie-laurens

The ultimate source for detailed information on all Stephanie's published books, including covers, descriptions, and excerpts, is Stephanie's Website www.stephanielaurens.com

You can also follow Stephanie via her Amazon Author Page at http://tinyurl.com/zc3e9mp

Goodreads members can follow Stephanie via her author page https://www.goodreads.com/author/show/9241.Stephanie_Laurens

You can email Stephanie at stephanie@stephanielaurens.com

Or find her on Facebook
https://www.facebook.com/AuthorStephanieLaurens/

COMING NEXT:
THE INEVITABLE FALL OF CHRISTOPHER CYNSTER
Cynster Next Generation Novel #8
To be released March 19, 2020.

Christopher Cynster has finally accepted that he does, indeed, want a wife and family of his own. But before he has a chance to even consider how to go about finding the right lady, the incursion of livestock into his family's hop fields puts him on a collision course with his aging neighbor's niece—a young lady who, with her doll-like appearance, is the epitome of the type of silly fashionable flibbertigibbet Christopher abhors. But appearances can be deceptive, and when Drake Varisey involves Christopher in a mission to expose a scheme threatening to destabilize the realm, Christopher discovers that Miss Ellen Martingale possesses qualities that command his respect, just as powerfully as, against his every expectation, she excites his interest in more personal ways.

Pre-orders available by January 1, 2020.

RECENTLY RELEASED:
A CONQUEST IMPOSSIBLE TO RESIST
Cynster Next Generation Novel #7

#1 New York Times *bestselling author Stephanie Laurens returns to the*

Cynsters' next generation to bring you a thrilling tale of love, intrigue, and fabulous horses.

A notorious rakehell with a stable of rare Thoroughbreds and a lady on a quest to locate such horses must negotiate personal minefields to forge a greatly desired alliance—one someone is prepared to murder to prevent.

Prudence Cynster has turned her back on husband hunting in favor of horse hunting. As the head of the breeding program underpinning the success of the Cynster racing stables, she's on a quest to acquire the necessary horses to refresh the stable's breeding stock.

On his estranged father's death, Deaglan Fitzgerald, now Earl of Glengarah, left London and the hedonistic life of a wealthy, wellborn rake and returned to Glengarah Castle determined to rectify the harm caused by his father's neglect. Driven by guilt that he hadn't been there to protect his people during the Great Famine, Deaglan holds firm against the lure of his father's extensive collection of horses and, leaving the stable to the care of his brother, Felix, devotes himself to returning the estate to prosperity.

Deaglan had fallen out with his father and been exiled from Glengarah over his drive to have the horses pay their way. Knowing Deaglan's wishes and that restoration of the estate is almost complete, Felix writes to the premier Thoroughbred breeding program in the British Isles to test their interest in the Glengarah horses.

On receiving a letter describing exactly the type of horses she's seeking, Pru overrides her family's reluctance and sets out for Ireland's west coast to visit the now-reclusive wicked Earl of Glengarah. Yet her only interest is in his horses, which she cannot wait to see.

When Felix tells Deaglan that a P. H. Cynster is about to arrive to assess the horses with a view to a breeding arrangement, Deaglan can only be grateful. But then P. H. Cynster turns out to be a lady, one utterly unlike any other he's ever met.

Yet they are who they are, and both understand their world. They battle their instincts and attempt to keep their interactions businesslike, but the sparks are incandescent and inevitably ignite a sexual blaze that consumes them both—and opens their eyes.

But before they can find their way to their now-desired goal, first one accident, then another distracts them. Someone, it seems, doesn't want them to strike a deal. Who? Why?

They need to find out before whoever it is resorts to the ultimate sanction.

A historical romance with neo-Gothic overtones, set in the west of Ireland. A Cynster Next Generation novel—a full-length historical romance of 125,000 words.

ALSO RECENTLY RELEASED:
The third volume in the Cavanaughs
THE BEGUILEMENT OF LADY EUSTACIA CAVANAUGH

#1 New York Times *bestselling author Stephanie Laurens continues the bold tales of the Cavanaugh siblings as the sole Cavanaugh sister discovers that love truly does conquer all.*

A lady with a passion for music and the maestro she challenges in pursuit of a worthy cause find themselves battling villains both past and present as they fight to secure life's greatest rewards—love, marriage, and family.

Stacie—Lady Eustacia Cavanaugh—is adamant marriage is not for her. Haunted by her parents' unhappy union, Stacie believes that, for her, marriage is an unacceptable risk. Wealthy and well-born, she needs for nothing, and with marriage off the table, to give her life purpose, she embarks on a plan to further the careers of emerging local musicians by introducing them to the ton via a series of musical evenings.

Yet despite her noble status, Stacie requires a musical lure to tempt the haut ton to her events, and in the elevated circles she inhabits, only one musician commands sufficient cachet—the reclusive and notoriously reluctant Marquess of Albury.

Frederick, Marquess of Albury, has fashioned a life for himself as a musical scholar, one he pursues largely out of sight of the ton. He might be renowned as a virtuoso on the pianoforte, yet he sees no reason to endure the smothering over-attentiveness of society. Then his mother inveigles him into meeting Stacie, and the challenge she lays before him is…tempting. On a number of fronts. Enough for him not to immediately refuse her.

A dance of subtle persuasion ensues, and step by step, Frederick finds himself convinced that Stacie's plan has real merit and that it behooves him to support her. At least for one event.

Stacie's first musical evening, featuring Frederick as the principal performer, is a massive success—until Fate takes a hand and lands them in a situation that forces them both to reassess.

Does Frederick want more than the sterile, academic life he'd thought was for him?

Can Stacie overcome her deepest fears and own to and reach for her girlhood dreams?

Impulsive, arrogant, and used to getting his own way, Frederick finds his answer easily enough, but his new direction puts him on a collision course with Stacie's fears. Luckily, he thrives on challenges—which is just as well, because in addition to convincing Stacie that love can, indeed, conquer all, he and she must unravel the mystery of who is behind a spate of murderous attacks before the villain succeeds in eliminating all hope of a happy ending.

A classical historical romance set in London and Surrey, in the heart of the ton. Third novel in The Cavanaughs—a full-length historical romance of 122,000 words.

And if you haven't already indulged:
PREVIOUS VOLUMES IN LADY OSBALDESTONE'S CHRISTMAS CHRONICLES

The first volume in Lady Osbaldestone's Christmas Chronicles
LADY OSBALDESTONE'S CHRISTMAS GOOSE

#1 New York Times bestselling author Stephanie Laurens brings you a lighthearted tale of Christmas long ago with a grandmother and three of her grandchildren, one lost soul, a lady driven to distraction, a recalcitrant donkey, and a flock of determined geese.

Three years after being widowed, Therese, Lady Osbaldestone finally settles into her dower property of Hartington Manor in the village of Little Moseley in Hampshire. She is in two minds as to whether life in the small village will generate sufficient interest to keep her amused over the months when she is not in London or visiting friends around the country. But she will see.

It's December, 1810, and Therese is looking forward to her usual Christmas with her family at Winslow Abbey, her youngest daughter,

Celia's home. But then a carriage rolls up and disgorges Celia's three oldest children. Their father has contracted mumps, and their mother has sent the three—Jamie, George, and Lottie—to spend this Christmas with their grandmama in Little Moseley.

Therese has never had to manage small children, not even her own. She assumes the children will keep themselves amused, but quickly learns that what amuses three inquisitive, curious, and confident youngsters isn't compatible with village peace. Just when it seems she will have to set her mind to inventing something, she and the children learn that with only twelve days to go before Christmas, the village flock of geese has vanished.

Every household in the village is now missing the centerpiece of their Christmas feast. But how could an entire flock go missing without the slightest trace? The children are as mystified and as curious as Therese— and she seizes on the mystery as the perfect distraction for the three children as well as herself.

But while searching for the geese, she and her three helpers stumble on two locals who, it is clear, are in dire need of assistance in sorting out their lives. Never one to shy from a little matchmaking, Therese undertakes to guide Miss Eugenia Fitzgibbon into the arms of the determinedly reclusive Lord Longfellow. To her considerable surprise, she discovers that her grandchildren have inherited skills and talents from both her late husband as well as herself. And with all the customary village events held in the lead up to Christmas, she and her three helpers have opportunities galore in which to subtly nudge and steer.

Yet while their matchmaking appears to be succeeding, neither they nor anyone else have found so much as a feather from the village's geese. Larceny is ruled out; a flock of that size could not have been taken from the area without someone noticing. So where could the birds be? And with the days passing and Christmas inexorably approaching, will they find the blasted birds in time?

First in series. A novel of 60,000 words. A Christmas tale of romance and geese.

**The second volume in Lady Osbaldestone's Christmas Chronicles
LADY OSBALDESTONE AND THE MISSING CHRISTMAS
CAROLS**

#1 New York Times bestselling author Stephanie Laurens brings you a heart-warming tale of a long-ago country-village Christmas, a grandmother, three eager grandchildren, one moody teenage granddaughter, an earnest young lady, a gentleman in hiding, and an elusive book of Christmas carols.

Therese, Lady Osbaldestone, and her household are quietly delighted when her younger daughter's three children, Jamie, George, and Lottie, insist on returning to Therese's house, Hartington Manor in the village Little Moseley, to spend the three weeks leading up to Christmas participating in the village's traditional events.

Then out of the blue, one of Therese's older granddaughters, Melissa, arrives on the doorstep. Her mother, Therese's older daughter, begs Therese to take Melissa in until the family gathering at Christmas—otherwise, Melissa has nowhere else to go.

Despite having no experience dealing with moody, reticent teenagers like Melissa, Therese welcomes Melissa warmly. The younger children are happy to include their cousin in their plans—and despite her initial aloofness, Melissa discovers she's not too old to enjoy the simple delights of a village Christmas.

The previous year, Therese learned the trick to keeping her unexpected guests out of mischief. She casts around and discovers that the new organist, who plays superbly, has a strange failing. He requires the written music in front of him before he can play a piece, and the church's book of Christmas carols has gone missing.

Therese immediately volunteers the services of her grandchildren, who are only too happy to fling themselves into the search to find the missing book of carols. Its disappearance threatens one of the village's most-valued Christmas traditions—the Carol Service—yet as the book has always been freely loaned within the village, no one imagines that it won't be found with a little application.

But as Therese's intrepid four follow the trail of the book from house to house, the mystery of where the book has vanished to only deepens. Then the organist hears the children singing and invites them to form a special guest choir. The children love singing, and provided they find the book in time, they'll be able to put on an extra-special service for the village.

While the urgency and their desire to finding the missing book escalates, the children—being Therese's grandchildren—get distracted by the potential for romance that buds, burgeons, and blooms before them.

Yet as Christmas nears, the questions remain: Will the four unravel the twisted trail of the missing book in time to save the village's Carol Service? And will they succeed in nudging the organist and the harpist they've found to play alongside him into seizing the happy-ever-after that hovers before the pair's noses?

Second in series. A novel of 62,000 words. A Christmas tale full of music and romance.

ABOUT THE AUTHOR

#1 *New York Times* bestselling author Stephanie Laurens began writing romances as an escape from the dry world of professional science. Her hobby quickly became a career when her first novel was accepted for publication, and with entirely becoming alacrity, she gave up writing about facts in favor of writing fiction.

All Laurens's works to date are historical romances, ranging from medieval times to the mid-1800s, and her settings range from Scotland to India. The majority of her works are set in the period of the British Regency. Laurens has published over 70 works of historical romance, including 40 *New York Times* bestsellers. Laurens has sold more than 20 million print, audio, and e-books globally. All her works are continuously available in print and e-book formats in English worldwide, and have been translated into many other languages. An international bestseller, among other accolades, Laurens has received the Romance Writers of America® prestigious RITA® Award for Best Romance Novella 2008 for *The Fall of Rogue Gerrard*.

Laurens's continuing novels featuring the Cynster family are widely regarded as classics of the historical romance genre. Other series include the *Bastion Club Novels*, the *Black Cobra Quartet*, the *Adventurers Quartet,* and the *Casebook of Barnaby Adair Novels*.

For information on all published novels and on upcoming releases and updates on novels yet to come, visit Stephanie's website: www. stephanielaurens.com

To sign up for Stephanie's Email Newsletter (a private list) for heads-up alerts as new books are released, exclusive sneak peeks into upcoming books, and exclusive sweepstakes contests, follow the prompts at http:// www.stephanielaurens.com/newsletter-signup/

To follow Stephanie on BookBub, head https://www.bookbub.com/ authors/stephanie-laurens.

Stephanie lives with her husband and a goofy black labradoodle in the hills outside Melbourne, Australia. When she isn't writing, she's reading, and if she isn't reading, she'll be tending her garden.

www.stephanielaurens.com
stephanie@stephanielaurens.com

Made in the USA
San Bernardino, CA
22 November 2019

60269238R00120